Trollope, Joanna
Leaves from the valley        12.95
                              1/84

DISCARD

# Leaves from the Valley

# Joanna Trollope

# *Leaves from the Valley*

St. Martin's Press
New York

Tro

**Library of Congress Cataloging in Publication Data**

Trollope, Joanna.
  Leaves from the valley.

  I. Title.
PR6070.R57L4   1984        823'.914      83-21096
ISBN 0-312-47729-5

First published in Great Britain in 1980 by Hutchinson.

First U.S. Edition

10 9 8 7 6 5 4 3 2 1

For Tory

# Acknowledgements

I should like to acknowledge my deep appreciation of Elizabeth Grey's encouragement and enthusiasm for this book. She also generously lent me invaluable material for it, as did Michael Casey and Bernard Stawt. I am most grateful to all of them.

J. T.

# Prelude — 1842

Inevitably, it was Aunt Price who caught them. They stood frozen where they were at the ominous approaching rustle of her skirts, Edgar actually up the ladder with a peach in his hand, Sarah steadying it since it was shakily balanced on the tiled floor of the orangery and Blanche holding out the stuff of her skirts to catch the tossed fruit. It was very awful.

'Thieves!' cried Aunt Price. 'Thieves! Greedy, sneaking little thieves!'

Blanche turned a calm blue gaze of scorn upon her. 'We are not greedy, Aunt.'

Aunt Price extended her voluminous, tightly cuffed sleeve and pointed furiously at the plunder in Blanche's skirts.

'Not greedy! Not greedy, when the evidence before me speaks such volumes to the contrary! What noble end, I wonder, can you hastily invent for those peaches, to disguise the undoubted fact that you intended to feast upon them yourselves?'

'We did not, Aunt,' Edgar said from the top of the ladder. Sarah could feel his trembling right down through the wooden shafts she held in her hands. 'They are not for us. They are for someone who is ill.'

Aunt Price advanced to the foot of the ladder. Sarah held on all the more tightly and shut her eyes.

'Would you, sir, add impertinence to gluttony? Would you presume to address me from that elevated position? Come down at once.'

Edgar came down slowly, his face pale and set, and although his glance never rested on Sarah as he passed her, his hand brushed hers for one moment.

'Explain yourself,' Aunt Price commanded. She leaned forward and plucked the peach from his hand as if she suspected him of being about to sink his teeth into its forbidden flesh.

'The peaches are for Miss Pelly, ma'am.'

7

'Miss Pelly?'

'She is ill, Aunt,' Blanche said reasonably. 'We have had no lessons all week because she is so ill and Cook sends up horrid food she cannot eat so we thought we would take her something pleasant.'

Aunt Price said with a wealth of scorn, 'Miss Pelly is a governess.'

'She is an ill governess,' Blanche said.

They were now, somehow, in a line before her, Edgar a head taller than Sarah, Blanche already grown past Sarah's shoulder. In her huge sleeves and tiny waisted gown, Aunt Price seethed malevolently before them like a giant wasp.

'And so you would put a governess, a mere governess, before your most blessed mother? These peaches, these white peaches, are grown for your mother alone. You know full well she is too delicate to take any but the most choice of foods, and you would openly rob her, would you, for some self-pitying rabbit of a governess?'

The complicated inaccuracy of all this made Edgar rigid with self-control. Sarah knew he would not be discourteous, but nor would he admit to anything unjust for the sake of peace, he would simply stand and stare before him and tremble from the effort of his own self-discipline.

Blanche looked up at the tree against the white wall behind them.

'Mamma cannot eat all those, Aunt.'

Aunt Price ignored her.

'Answer me, sir! It is you who are the most culpable since you are bound to lead your sisters. Answer me!'

It was clear Edgar could not. Sarah said in a rush:

'Aunt, Mamma would not wish to eat all those peaches. So many would make her worse! She would not grudge Miss Pelly a few –'

'Ah! So you have a tongue, miss, have you? Cowering behind your brother as usual. No, do not suggest to me that your sainted mother would grudge her last mouthful to a needy soul, it is not *that* that is in question. But you would rob her, do you hear me, rob her!'

Blanche thought briefly how absurd Aunt Price looked in her rage, her great garden hat with its lugubrious black streamers perched on her sausage-shaped curls, and shaking on its nest with every vehemently uttered syllable. At the same moment Sarah tried to envisage her languid, indolent mother rising gracefully from her sofa in a cascade of ruffles and ribbons to present her last slice of peach to a beggar who had appeared incongruously but opportunely in the drawing room. It was not an image in which she had any faith, and it was soon obliterated by the more realistic one of poor Miss Pelly, thin and hot and wretched in her disagreeable little room overlooking the kitchen yard.

'Miss Pelly is needy, Aunt. She is homesick for Northumberland. She tells us how she misses the moors and the water and the wildness. And now she is ill.'

'I should be ill, I think,' Blanche said reflectively, 'if I had to wear such nightgowns.'

Sarah had to look down. She longed to smile, just a tiny smile, in the midst of the awfulness. She shot a sideways glance at Edgar to see if Blanche had lightened his load a little, but he was still too occupied with himself to do anything but stare woodenly before him.

'I shall go in now,' Aunt Price announced, 'Blanche shall accompany me with the fruit and we shall go straight to the drawing room. God is to be thanked that your mother is a little stronger today and may bear the grief you will cause her. I shall inform your father of course. Edgar and Sarah, you will follow and wait in the dining room. You will not speak.'

She swirled around majestically and began to stalk back along the orangery, her dark, stiff skirts hissing over the black and white tiles, and her hand clamped upon Blanche's shoulder. Despite the discomfort of this, Blanche could not but derive some pleasure from the knowledge that as she still held her skirts up in a sort of hammock to cradle the peaches, her pantaloons were immodestly visible to well above her knees.

Sarah and Edgar trailed behind them. Sarah could tell from the way Blanche held her head that she had found some private relief from her predicament. Personally, Sarah could see none : they would be scolded, probably punished and at the end of the day not only would Miss Pelly be deprived of her peaches, but Aunt Price would surely contrive to see that the food sent up to the ailing governess was as barely edible as possible. Aunt

9

Price had a talent for irrelevant punishment. Indeed, Sarah had thought how useful Aunt Price would have been on a witch hunt, so ingenious was she in the plausible invention of guilt. Sarah gave one brief glance at Edgar before they entered the house, and felt a surge of pity. His ramrod back had stooped, his fiery gaze had dimmed, the depression after the failure of attempted splendour had set in, as it always did. She shot out a hand and gave his arm a brief squeeze. He answered her by sighing.

Lady Drummond was lying on the sofa in precisely the attitude of indolent hypochondria she had adopted since Blanche's birth eight years before. She wore a blue robe which Blanche much admired, fastened with cream silk frogging, and her gaze, which she swung slowly from her Pekinese to her daughter, was entirely empty. She peered dubiously into Blanche's skirts.

'I cannot possibly eat all those, Sister.'

Aunt Price swelled visibly.

'Shall you tell your injured mother yourself, Blanche, or must I confess your guilt for you?'

Blanche gave the smallest shrug.

'Miss Pelly is ill, Mamma – '

'Miss Pelly, Sister?'

'The governess,' Aunt Price said witheringly.

'She is ill, Mamma, and cannot eat the nasty things she is given, and we – '

'We?' Aunt Price interrupted terribly.

'It was Sarah who thought of it, but we all agreed. Edgar said that as she is so poor and ill and you had many pleasant things to eat, it would not be wrong to take her some peaches. He said,' Blanche repeated with emphasis, 'that it would not be wrong.'

Aunt Price began a tirade. Under cover of it Blanche gazed at her mother's jewels, and the improbable luxuriance of the curls piled above her brow; and Lady Drummond began to wish, as powerfully as she ever wished anything, that they would both go away and leave her. Sister Price was so noisy, though undoubtedly useful, and Blanche's fingernails were offensively unclean. She yawned a little.

'It is terrible to contemplate what ill-effect this wickedness may have upon you,' Aunt Price declared.

It occurred to Blanche that if that were the case, what was the object of Aunt Price's bringing her here, in her schoolroom clothes, to confess to her mother? If she had been Sarah, she knew she would have said nothing, but she was not Sarah.

'Does Aunt Price wish to make you ill, Mamma?'

There was a whirlwind of fury behind her. Her arm was seized so that she was forced to release her skirts on one side and the pale velvety fruit tumbled softly on to the rug at her feet. She found herself being propelled back across the drawing room at great speed and thrust outside with violence. Behind her, Lady Drummond resumed her gazing into space, and the Pekinese flopped off the sofa to nose at the scattered peaches.

In the dining room, seated on hard chairs against the walls, Edgar and Sarah heard the drawing-room door being opened, and then a flurry of feet as Aunt Price's furious voice swept past the closed dining-room door and up the staircase. Had Blanche been very outrageous? Sarah looked hopefully at her brother, but he was gazing mournfully at the picture over the chimney-piece, a picture of their grandfather who had been killed fifteen years before, riding with the — Hussars at Waterloo. He had been fifty-five, and his son, at nearly thirty, had refused to go. Edgar could not but feel that decision was ignoble. He looked up at the portrait with hope, trying to see in it some feature that would strike an especial chord within his own tormented breast. He had always wished to say in term time, at Harrow, that he was supposed to bear a great resemblance to the Sir Edgar Drummond who had died so splendidly after capturing a French gun. But nobody had ever observed a likeness between grandfather and grandson and Edgar could not, of course, invent one.

The door opened. Aunt Price, flushed from some violent exertion, whether physical or emotional it was impossible to tell, stood breathing deeply on the threshold.

'Your father wishes to see you, Edgar.'

Edgar rose, and Sarah with him.

'Alone, miss. You will remain here for the moment. Martha has work to do in here so do not suppose you may slip away.'

She stood slightly aside so that Edgar might pass out and a subdued little housemaid might dart hastily in. The door closed loudly behind her.

Sir Thomas Drummond had his face to the window when Edgar was announced. His gaze lingered upon gentle green parkland, dotted with elm and oak and sheep, the former planted by his forbears in the previous century, the latter a source of dwindling income to himself. Northamptonshire was not notable for sheep country, but his father had been, for his time, a professional soldier, and Sir Thomas had inherited farms unchanged since 1780. In some ways he had not minded this state of affairs since it enabled the labourers to be paid, in years of poor yield, in bad corn and worse beer, but it had become apparent over the last few years that the supply of labourers to be recompensed in this expedient manner was dwindling. The broad acres from which his father had taken seventy able-bodied men to the field of Waterloo would hardly yield up that number of women and children now. They were drifting north, it seemed, to the cotton mills of Lancashire, the potteries of Staffordshire and south to heaven knew what end in London. There had been times when Sir Thomas had felt the beginnings of anxiety as to his future way of life. He did not care to hunt or to shoot, but he liked to be comfortable and he wished to be comfortable easily. A solution had come, of course, as solutions must do to the blessed who hardly stir themselves to seek for them. The solution was the railways.

Sir Thomas's younger brother had brought the solution to him. The brother had been left a small and barren piece of West Yorkshire, the Northamptonshire lands having gone to Sir Thomas with the title since the Scottish estates from which the Drummonds all came had vanished after some discreet manoeuvring with the Duke of Cumberland after Culloden. The brother had surveyed his inheritance with distaste, but out of the sow's ear had sprung a silk purse since the tract of empty moorland held a rich seam of coal in its depths. The brother had become not only rich but an expert and innovator in mining techniques and had held out staunchly, in the twenties, for the progressive method of drawing coal along rails by means of a locomotive rather than by horses. He went further than that, and laid down the first local line for passenger as well as coal transport in his district. He became a friend of the Quaker family of Bradshaw, and through them involved in the first plans for a line that would run south to London from the Midlands. One way in which the line could be laid was across the western edge of his brother's Northamptonshire land, conveniently south-east of Leicester. The chosen ten-mile stretch lay two miles from the house, and there was no shortage of eager investors to buy up the land in those first days of railway fever. The brother was instrumental in the affair, and Sir Thomas was delighted.

He could now regard his green acres with tranquillity. The quietly undulating land stretched away to the dark blot of a patch of woodland beyond which the reason for his future income would profitably run. Advised by his brother, Sir Thomas intended to invest himself. He was assured that by the fifties, England would be latticed with railways, it would become the greatest transport system in the world and thus early investment could bring nothing but gain. The contemplation of this caused Sir Thomas to spend long hours at his study window and rendered him, on this occasion, oblivious to his son waiting patiently in the shadows by the door.

Edgar did not like to speak. He knew nothing of what preoccupied his father since his father never spoke to him in confidence nor, for that matter, in conversation. Even Harrow appeared to provoke no nostalgic common ground, so Edgar stood straight and still, and worried and gnawed at his sense of injustice until his feelings seemed to bleed within him.

'Ah, sir. And what brings you to me?'

Edgar advanced two paces across the Turkey carpet.

'Aunt Price sent me, sir.'

'Ah yes. Peaches. You were caught red-handed stealing peaches. What have you to say for yourself, sir?'

Edgar would not plead his cause.

'You know, do you not, that those peaches in the orangery are solely for your mother?'

'Yes, sir.'

'Then as you have deprived your mother, we must, to remind you, deprive you somewhat. I shall speak to your aunt.'

Edgar thought wildly of those cursed peaches, at least thirty of them simultaneously ripe, hanging creamily on their tree, and of Sarah's impassioned plea for poor, sick, lonely Miss Pelly and of Blanche's assurance she had seen Aunt Price go into the linen room, an occupation that always took her at least half an hour. He quelled rigorously the urgent desire to speak and justify himself.

'It is not,' his father said, 'that I consider you too old to thrash, but merely that an act of such greed must be punished in the same terms. Do they make such gluttons of you at Harrow?'

'No, sir.'

Indeed they did not; what few edible comforts Edgar managed to acquire either by gift or purchase were invariably wrenched or bullied away by older boys. He accepted that, just as he accepted that at Harrow at large the boys were left to form their own society and he must take the consequences of that just as much as he must take those of Aunt Price's whimsical vindictiveness. He clung faithfully to such rules as were laid down by a higher authority, since they seemed to him to provide the only means to save oneself from drowning in an ocean of other people's arbitrary desires. Thus he would abide honourably by whatever punishment his father and aunt meted out to him, for such things constituted the only order in his world that was not of his own shy making.

'How old are you now?'

'Fourteen, sir.'

'And what is to become of you?'

This was no question, Edgar knew. His father had never consulted him on the smallest point in all his life, so why should he do so on a subject so important? Despite his disgrace over the peaches, therefore, Edgar felt there was no harm in making his own suggestion since there was not the smallest chance of its being attended to.

'I should like to join the army, sir.'

Sir Thomas never laughed, but he now gave a cold yelp that might pass as a sign of amusement.

'Absurd!'

'My grandfather was a soldier, sir.'

'And look what became of him. The army is finished, quite finished.'

Edgar took two more steps across the carpet.

'Might there not be another war, sir?'

'No. Most indubitably no. The French are become allies. There is no one left to fight, nothing worth fighting for. If you imagine I am going to spend ten thousand pounds to purchase you a regiment in fancy uniforms so that you may idle and drink and gamble away your time, you have never been more mistaken.'

Edgar was shocked. The idea of drink and gambling had never entered his head, indeed he was dismayed to find it regarded as inseparable from army life. His own notion of army life, gleaned from avid reading of despatches from the Peninsular Wars and Waterloo, and from treating as gospel truth every syllable uttered by the ageing Duke of Wellington, was a mixture of order, glory and honour; for him the army was peopled with noble heroes of impeccably blue-blooded stock, aristocrats who wore their right to command as beautifully as they wore their elegant uniforms, and whom the common soldiers – a vague, humble, biddable mass of humanity containing, in Edgar's mind, no individuals – looked to as both fathers and leaders.

'You see yourself, I assume, as another Brudenell, unhappily born into the wrong family?'

Edgar blushed deeply; it was an unkind dig. Some years ago, when he had been only nine or ten, a tutor had been engaged for him whose previous career had included a brief and tempestuous spell at Deene Park, seat of the Earls of Cardigan, which lay not above eight miles from the Drummonds' humbler house. The doings of those seven lovely girls and that wild, doted-on, ruinously spoiled and savagely tempered son at Deene Park had been legendary in the second decade of the century. The tutor saw little enough of the son, James Brudenell, during his few months at Deene, but what he had seen had been unforgettable, and he regaled an awestruck Edgar with tales of wildness and violence and superb horsemanship, tales even then nearly twenty years old. James Brudenell had gone on to be a soldier, and Edgar, knowing nothing of what manner of soldier he was, but simply that he was one, and that he and Edgar came from the same corner of the same county, had unwisely confided to his father, in a burst of infatuation with his

15

strangely chosen hero, that he wished he were exactly like James Brudenell. Sir Thomas Drummond, instead of pointing out that James Brudenell, by now the seventh Earl of Cardigan, was probably the most dangerous and stupid man in the British army, merely grimaced with cold amusement at his son, and kept the embarrassing confession as a goad to apply painfully when opportunity offered.

'No, sir. I wish no such thing. I do not wish to be bought an expensive regiment. I would not mind serving as major or even only captain for thirty years, but I do want to enter the army.'

Sir Thomas looked out of the window again and thought with satisfaction that this alarming contemporary of his, this seventh Earl of Cardigan, would at least be able to make no money out of the new Midland Railway. Deene Park lay far too far to the north and east, whereas Oakley Park, snug between Corby and Kettering, was precisely on the projected route. He threw a glance at Edgar over his shoulder.

'You have hardly the physique.'

Was this a yet more oblique reference to his brief desire to be a Brudenell? Brudenells were tall and beautiful and golden-haired, Drummonds of middle height and brown, except of course for Blanche who was as fair as her name.

Edgar said bravely, 'I think that will not matter, sir. You said there would be no more fighting. Perhaps I might be a regimental paymaster.'

It cost him something to say it. What he really wanted was to be talked of as the star of a crack cavalry regiment, but his father's attitude would be an impossible obstacle to such splendour. All his father cared for was money, so all approaches must work upon this preoccupation, and glamour must be sacrificed for expediency.

'The soldier tradesman,' Sir Thomas said unkindly.

'It would not be – dishonourable, sir.'

'I fail to see what honour has to do with it. It would be a reasonably practical move. Indeed, reports from Harrow give me little hope to think you will leave your mark upon the world, so we may as well, I suppose, make you useful.'

He turned from the window and seated himself, staring down for some minutes at his clasped hands lying on the desk top.

Edgar waited. He did not look at his father, or round the room, but stared unwaveringly at a spot on the carpet until the bright geometric design seemed to quiver and squirm.

'As to the matter of the peaches, I may tell you that I am grossly displeased. Ask your aunt to be so good as to spare me a moment that we may devise a diet that will make your greed memorable to you. Bread and water is perfectly nourishing and its monotony may jog your conscience. Go.'

Edgar did not raise his head. He gave a small bow to acknowledge having heard his father and went quietly from the room.

Sarah sat on, forgotten. It was a warm day but the dining room, on the sunless side of the house, was cheerless and tank-like with its high dark walls and stiff furniture. Sarah admired the furniture, it was slender and elegant and made of rosewood, but apart from the table, it was all pushed back against the walls, just as it had been in her grandfather's time, and it gave the room an unwelcoming, formal air. The pictures were better, especially her grandfather in his lovely uniform and her grandmother in a pretty, gauzy high-waisted dress, and some earlier uncles and aunts in plumed hats and luxuriant curls, but they all looked haughtily across the room at each other, over her head, and that was hardly comforting. The only homely object she could see from her seat was a silver leaf full of walnuts on the sideboard, walnuts gathered from the crooked tree in the shrubbery where Edgar had once made a nest for her and Blanche out of bent withies and creepers.

After a while, very cautiously, she leaned sideways so that she might lie across two chairs instead of remaining endlessly, achingly upright on one. She acted with circumspection not because she was afraid of being caught, but because she knew Edgar would feel it was very wrong not to accept and endure the precise terms of punishment. If the punishment had stated, 'Sit in the dining room', sit one must. The facts that the punishment was unfair, that nobody would listen to the truth, that poor Miss Pelly would never get a peach, Edgar would dismiss entirely once it was evident nothing would be done about any of them. He would, Sarah knew, expect her to endure and obey implicitly, just as he would do. For him, she would endure and obey – well, almost, and she would confess to him that she had

17

rested her back for a little while by lying sideways and he would forgive her for her honesty.

She pillowed her cheek as well as she could on the hard, smooth, satin-striped surface and surveyed the peculiar sideways dining room, bisected by a hard long line of table edge with uneven oblongs of window either side of it and forested in one half by elegant furniture legs. It was not a good position to be in, either physically or emotionally, but at least it offered her the unique chance of time to herself. If she were free, of course, she would put that time to good use and write minutely in her journal of all the day's happenings and consequences. Even Edgar did not know she kept it, for he would feel the emotional comfort it afforded her to be very wrong, so she wrote it at night when Blanche was asleep, by the light of candle ends stolen from the schoolroom candlesticks. It would be unimaginably wonderful to be able to write it using that magnificent table as a desk, by daylight, not crouching on her pillow with an ear always strained for the coming of the nursery maid to rake apart the coals in the fireplace. Tonight she would tell the journal just what she thought of Aunt Price, and then she would pray as she always did that God might make Mamma well and able to run the house again so that Aunt Price would return to Shropshire and never come back.

There was a faint tapping on the nearest window. Blanche was out there, without a bonnet as usual, holding up a piece of paper against the glass. Reflecting that Aunt Price could not know which chair she had confined herself to, Sarah moved two along quickly and peered at the message.

'No supper today,' it said, 'but DO NOT DESPARE. Edgar won't speak. Are you crying?'

Sarah smiled and pointed to her dry eyes. Blanche looked relieved, and after a hasty glance round, hitched up her skirts and revealed a bag of apples slung round her waist on a piece of tape.

'Be careful!' Sarah shouted through the window.

Blanche nodded, screwed up the paper, thrust it hastily among the apples, and scampered off towards the rose garden.

Sarah was not at all surprised to see that she was free. Blanche usually evaded retribution, and nobody seemed much to notice or to care. Sarah watched her skipping figure lovingly and won-

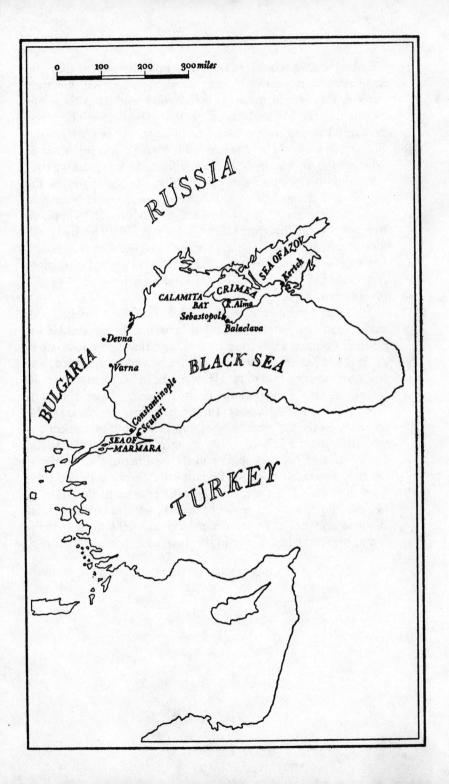

0    100    200    300 miles

RUSSIA

SEA OF AZOV

Kertch

CRIMEA

CALAMITA
BAY

R. Alma

Sebastopol

Balaclava

Devna

BULGARIA

Varna

BLACK SEA

Constantinople
Scutari

SEA OF
MARMARA

TURKEY

dered what they would do with the apple cores when they had scrunched them secretly in bed that night; perhaps if they were careful, they would tiptoe to the window and drop them one by one into the Michaelmas daisies that grew below. They must be careful not to eat too many or Blanche would have a pain. She lay down again and wondered if Blanche was still alone or whether the nursery maid had found her and was looming over her inhibitingly while she played. She liked playing, at the moment, at being Mamma before she was so weak, but it was not a game that was very satisfactory without Sarah to applaud her and invent imaginary clothes for her. Blanche had such lovely hair, just like Mamma's must have been, and although her face was not as pretty as Sarah's it was a good deal more memorable. Sarah had observed in church how often people glanced covertly at Blanche.

It was only to be expected that Edgar would not speak; Sarah understood completely that he felt himself to be responsible for all their disgrace and supperlessness, and that he was also now, since the injustice of their accusation had to be accepted, setting an example of stoicism. He would be in his room, she could picture it, on the single hard chair, refusing himself the comforting distraction of a book, simply enduring. For his sake, she must try to do the same. She sat up briefly out of respect for that stiff, self-disciplined figure upstairs, but realized that the conjunction of her thin spine and the beading of the chairback made it impossible even for Edgar's sake. So she subsided sideways for the third time, and closed her eyes to dream of a perfect house, set in a wood by a lake, with only herself and Blanche and Edgar to inhabit it, and there the nursery maid found her, three hours later in the dusk, smiling and fast asleep.

# One – 1854

The winter had been an active one for Fleet Street. Frederick Hope, editor of *The Clarion* and arch rival of John Delane of *The Times*, had been heard to say that he believed England's printing presses would have ground to a halt, weighed down by trivia and commonplaces, if it had not been for the timely announcement of a British expeditionary force being sent to save the Turks from the Russian bear. The note of relief in his voice had been unmistakable. The past three years of *The Clarion* showed nothing but a self-satisfied catalogue of good effects stemming from the Poor Laws, the repealed Corn Laws, the Reform Bill, and an even more complacent charting of the prosperity brought by the railways and industry. The English, Hope had declared in the autumn of 1853, were gorged, and sick of their own success; there had been no call to arms since Waterloo; the great British public was bored with peace.

His assistant editor, a man concerned more with honest than dramatic reporting, was sceptical.

'And was it not in these very pages, but three years since for the Great Exhibition in Hyde Park, that you were among the loudest voices in praise of pacifism? Sure, there were plenty to second you, plenty in Parliament too, but are you supposing they'll be keen to change their tune to suit your new one?'

Hope had laughed.

'They are thankful to. Nothing stirs up a nation like the call to arms, and this nation is in danger of drowning in its own self-satisfaction. The bourgeoisie of this country are ripe to be whipped up into a crusading ardour on behalf of the Turks and *The Clarion* shall assist at the rites.'

There had been plenty of material for the campaign. The collapsing Turkish Empire looked like being appropriated by the expansionist Tsar Nicholas I; Hope pointed out frequently in his paper's pages how the Russians craved a port on the

Mediterranean and how disastrous that would be for England's supremacy on the seas. Editorials poured from him roundly declaring that Britain, arm in arm with her new ally in the form of Napoleon III and his avowed intent to defend the Roman Catholics of the Eastern Mediterranean from the contamination of Russian Orthodox Christianity, were honour bound to offer help to the tottering Turkish government. On the day, October 5th, 1853, that the said government actually declared war on Russia, Hope's eloquence knew no restraint.

'May providence protect the Turks and massacre every Russian! May the strong red arm of British soldiery support the weak, and put to flight the unlawful! May the Tsar be shown that he may not again seek to infringe the right to live and worship as free men in a free land, a right every man in the British army would gladly die for!'

It was noted by the assistant editor that *The Times* was profoundly unenthusiastic about the project and he was extremely suspicious that the pro-Turkish Fleet Street faction that took to calling *The Times* 'The Russian Organ of Printing House Square' owed its foundation to his vigorous editor. The feelings of the august rival to *The Clarion* seemed to be shared by the Queen and her consort, but Hope was undaunted. Throughout the winter of 1853 the offices of *The Clarion* virtually silted up with enthusiastic letters from the general public supporting the paper's stand.

'Parliament may be against it, the Queen may not care for it, even our ally may waver, but the British public is behind the Cause for Right to a man!'

The circulation of *The Clarion* increased by fifteen thousand. Its nickname in Fleet Street became 'The War-Monger' and that of its editor, 'The Crusader'. Hope rode high. Damning *The Times* for its faintheartedness, he set out to give *The Clarion*'s readers what they so clearly wanted, a detailed and prompt report of the campaign that would show England to be not only keeper of Europe's conscience, but also an invincible fighting force. His assistant editor pointed out that the same fighting force had had no practice for forty years and thus might be sadly antiquated; but Hope, aglow with fervour, brushed him aside and set out to find a man whose reports would prove him wrong and, at the same time, outshine those sent back from the front by a Mr Russell, war correspondent appointed by *The Times*.

Robert Chiltern was surprised to find himself selected. He was a loudly proclaimed new Tory, a disciple of Peel and a supporter of John Bright, and all his recent contributions to *The Clarion* had in fact been discarded since they were no support to the paper's declared views on the Turkish question. The summons to see Hope he took as a prelude to his dismissal.

He found Hope humming before a roaring fire, the tails of his pepper and salt coat over his arms, his plaid waistcoat ablaze with seals and his moustache fairly bristling with energy. Robert surveyed him with a certain amount of apprehension.

'You are wasting your energies, Chiltern!'

'On the contrary, sir,' Robert said, feeling that as his last days as a journalist were inevitably numbered, he had nothing to lose, 'you waste the fruits of them for me.'

Hope barked approval.

'I can't sanction your views! Indeed I cannot. Do you think I'm to toady to *The Times* by printing the milksop stuff you write for me?'

'It is not merely the opinion of *The Times* that this will be a rotten war fought for a rotten cause.'

'Sit down, Chiltern.'

Robert chose a red leather chair by the great mahogany desk. Hope continued to stand and roast his buttocks, arms akimbo.

'You say it's a rotten cause and it will be a rotten war. I'm bound to disagree with you about the former and I hope to be proved wrong about the latter. What proof I shall obtain, Chiltern, you will provide for me.'

Robert stared.

'Have you met W. H. Russell, Chiltern?'

Robert nodded. He had met him several times, a large, noisy Irishman capable of great eloquence and of drinking extraordinary quantities of other people's brandy. They had been parliamentary reporters together at Westminster and then Russell had gone off to report some bloody little skirmish in Schleswig Holstein and had come home with a wound. He was now bound East with the army.

'I know him, sir.'

'I want reports better than his will be, Chiltern.'

Robert rose from his chair. Because of being so tall, he felt always at more of an advantage when on his feet. Standing, he topped Hope by at least four inches.

'Are you sending me to Constantinople, sir?'

Hope beamed.

'I am indeed. You are *The Clarion*'s war reporter. The British public looks to you to enhance our reputation worldwide, and to prove to them that their faith in England as defender of the weak is more than justified.'

Robert's long, dark face did not lighten.

'I would have thought, sir, that from the quantity of my efforts you have used as tapers, you were not only aware that I oppose this venture but that I am not hypocrite enough to pretend otherwise. Even,' he added sternly, 'for professional advancement.'

The hope of the latter was sweet to him. Success in his profession would serve to show his astounded family that he was not entirely insane to refuse their traditional involvement with the army.

'You are my choice, Chiltern. Take it or leave it. You are easily the most acute reporter I possess, and I would depend upon your professionalism not to let your observations be coloured by your principles.'

'Why am I your choice?'

Hope struck his broad forehead theatrically.

'Good God, man, it would be supposed from your cold, suspicious manner that I were dismissing you from the paper's staff, not offering you the choicest plum for the asking!'

'I am not cold, sir. But I am suspicious. The chance to go to the Eastern Mediterranean is better than anything I have ever hoped for, but I cannot see why I should be chosen. You have destroyed every editorial sentence I have written for the last few months, and you cannot suppose I should be turncoat enough to change my views in gratitude simply.'

'What a prig you are, Robert,' Hope said sadly.

'I hope not.'

The editor crossed to his desk and sat down heavily behind it. He looked discouraged for a moment, then he seemed to make some sort of resolve and his countenance cleared again.

'I'll be frank with you, Robert. The Government doesn't want reporters. I tried to send Lacey, who is a staunch supporter of the whole affair, but his "permission to sail" has been refused and Lord Hardinge returned his letter of introduction without comment.'

'The commander-in-chief of the army?'

'The same. So I am forced to use what connections I can find, and you happen to have what I need. Your family have been cavalrymen for generations and the present colonel of the —th Hussars has been gracious enough to say that in view of your family's long connection with the regiment, you may go with them on the condition that your reporting in no way causes embarrassment or discredit to the regiment or its officers. Because of this official protection, the Government cannot withhold permission for you to go. May I point out, before you honour me with some high-minded refusal, that if you do not go, *The Times* will have the field quite literally to itself?'

Robert, who had remained standing throughout this revelation, now moved to the window and gazed out at the yellow February fog that filled the street outside.

'I shall not refuse, sir. I'll be glad to get out of London to tell the truth. I may even,' he turned and smiled at Hope, 'have a chance to prove that my politics are no heresy.'

Hope bounded up in elation.

'Capital, my dear boy, capital! The gallopers may yet turn you into a plunger like themselves!'

Robert pulled a face.

'Unlikely. I've a low opinion of the cavalry, about as low as their opinion of themselves is high.'

'Is there anything in this world, Chiltern, that you have a high opinion of?'

'Plenty, sir, but I shall not confide in you for fear of being called priggish again. When do I leave?'

Hope came round the desk, rubbing his hands.

'February the twenty-third. Gives you two weeks. The army say they'll see to your accommodation. In fact, I've a fellow to meet you, the regiment's paymaster. Likable fellow, very reliable if a bit on the stiff side – '

'So you did not suppose I would seriously consider refusing?'

'Certainly not! You would have been mad. I knew my luck

in the matter had turned when Colonel Lowe said he would take you on. Russell has had no such luck.'

Robert suppressed a faint smile and moved towards the door.

'Am I going out to report whatever action there is or to score off *The Times*?'

Hope shrugged.

'It is to be desired that the former automatically achieves the latter. I hope you will be civil to the paymaster, Robert, and remember that your ideals are quite foreign to him. He has requested that you call on him in Mount Street, and as they are being so accommodating about taking you, I feel you should go immediately. He is a Captain Drummond, a Captain Edgar Drummond.'

The house in Mount Street wore the dejected half-alive air of all houses which know they are not their owner's principal dwelling. Oakley Park took all the life of the family, Mount Street was merely a convenience. Late afternoon light in February did nothing to enhance the flat grey front of the house, and when the black painted door was opened by a lugubrious manservant and revealed a shadowed hall beyond, Robert held out few hopes of finding Captain Edgar Drummond congenial. The footman led him across the gloomy hall, up a curving staircase carpeted in plum colour and lined with views of Scotland all apparently painted under the most adverse weather conditions, and announced him without enthusiasm at the double doors of a drawing room.

There was a young man in civilian clothes writing at a round table, a slight young man, quietly dressed, with a firm and noble expression. He came forward to greet Robert immediately and led him down the length of the room to a window overlooking the small garden. To Robert's amazement, the window was flanked by two young women.

'May I present my sisters, Mr Chiltern. Both Sarah and Blanche will accompany me to Constantinople.'

Robert looked at the sisters with admiration, and then turned to Captain Drummond.

'Do you intend to take your mother also, Captain Drummond?'

There was a small gasp. Robert looked across at the darker

26

sister and saw that she had shot him a glance of extreme indignation. Edgar Drummond himself had blushed slightly beneath the mild mockery.

'My mother is an invalid, Mr Chiltern. My sisters are to come because we prefer not to be separated and also because this will only be the smallest of skirmishes. We will all be home for Easter.'

Robert looked at the blonde sister but she was gazing away from him out of the window as if he were not in the room. Despite her glance of reproof seconds before, he decided to address the dark one.

'Have you ever been on an – an excursion of this nature before, Miss Drummond?'

'No, Mr Chiltern. I have never been out of England.'

She had a lovely voice, a deep, soft, flexible voice.

'I am told Constantinople is most picturesque, Miss Drummond. Do either you or your sister care to draw?'

His tone was still uncomfortably teasing. Sarah did not reply, but Blanche said, unexpectedly from her reverie, 'I do.'

'My sisters,' Captain Drummond said proudly, 'are accomplished in many ways. They are both extremely musical, their French is quite flawless I am told, and their sketches are often begged for.'

Blanche looked extremely gratified at this tribute but Sarah appeared to feel a twinge of confusion and did not glance in thanks at her brother.

'You are a fortunate man,' Robert Chiltern said.

'I hope, Mr Chiltern, that you will assist me in the protection of my good fortune. It may be that in the course of my duties I shall not always be able to accompany or amuse my sisters, and I shall be most grateful for your help in the matter.'

It was the second time that day that Robert had quelled a smile.

'Forgive me, Captain Drummond, but though my profession may not be as – exalted as your own, I am accompanying your regiment with a job to do. I am not,' he glanced briefly at the sisters, 'a sightseer. I can think of nothing I would prefer to do with my spare time than to spend it in such delightful company, but I cannot promise unlimited leisure to indulge myself.'

The three Drummonds exchanged glances. Robert felt

himself excluded from some private sympathy, as if he had broken a rule he knew nothing of.

'I cannot provide you with a horse,' Edgar Drummond said, as if he had not heard Robert's speech. 'We are a cavalry regiment it is true, but even though Colonel Lowe might sanction your drawing supplies from our stores, I fear a horse cannot be included.'

'I must fend for myself, then. I am most grateful to you for your kindness in allowing me to attach myself to your regiment.'

Sarah said suddenly, 'It might have been your regiment also.'

'Indeed it might, Miss Drummond. It was my father's, but I fear I have disappointed him by choosing the pen rather than the sword.' He stopped and looked at her. She was pleating the silk of her flounced skirt between her fingers in a restless way and her head was bent. 'You feel my decision was an ignoble one, Miss Drummond?'

She shot a look at her brother. 'Yes,' she said.

All three Drummonds now looked earnestly at him evidently expecting him to respond in kind to their standards of honour. Robert, confronted by three remarkably similar pairs of blue eyes in three remarkably dissimilar faces, merely laughed. The sisters looked down again at their silken laps, and their brother, seeing that Robert Chiltern represented yet another of those difficult orders that his nature so loved to subdue itself to and obey, rose and drew him back to the round table where they might discuss practical matters. A horse would not be forthcoming, a tent would not be necessary, a soldier-servant might be allotted at Colonel Lowe's personal discretion. Food the army would provide, pistols and writing materials it could not. Robert was to bring his own bedding and any article he might need for the voyage between Plymouth and Malta, the first port of call. He was to be in Plymouth in ten days.

He retraced his steps down the long room to say good-bye. Blanche smiled and offered her hand, but she looked abstracted still. Sarah's expression he could not fathom, she seemed to look both troubled and reproving.

'I am sorry to fall so far short of your standards, Miss Drummond.'

She bowed very slightly.

'We shall see you in Plymouth, Mr Chiltern.'

We gained a queer regimental mascot today, a war correspondent from *The Clarion*. He came at a very odd time, not at all conventional, just as Blanche and I were about to dress, but Edgar was very civil with him and I think he was grateful though his manner was hard to make out. He is to sail with us on the *Hercules*, all at Edgar's arrangement. Of course, Edgar says he will be very idle for there will be no more than a little skirmishing before the Russians are routed.

I do pray that he is right. I am so ashamed of myself but I do not want to go. If there should be fighting I should feel so useless, so out of place. Edgar assures me that there will be none and that I am always of service to him and in that I must and *shall* take comfort. I do not think Blanche is daunted by such thoughts. She read in the *Military Gazette* that Lord Raglan is sixty-five, and Lord Lucan and Lord Cardigan both over fifty, and she very much fears that the whole army will be of a similar age and that there will be nobody younger to dance with. I wish I could think of dancing.

I wrote to Papa today. I think he could not but be gratified to see Edgar's pleasure in his position and I told him of all the compliments I had heard about Edgar's competence. Five thousand pounds is certainly a considerable sum, but I think many pay more for commissions in cavalry regiments and, after all, Aunt Price did stipulate in her will that her legacy to Edgar was to further him in life. It still astounds me that she left him a single penny. He would think it very wrong of me, but I am firmly of the opinion that she repented of her steady cruelty to him in childhood.

Six more days in London. The splendour of the regiments daily marching through for embarkation is indescribable. I would not have believed there was as much gold lace in the world as I have seen on the jackets. Blanche and I stood on the steps of St Martin's Church today and watched the Coldstream Guards march through Trafalgar Square, and the band played 'Rule Britannia' and we could hardly see for crying. There were poor women and children running desperately beside the column and a wretched pack of scarecrow females behind it weighed down with bundles. They are to go too, I was told, to wash the soldiers' linen. They get a halfpenny a day from each customer and their menfolk earn a shilling. A shilling! It does not seem possible to risk losing your life for a shilling. I dropped a shilling in Hyde Park on Tuesday and because it was coming on to rain I did not trouble to stop and find it. It shames me now.

Tomorrow we are to choose new parasols, for Malta will be hot and Blanche freckles so easily. My new evening mantle is a great pleasure to me, just the deep rich blue of the night sky.

I did not feel comfortable with Mr Chiltern today. I hope he did not observe my confusion.

# *Two*

It is generally accepted that the pen is mightier than the sword; I now have evidence that it is also mightier than the stomach. The whole of our ship is draped with the suffering forms of our gallant soldiers and I am the only one, it seems, able to ride out the storm. I can only suppose that my occupation of writing is proof against sickness by the very demands it makes upon the system. There are no energies left for weakness.

Robert stopped and laid down his pen. He had stowed everything he possessed that was compassable under his bunk since he found the crash of objects careering about his jerking cabin a severe deterrent to concentration. The servant allotted him was too sick to move, which gave Robert the advantage of perfect solitude at least. The ship was disagreeable in the extreme now, there was no incentive to stagger along the heaving decks unless one took a sadistic pleasure in seeing so many so wretched. He yawned, pulled his cravat a little looser and bent to his task once more.

If the men suffer, the horses take an even harder toll. A visit to the stifling heat of the hold, rendered an inferno by the proximity of the boilers, is not for the weak stomached. The horses are tethered in a double row down there in the gloom, loosely secured by canvas slings around the belly which provide no support whatever when the ship plunges in high seas. When I saw them all but yesterday, the majority were mad with terror.

He did not add, for the benefit of the readers of *The Clarion*, that he had almost had to carry a most distraught Miss Drummond from that dreadful place. He had gone down to the hold in the same spirit of inquiry as had driven him into almost every other nook and cranny of the *Hercules* and had observed in the clamour and dimness the unmistakable figure of a lady clinging

31

to the row of wooden mangers that divided the lines of horses. It had transpired to be Miss Drummond. She had come down, unescorted, to bring sugar to the horses she and her sister had brought with them, and had been quite overwhelmed by the panic and chaos and powerful stench of ammonia. She clung, eyes almost closed, her wide plaid skirts littered with straw, ignored by the soldiers who were most desperately preoccupied with their terrified and thrashing charges.

Robert had put his arms about her and virtually carried her out. It was no easy matter, for the ship had bucked and heaved as if it were no more than a toy upon that stormy sea. Conversation was almost impossible, but before he had seen her to the safety of her cabin, Robert had ascertained that she had gone alone because her sister and their maid were both laid low and that her brother was, of course, too much occupied to escort her.

'I beg you will tell him nothing of this escapade, Mr Chiltern. He told us that we should not leave our cabin alone, but I could not sit there hour after hour and I had no idea of how terrible the hold would be.'

He had, of course, promised silence, but was puzzled to know what Captain Drummond could possibly have found to occupy him so intently. His job was surely one that took up but little of his time. Robert sighed. Contemplation of Edgar Drummond's business would get him no further forward in his own.

Our journey will take ten days. We have something under a week left to endure, and I think we will greet Malta as if it were the Gates of Paradise. It is to be hoped that Malta will prove an island of plenty, for it seemed to me that as we left Plymouth in the darkness four nights ago, a considerable quantity of boxes and equipment remained upon the quayside. Perhaps they did not belong to this regiment, perhaps not even to the army, but on the other hand perhaps some may suffer by their absence. On this voyage the men are allotted fourteen inches in width to swing their hammocks, a space which can hardly be called luxurious, and their bedding is one blanket and one military greatcoat if they choose to use it. It seems that after ten days of such cramped accommodation and misery, they must be recompensed by all the care the commissariat can give them.

He stopped again, his thoughts reverting once more to Edgar Drummond. They had in fact met but twice since that brief encounter in Mount Street, once at a luncheon party given by the regiment for its ladies the day before they set sail and once in the mess on the first day out before storms had sent most of the officers tottering to their cabins. At the regimental lunch, Captain Drummond had appeared quite composed, owing, Robert supposed, to the success of the occasion and the perfection of the arrangements. Robert had not known whether in truth he was himself welcome or not and he had spent some time out on the deck of the *Hercules*, watching flowers and wine and hot house fruit being hauled up the sides in baskets and wondering if all these luxurious tributes were for the Misses Drummond. Miss Blanche Drummond certainly seemed in her element. Her strange and fascinating face was to be seen in circle after circle of tight-waisted, moustached and drawling admirers, her fair head like a torch among all that red and gold. Her sister never lacked for escorts either, but Robert saw how often her glance would search about until she had found her brother and reassured herself that he was at ease. Robert wondered if she observed how unremarkable Captain Drummond managed to look among those peacocks of the regiment; he was certainly dressed like them, but his constant preoccupation to do what was correct was death to achieving their air of superb nonchalance. For it was superb. However much Robert felt indignant stirrings within him that these swells with their blue blood and great fortunes should command the army with no more experience than the rawest recruit, he could not but acknowledge the power of their allure.

Blanche Drummond certainly felt that allure, but did Sarah? She did not laugh as much as her sister, although Robert thought he had seen a glimmer or two of private amusement in her face as the young officers shouldered their way into her notice. She seemed remote from them in a way, indeed remote from almost everything that did not affect her brother or sister. She seemed to look for guidance from the one and to regard both with a protective passion.

Robert flung his pen down and stretched. Heaving or not, he must try the deck and a little air. He stood and re-tied his cravat, exchanged his slippers for boots, his smoking jacket for a greatcoat and weighted his papers with his mahogany writing case. Ships, he reflected, as he stepped stoopingly outside, were not constructed for the convenience of men over six foot.

Once outside in the raw grey light, it struck him that it would be pleasurable to oblige Captain Drummond by entertaining his sisters. He would go to their cabin and invite them to walk with him upon the deck, and they might cling to him most delightfully for safety. He made his way towards the foredeck, stepping carefully among the drooping forms of seasick soldiers as he went, and knocked smartly. There was no reply. Convinced that they could be nowhere else on such seas but safely within their cabin, he rapped again. A voice spoke this time, but faintly. Robert opened the door and stepped in.

Blanche was alone in the cabin. She lay in bed, as white as the confusion of sheets and nightclothes in that narrow space, and surveyed him without expression from dark-circled eyes. Robert made instantly as if to go. There was no one else in the room, no maid even, and he had entirely forgotten that Sarah had said her sister was unwell. It was unthinkable that he should stay. He put his hand upon the doorknob and said, 'Do forgive me, Miss Drummond. I had no idea – I had entirely forgotten that you – I am so sorry to find you unwell.'

Blanche thought that he did not sound it. She said nothing but continued to stare at him with her empty gaze.

'Is there anything I can do for you?'

She felt determined suddenly to punish him for the reluctance of his tone. She pointed to some billowing heaps of material, dresses which had slipped from their pegs on the swaying walls. 'You might pick those up.'

Gingerly he bent to retrieve the armfuls of silk, uncertain what next to do with them, holding up first a sleeve, next a flounce as he sought some guidance as to how to hang them. Blanche surveyed him unblinkingly, and when at long last he managed to attach the dresses somehow to their moorings she flung herself over on her side, presenting him with her back adorned in crumpled white pintucking and a tangle of damp pale hair. The sight was both intimate and disturbing. With her face to the wall, Blanche said, 'Sarah is walking on the deck. It is hardly kind to leave me so long.'

Robert reached again for the door handle.

'Allow me,' he said in some relief, 'to fetch her for you.'

Sarah had walked for ten minutes or so, enjoying the difficulty
of doing so on the slanting deck, and the wild pale sky above
her. There were gulls following the *Hercules*, and she could
hear their screams above the wind. Holding the rail with one
hand and her shawl with the other, she crept along the slippery
surface while the wind whipped her bonnet ribbons across her
face.

A hand plucked suddenly at her skirt. Sarah looked down.
There was a woman down there, crouching in the shadows,
bundled up in a tattered shawl, a hard-faced woman, her
appearance raw with poverty. Sarah shrank back.

'Help me, lady!'

Sarah looked about her helplessly. There were a few sailors
busy at the end of the deck, but she was as alarmed at the
thought of contact with them as she was with this collection of
rags at her feet.

'What – what do you want?'

The woman crept an inch or two forward.

'Hide me, lady!'

Sarah gasped.

'Hide you!'

'I shouldn't be 'ere. I crep' on at Plymouth when the officer
weren't lookin'. There were a ballot to see who'd come. Only
eight to come, lady, eight wives for the whole regiment. I crep'
on. My man's with the regiment. Evans, 'e is. What 'ud I do
at 'ome wi'out 'im? Like to starve, I am. Hide me, lady, and
I'll serve you. Truth I will.'

'I cannot –' Sarah began desperately.

'I'm beggin' you, lady. I won't touch a drop till we lands – '

There was a steady step on the deck and the woman melted
back into the shadows. Sarah stood in perfect indecision for a
moment, and then her arm was taken and Robert Chiltern's
voice asked her what she was doing, unescorted on a troopship
for the second time in two days.

'There is a woman down there, a ragged woman, who has
hidden herself on the ship to be with her husband. She says the

army would not let her accompany him so she has stolen on board. She asked me to help her.'

She spoke rapidly, looking down all the time, but the arm he had drawn within his was shaking.

'And shall you?'

'I – I do not think that I can.' She wanted to say that the woman was dirty and malodorous and that Edgar would never countenance such unofficial charity but found she could not utter these things.

'There are several army wives on this ship,' Robert Chiltern said. 'They are battened down like cattle and one is expecting a child shortly. The army makes no provision for them.'

Sarah thought of those weeping running figures in Trafalgar Square, the women and children scattering beside the marching columns.

'I cannot help her. I do not know how.'

'Should you like to?'

'I should like to – know how. I should like to know what to do.'

'She is one of thousands, Miss Drummond.'

Sarah took a step or two away from the dark corner where the woman still crouched.

'Shall you write about her?'

'I have.'

'Did – did you blame anybody?' She seemed to speak with difficulty.

'No one in particular.'

'I will ask my brother to intercede for her, Mr Chiltern. I cannot – do anything myself. I must do what he thinks best.'

He conducted her back to her cabin in silence. At the door they met her brother who wore a harassed look and did not seem pleased either to see Sarah and Robert together, or Blanche alone, even for a quarter of an hour. Robert surrendered his charge and had turned away before he could see the pleading, almost yearning glance she gave him.

In Malta, the wife of Trooper Evans, who had been discovered hiding on the foredeck of the *Hercules*, was almost sent home. The allotment of wives for the regiment was not to be exceeded, but through some intercession by an unnamed person, Colonel

36

Lowe was prevailed upon to relent and allow her to remain under oath of good and useful conduct. It was also discovered that Malta was a rocky and unproductive place and could not supply the deficiencies in the army's stores. There appeared to be insufficient fodder for the officers' horses among the regiment, the consignment of coals had been left behind, and the troops, unwarmed, were to spend the first few nights on Maltese soil under canvas in driving March rain. Reports of all this appeared, to the writer's surprise, almost unedited in *The Clarion* and the only letter he received from the editor, far from chastising him as he had anticipated, merely congratulated him on his efforts thus far and requested sufficient further material to fill a daily column.

Tonight we are moored off a place called Scutari. Tomorrow we land. I could wish it was Constantinople we were going to for it looks enchanting, a magic prospect of domes and minarets, painted houses and balconies, all entwined with flowers and creepers. Blanche sat on the deck all afternoon to sketch it and the competition to sharpen her pencils was keen. Edgar says we may go on a tour to visit it, but we must wait until he has a proper escort for us.

Edgar seems much preoccupied. It appears the French got here before us and all the best billets are taken, and there is terrible difficulty in finding quarters for everyone. It is like Malta all over again except that the weather is fine and warm. Blanche and I are to stay on board, he says, which I am not happy about. I begin to feel out of place here, a trouble and a nuisance, and I do not want to be allotted a special category, better than that of the men who must do the work. I confided this feeling to Mr Chiltern who laughed and said there was nothing I could do but washing and he had little confidence that I should know how to do that; sadly he is quite right. I repeated my wish to Edgar, and Mr Chiltern's reply, and he looked most astonished at me and said I must remember Mr Chiltern is only a journalist.

I suppose we must buy ponies since our poor horses died at sea, for even if we were only to be here a matter of weeks, we cannot stay on board the whole time. In any case, I should like to explore, for although it was dusk when we moored, I could see just enough to judge that Scutari is most picturesque, crowned with a magnificent barrack building. All in short promises extremely well except for a most disagreeable smell in the air whose source I cannot trace in the darkness.

Mr Chiltern went ashore the moment we dropped anchor, and is not returned. I have not seen him without his notebook since we landed in Malta and it seems he knows huge numbers of the men by name. Being with him is like being with someone who constantly turns up great stones on damp ground revealing shocking, unpleasant, hidden things but also sometimes things of great beauty. I should never have seen so much in Malta without him, nor learned so much of its history, nor should I begin to understand the life of the common soldier so clearly. I begin to think that the officers do not see them as people at all.

There is to be a ball in Constantinople, and Blanche and I are to be presented to Lord Raglan, Lord Lucan and Lord Cardigan. The British ambassador is to give the ball and all the officers of all the cavalry regiments are to attend, with their ladies. It will be fascinating to see company other than our tight little group on this ship, and it will divert my thoughts which will not cheer themselves up whatever I do to aid them.

It is past midnight and Blanche is already sleeping. Captain Blane has brought a French chef with him and a quantity of supplies from Fortnum and Mason and tonight we dined with him. It was inexpressibly delicious after food that has become too dull to be bothered with. I wore the pale green silk trimmed with lily of the valley, and lilies of the valley in my hair, and Blanche wore cream with roses. She looked so happy, as happy as she always is when things are pleasant and easy. She is smiling even now, in her sleep.

I can see little lights burning in Scutari. I wonder if Mr Chiltern has found himself lodgings? He had to in Malta for there was no tent for him. I wish he and Edgar could look more warmly upon each other, but I fear poor Edgar has no time to spend upon other people, he is so desperately busy about his arrangements. I hope he will let me go ashore with him tomorrow while he helps in searching out billets for the officers.

# Three

There was nothing pleasant about Scutari after that first heady glimpse in the dusk. Edgar took much persuading to allow his sisters ashore, once he had taken his own first horrified glance at the place, but eventually agreed that they might look at it if heavily escorted. Immediately a group of young officers presented themselves and their horses at the Misses Drummonds' service and a boat was lowered to row them ashore.

If Sarah had wondered what the smell was, in the air, that first evening off Scutari, she could be no longer in doubt. The harbour at Scutari was filled with the most revolting refuse imaginable, much of it blown across the Bosphorus from Constantinople, which choked the still water and rendered the air almost unbreathable. Stifling gasps into their handkerchiefs, Blanche and Sarah bowed forward as the boat lurched among the drifting rubbish, staring fixedly at their own laps. The *Hercules* had been bad enough during the storm in the Bay of Biscay but this was abominable, impossible.

The boat ground at last into the beach, where gaunt and hideous dogs prowled among the debris. Sarah was swung up unceremoniously into a sailor's arms and carried ashore to a waiting pony; she could hear Blanche laughing behind her as she received the same service. They rode up the littered beach, watched admiringly by lounging Turks, many of whom pressed closely enough to the girls to touch the hem of their habits; and it became increasingly and unpleasantly evident that Scutari belied its pretty appearance from the sea in every way. The houses that looked like whitewashed sugar knobs from a distance were low, windowless, poorly built and filthy; the streets were rutted and pitted and strewn with the carcasses of rats; oily water ran down open ditches or gathered in sinister puddles here and there and the smell which hovered over the harbour persisted after them.

Sarah looked over her shoulder. Blanche was staunchly look-ing down at her horse's neck, her face very white. Sarah drew rein and fell back beside her sister. She knew what had hap-pened, that Blanche had taken one appalled look at the rotting squalor round her and had decided not under any circum-stances to risk a second.

'Do you wish to go back?' she whispered.

Blanche nodded.

'I did not know it would look like this. It looked so pretty from the sea. Do you think Edgar would let us go to Con-stantinople instead?'

Sarah considered.

'I doubt it would be any better.'

'It must,' Blanche said desperately, 'it *must*.'

They were now almost at the walls of the old Turkish bar-racks, a vast and splendid building constructed in a huge hollow square, solid and magnificent and now swarming with the red coats of the British Army. Sarah looked up at it with an expres-sion of genuine admiration.

'Do look up, Blanche, do! It is a most handsome building, indeed it is!'

'Then it is a sham, Miss Drummond.'

A voice spoke at her knee. She looked down and saw Robert Chiltern there in the dust, dishevelled and weary, his forage cap in his hand, and a day's dark growth on his chin.

'I've spent the last three nights there, Miss Drummond.'

'Was – was there no other lodging?'

'I did not look for it. I went to see what the men must endure, and a more filthy, verminous, decaying hell of a place I cannot imagine. If you can believe such utter folly, this rat-infested plague pit is to be used for the British hospital!'

Sarah glanced from his exhausted face to the yellow walls towering so impressively above her.

'Hospital?' she said stupidly.

'Yes, hospital, Miss Drummond. I have discovered that our splendid army of thirty thousand men has but one thousand rolls each of lint, adhesive plaster and tow and a couple of hundred old sheets, and these truly impressive supplies are to be used in this crumbling insanitary ruin. Let us fervently hope we have little need of them.'

'But – but my brother says there will be no fighting worth speaking of, that we shall be home by Easter – '

Robert said gently, 'Miss Drummond, Easter is now three weeks past.'

Sarah's face clouded with confusion. She turned away from Robert Chiltern and seemed to be looking keenly about her for someone.

'Your sister is safe with her escort, Miss Drummond. Entirely surrounded one might say.'

Sarah turned back to him. She said rather hurriedly, 'Perhaps I should persuade my brother that we should find lodgings on shore.'

Robert's expression became more gentle. He laid his hand on her mount's neck.

'No. No, my dear Miss Drummond. I promise you that it would achieve nothing but your own misery. Every dwelling in this horribly uncomfortable place is entirely infested with vermin. I heard of one intrepid lady only today who sleeps in a ring of lighted candles as the only way to defend herself. I am myself as covered with fleabites as if I had the measles.'

'And the men too?'

'I am pure and wholesome compared to the men, but no doubt I shall acquire my fair share of lice in due course. I have, as you see, the distinct advantage of comfortable clothes and am not half choked by a leather stock as they are in this heat. You, I may say, look like a vision from heaven after what I have been gazing upon.'

She smiled down at him delightedly.

'Shall you come back to the ship, Mr Chiltern?'

He shook his head.

'Regrettably, no. I would be too far away from things. I have found myself a hovel on the shore and an old hag to serve me brown rice and eggs and the sourest wine in the world. Don't drink any water, Miss Drummond, that hasn't been boiled. I must bid you farewell. The sight of you has done me immeasurable good and I look forward to its benign influence again in the near future.'

He took a step away into an idly curious group of Turks in bright pantaloons. Sarah leaned forward and said with a note of eagerness in her voice, 'Shall you come to the ball? The

British ambassador is to give one and we are all to go. His house is said to be as splendid as a palace. Shall you come?'

He smiled and waved at her.

'Certainly I shall. I'm not one to miss the chance of a fight between our cavalry lords. May I extract the promise of a dance here and now?'

Sarah laughed. It seemed so absurd to be asked for a dance here, on a pony in a swarm of flies and Turkish peasants, absurd but so reassuring.

'Of course,' she said. She looked around and saw that Blanche was staring coldly past her at Robert Chiltern. She turned quickly in surprise to see what Robert himself had made of such animosity, but he had not seen it, had not even noticed, but was striding away through the crowd.

They did not go to Scutari again. Blanche confided to Edgar what a shockingly horrid place it was, and he had seemed to find her reaction entirely suitable.

'I do not see why you should wish to go again, my dear Sarah. It only provides the most unfitting sights and I cannot think what is to be gained from going again.'

'But it is so stifling to remain upon the ship, Edgar! Scutari may be disagreeable but it is interesting, very interesting, and I would so much rather have the discomfort of being somewhere unpleasant and stimulating than somewhere pleasant and dull!'

Edgar glanced at her anxiously. He had come to feel a grave unease about the principles of Robert Chiltern, but had supposed, since Chiltern was a gentleman, that he would naturally refrain from any attempt to influence the ladies with his liberal notions. Edgar had at first been profoundly grateful for Chiltern's presence, for during that nightmare voyage when so many of the regiment's essentials appeared not to have accompanied it, he had had no time to spare for his sisters. They had – or at least Sarah had – seemed to like Chiltern and one could not complain of his manner to them or his appearance. But there were elements in him that made Edgar uneasy, radical elements that he clearly made no attempt to hide. Though she had not named him, Edgar was sure Chiltern had been behind Sarah's curious and uncharacteristic request for clemency to be shown to a female stowaway, and in Malta she had spent an almost unseemly amount of time with Chiltern and imbibed while with him a very peculiar, to Edgar's view, version of the siege of Malta. As the English had hardly been involved it was not, to Edgar's mind, a particularly significant episode, but Sarah, inspired by Robert Chiltern, claimed that Europe owed its autonomy to the siege, quite as much as it did to Trafalgar or Waterloo. Edgar had attempted to explain that England's supremacy was an unquestionable and essential fact, but Sarah, usually all desire to please, had suggested that it might be to England's advantage to consider herself indebted in some measure to other countries for her continued freedom and Edgar was certain such an extraordinary view could not be her own.

Now she was wanting to see Turkish life at close quarters, and was claiming that life on the ship, which was as near a resemblance to home life as Edgar could arrange in such cramped circumstances, bored her. Sarah had never complained of dullness before, he had always relied upon her as a model of self-sufficiency. Blanche was another matter of course, and had been so from childhood, always needing amusement and society, but Sarah had never so much as hinted that her life was monotonous.

'May we not go to Constantinople, then?' she asked. 'I am sure that – that some of the officers would take us if you are too much occupied.'

Edgar fussed a little. Men who had been to Constantinople reported that like Scutari, its fairy-tale appearance from a distance belied its reality enormously. The streets were pitted, narrow and filthy, and the Turks had a disconcerting habit of peering with intense interest at any European woman who walked in their midst, so intriguingly barefaced and slender by comparison with the veiled opulence of their own women. It was also unbearably noisy, hot and foul-smelling, and only to be approached across a harbour many times as disgusting as that at Scutari.

'I hardly think you will like it, Sarah. From what I hear it is by no means a salubrious place and bears no relation to anything familiar to you –'

'That is why I want to go!' Sarah cried. 'What is the point of our being here if we are to remain like birds in a cage? We might just as well have stayed at home!'

Edgar felt it would undermine his position of authority to admit that he had had no notion of the squalor of Turkish life himself.

'I am very sorry you are so – so weary of your own company. I brought you with me because I believed that the three of us are always best contented together, but I am sorry if our shared life is no longer enough for you.'

Sarah looked instantly contrite. She put her arms about her brother's neck and kissed him warmly, and said there was no company on earth she would prefer to his and Blanche's and that not for all the world would she have stayed behind. Blanche watched, as she had watched the whole conversation, in silence.

When Edgar had gone, the visit to Constantinople tacitly shelved, Sarah turned to her sister.

'Blanche, are you not chafing at being ever and always on this ship? Do you not long for something to do? I hear that Lady Erroll who has come with the Rifle Brigade is living with her husband in a green marquee put up in the camp on the shore. Would you not much prefer to be there and in the midst of things?'

'No,' Blanche said vehemently, 'a thousand times no. I hate it here, Sarah, I wish to God we had never come. I never saw anything so dirty or terrible as that place on the shore. I never want to go there again, never. You can arrange what outings you like, but I shan't come, I shan't. I want to go home, Sarah, I want to go back to Oakley, where things are safe and pleasant. Would you come with me if I went home, for I could not go alone?'

'And leave Edgar?' Sarah sounded horrified. 'We have never been apart except when he was at school, not once! We cannot leave him now!'

'Why not?' Blanche demanded.

'He needs us. His job is not always easy and he needs us to ease him.'

Blanche seemed close to tears.

'Do you think he suffers as much as I do? Why should I stay in this horrible place? Why should I waste even a few months of my life? I would do anything for Edgar, you know I would, but what point is there in such sacrifice when he is as preoccupied as he has been lately?'

Sarah came and knelt by her sister in the small space left between her chair and the cabin wall.

'Do you not see, Blanche, how much he would be shaken if we were to go? It would quite rock him, I know it would. To a certain extent I share your feelings, but although I agree the place is not the most desirable, it does fascinate me too. What I hate is to feel so useless. Everyone here has an occupation, even those poor women who follow the army can cook and wash for the soldiers, but we can do nothing at all. The only duty we have to perform is to support Edgar as best we can so that he may do his job as best *he* can. And we must do it, Blanche, we must help him. I have not helped him by being so complaining, but I repent of that and I will not complain again. You must help him by not seeming to blame him for being here, and if we both suppress our dislikes, I feel sure we shall be happier for it and more help to him.'

Blanche sighed and said indistinctly, 'I will try. If you will not come with me, I cannot go alone, so I will try to bear it.'

Sarah kissed her and said no more. Instead she called their maid and asked her to bring out their ball gowns. They would, she declared, decide if any re-trimming were necessary before the ambassador's ball.

# *Four*

On the night of the ball in May, they did not leave the *Hercules* until after dark. The ship, in company with several others carrying cavalry officers, had steamed slowly towards Constantinople during the day and Sarah, denied a visit still by Edgar, had strained her eyes from the foredeck to see the leprous reality of the city. She had stayed there until dusk, watching the storks flap lazily over the towers and minarets in the apple-green sky of twilight, and lamps light up like jewels among the darkening buildings, and had managed to make Edgar feel that he had been needlessly overbearing.

They were taken inshore by small Turkish caiques, each with a lantern swinging at the prow and rowed by garlic-scented sailors who made Blanche bury her nose in a bunch of rosebuds and myrtle. They had a caique each, to allow for the vastness of their skirts, and an escort of officers, marvellous in blue and gold, and scarlet overalls so tight that fellow officers doubted they could sit down. Edgar accompanied Blanche, it being understood that her need for protection and moral support was greater than Sarah's.

'I had hoped Mr Chiltern might escort you, Sarah.'

Edgar heard her catch her breath.

'Oh, is he coming? Did he remember? I wonder that he has not been back to see us, not once. I hope he is being properly cared for, properly fed – '

'Mr Chiltern is well able to take care of himself, Sarah. It would benefit everyone a good deal if he were to think of taking care of others upon occasion as well.'

'He has much to think of!' Sarah said, and her voice was thick with indignation.

Edgar maintained a reproving silence as a reply to this foolishness.

There were sedan chairs waiting for them on the shore, to

Blanche's delight. Antique, still bearing faint memories of the painted wreaths and flowers they once bore, Edgar had found them at the house of a French nobleman living in Constantinople who had been delighted to lend them for such delicate use. Their skirts were compressed inside with difficulty, the doors were shut against the smells of the city, and they were borne away between a double column of cheering officers, swords on their hips, nosegays in their hands.

A cobalt blue dusk hung over the city. They were carried from the quayside, littered with coarse nets of oranges and baskets of fish, bundles of humanity wrapped in black and sailors barelegged and baggy-breeched among the slime and debris of the wharf, up innumerable alleys as stifling as tunnels. The cobbles of these dark passages must have been slippery and evil from the sudden jolts and starts of the chair bearers, and it seemed to Sarah and Blanche that they were struggling uphill, climbing away from that filthy shore and filthier sea. Red-lit doorways swung past, giving glimpses of shadowy interiors and fires, and moustached faces under felt Turkish caps pressed themselves like grinning moths to the windows of the chairs.

After ten minutes or so of this alarming and mysterious progress, the chair bearers swung right, away from the black and red of the alleys and into a thoroughfare altogether more familiar and comforting. Night had not fallen so thickly that it was not possible to make out a wide white dust road and the recognizable pointed leaves of oleander in great dark clumps on either side. Every so often a gateway, part Oriental, part European in design, with lamps and sentries and a gravelled drive, gave glimpses of a lit house below and beyond it the pale reflecting glitter of the Bosphorus.

Cautiously Sarah lowered a window. Damp evening air surged in, salty and spicy and warmer than England could ever be until high summer. There was a light wind blowing, rustling the shrubs by the road and sending up little aromatic puffs of dust. The houses they passed behind were becoming more and more magnificent, seeming to be, silhouetted as they were against the gleaming water, like perforated palaces of paper and lace. In daylight they would reveal themselves to be of wonderfully carved and fretted wood, stained deep red and hung with shutters and balconies, but at night, illumined by a thousand oil lamps, they were as insubstantial as the turreted castles of fairyland.

Forgetful of the chair bearers, Sarah craned out in her excitement, tilting the sedan severely. The air became thick and sweet with the scent of orange blossom and a gateway of cream stone gigantic enough to be worthy of an emperor and flickering with leaping flares in iron brackets, blocked the roadway. There were guards here too, resplendent in livery, and the soft dust of the roadway gave place to a paving of smooth slabs. Encouraged by their journey's end being almost in sight, the chair bearers quickened their pace and almost trotted down the great avenue lined with fragrant shrubs to the lights and music that awaited them on the water's edge.

The embassy was very wonderful, indeed almost a palace. The ambassador was a man of enormous influence who had a passion for grandeur, and his vast house, lit with thousands of lanterns and set among a veritable forest of roses and myrtles, seemed like a dwelling of another planet after the cabin on the *Hercules*. They walked down long white corridors ablaze with lamps and hung with flowers into a drawing room festooned with garlands and echoing softly to the music of a regimental band. Sarah looked sideways at Blanche and saw her whole being illumined with pleasure and relief. She touched her arm and Blanche turned upon her eyes full of delight.

'Oh, Sarah, Sarah, it is like coming home!'

The dresses were fabulous, the jewels and uniforms unbelievable. Robert had told her somewhat sardonically that this was the best dressed army England had ever mustered. Seeing it now in all its splendour one could not doubt it.

The national anthem began, and the voices in the room died to whispers, then to silence. Between the rows of coloured silk and scarlet cloth, diamonds and gold braid, flower-woven curls and plumed moustaches stalked the ambassador and his lady, his daughters, Lord Raglan, and the two commanders of the cavalry, both tall, both magnificent and both quite evidently furious to be together. They moved down the huge room stiffly, gazing immovably before them, and Edgar, recalling his boyhood infatuation for Lord Cardigan, felt a mingled twist of shame for that feeling, and undying admiration for authority and aristocratic splendour. He knew now all Lord Cardigan's violent and dangerous career, the cavalry was full of it, but for all that, he watched the striding figure in its cherry-coloured overalls and felt himself consumed by excitement and envy. He turned to speak to Sarah in order to hide his confusion at his own feelings, and as his eyes swung round they caught, very briefly, the amused gaze of Robert Chiltern from across the room.

Sarah and Blanche were presented to Lord Raglan. It was an impressive moment. He had known their grandfather, had been present at Waterloo when he had fallen, had heard the Duke of Wellington commend him as one of the most gallant officers his regiment had ever possessed. He told them of all this, holding a hand of each, overwhelming them with his manner and his charm. He looked long at Sarah.

'You remind me of him, my dear. Very strongly. Very strongly indeed. You have the same decided look.'

Still holding their hands, he turned to Edgar.

'And when we leave the Bosphorus and sail up the Black Sea to Varna, so as to be closer to the Russian army, what shall you do then with these charming charges?'

'Varna!' If Blanche had said Hades, she could not have said it with more horror.

'Indeed yes, Varna. A most delightful and pretty place. A valley full of birds and butterflies. Should you not like to see it?'

'Are you – are you giving us permission to go with the army?' Sarah said clumsily, seeming to forget courtesy in her eagerness. 'Are you saying we may go?'

Lord Raglan bent towards them, smiling.

'We must not tell our cavalry lords, for they do not think women are fitting for the army. But if it is your wish to go, I would not oppose that wish.'

Blanche opened her mouth to protest that the last thing on earth she wished to do was to follow the army any deeper into this loathsome country, but she was startled to feel Sarah's slippered foot come with surprising force upon her ankle.

'You have an objection, my dear?'

Sarah's foot struck again.

'No, my lord, not at all. My sister is like myself, astonished at your goodness. We – we do not like to be separated from our brother and would be deeply unhappy to be sent home without him.'

Lord Raglan considered Edgar gravely. Why, with his grandfather's reputation for gallantry, he should be merely paymaster in his regiment was surprise enough, but this display of sibling devotion among the Drummonds, though touching, was a further puzzle. Both girls were charming to look at, the blonde one had a curious but memorable face, and the darker one seemed a girl of decision and spirit, but Edgar himself, slight, anxious-looking and restrained, seemed not at all the type of brother to rouse passionate fondness in any sister. A member of his staff touched his arm.

'You have done us all a great favour, my lord, by your permission to Captain Drummond to take his sisters to Varna.'

Lord Raglan beamed upon them both.

'I have?'

'Indeed yes. They have been kept prisoner on the *Hercules* by their jealous brother, sir, and the army has thus been deprived of the two fairest sights upon the Bosphorus.'

Lord Raglan held up a warning finger to Edgar.

'Ah, dear boy, most unwise. I am sure your sisters possess the most excellent sense, and you will kill them with dullness if you do not allow them some freedom. Mind you,' he said, turning his gaze back to Sarah and Blanche, 'you were best on the ship, my dears, much best. My quarters at Scutari are furiously hot and most unpleasant. I have had to take to working in my bedroom to be further from the stench of the water. Now you must dance, indeed you shall. My own dancing days are gone, but there are plenty to supply my want of agility.'

Sarah saw, out of the tail of her eye, Lord Cardigan swoop down upon Blanche like an eagle and carry her irresistibly off. Blanche's face shone with pleasure, her eyes seemed bluer, her hair paler.

'I hope promises made in unconventional circumstances are still to be honoured, Miss Drummond?'

Robert Chiltern was at her elbow, in the uniform of the Rifle Brigade.

'Mr Chiltern!'

'In sheep's clothing, you see, lent by a kindly captain since

51

my clothes are hardly suitable now for society. Will you still dance?'

There were cries of outrage all round. What, dance with a civilian, a mere scribbler, when the choice among those glittering swells was so infinite? Sarah smiled, and put her hand into Robert's and was led away.

'You are in a sought-after minority, Miss Drummond. Perhaps four hundred officers and not above fifty women, most of whom are hardly of dancing or flirting age. I am most relieved to see you. I had begun to think you were mewed up in that ship for life.'

Couples were beginning to form up for a quadrille. Robert swung her round to face him across the set.

'I – I felt a little like a hermit,' she confessed reluctantly.

'To do your brother justice,' Robert said with quick inference, 'there is little to do in Scutari but shoot rats and squash lice, but did you know we are to move?'

'Oh yes! Lord Raglan has just said we may go with the regiment.'

Robert looked across the room with amusement at a very golden head in a crowd of Highlanders.

'Don't tell Mrs Duberly, Miss Drummond. The pride of the 8th Hussars has just been told she may not go. Lord Lucan won't have it. I feel, however, she may well be a match for him.'

'I did not know there were any other ladies with the cavalry?'

The fiddles struck up. Robert bowed.

'Very few. You are a select band and I hereby appoint you queen of it.' He moved across the set and took her hand. 'I wish to talk to you as well as dance with you. Will you spare the time between compliments?'

Lord Cardigan and Blanche moved down the set between them, Blanche smiling radiantly, Lord Cardigan magnificent and smelling strongly of wine.

When they had gone and Robert moved to her side again, Sarah said, 'Oh yes. Yes, indeed. Yes, I shall be delighted.'

The moment the quadrille was over, Sarah was captured. To her surprise her captor was a Frenchman, who had outmanoeuvred his English counterparts with guile and speed, and who separated her so swiftly from the crowd that she had not even time to make a place or time of assignment with Robert.

'Henri de la Haye, mademoiselle.'

She held out her hand to him, still a little breathless from the dance.

'I do not recognize your uniform, Monsieur de la Haye.'

'Ah! You would not, it is so strange. I command the Zouaves from North Africa, mademoiselle, and it is intended that you find my uniform both picturesque and graceful.'

'But hardly practical,' Sarah said tartly.

He wore an open jacket of blue and red, wide breeches held up by a broad sash and tucked into kneeboots of embroidered leather. He grimaced at her remark.

'Are you not a romantic, mademoiselle?'

'I have hardly had the chance.'

'I must regard that as a challenge! I am a romantic, mademoiselle, through and through! Why else should I abandon a most comfortable life in Paris to attach myself to this regiment of brigands if it is not for the romance of the thing? But tell me,' he drew a little nearer in confidence, 'is that charming blonde in eau-de-nil your sister?'

'Yes.'

'Do you not think it a great shame that one so young and charming should dance with a man, however gallant, who is old enough to have sired her?'

'No,' said Sarah, 'and if you kidnapped me merely to insinuate yourself into an introduction to my sister, you are wasting your time.'

'Are all the beautiful ladies of England so severe?'

'Yes,' said Sarah, 'every one.'

Henri de la Haye looked at her delightedly.

'The English are a challenge, are they not? Come now, forgive me just a little and present me to your sister.'

Sarah did not return his smile. She moved towards the drawing-room door, saying as she did so, 'You may present yourself if you wish,' and then she escaped into the wide, white passage beyond. He made no attempt to follow her, and when she was retrieved by a major of the Lancers and brought back to the dance floor, Lord Cardigan had found Mrs Duberly it seemed, and Blanche was on the arm of Henri de la Haye.

53

At supper, Robert found her again. She was seated in an arbour, a niche decorated with swags of ribbons and roses, and as heavily escorted as she had been all evening. Beside her was Colonel Lowe, Edgar's commanding officer, a man of fifty who had distinguished himself in the service of the Nizam of Hyderabad and had later served for eight dangerous years on the North West frontier. He was lean and brown, his face lightly crossed with a hundred lines, and he was relating a story to her about a maverick elephant in the Nizam's army. Sarah was laughing and eating an ice.

'I'm come to ravish you away for the second time in one evening.'

Sarah was loudly advised not to go with him. What could he possibly offer that they could not outshine immediately? Damned if they knew why the fellow had been asked in the first place.

'Family connections,' Robert said airily, holding his hand out to her.

He found a secluded seat on a terrace with a view of the water. There was no doubt that both the city and the Bosphorus were at their best under pall of darkness, the decay blotted out and only the lights glittering in the velvety blackness. Before she seated herself where he indicated, Robert saw Sarah look quickly and covertly round for Edgar. He was not to be seen.

'Your brother is supping with a covey of fellow officers, Miss Drummond.'

Sarah blushed in the dimness.

'I hope you feel you can talk to me without first gaining his permission?'

She said indignantly, 'Of course! Indeed I may! You have quite a mistaken view of him!'

'Perhaps.'

She said stiffly, 'He is ever mindful of our safety and happiness, that is all. He has been our guardian since we were small, he has always looked to us.'

Robert said nothing. He did not wish to tease her any more and he wanted a moment to elapse in silence to make a change of mood possible. When at last he spoke, his mocking tone was quite gone.

'I do not in the least wish to offend you or your feelings for your brother. But I see in you something that makes me wish to speak to you quite openly and I cannot be frank if I must be constrained by mere social delicacy.'

'Of course,' she said, her voice loud with relief, 'I quite understand.'

He touched her hand lightly and smiled.

'I will believe you. I have a view of life, Miss Drummond, very different to your brother's and I would like very much to feel that you might consider it, since I believe, having seen a little of your actions, and reactions, that the adoption of it, at least in part, might be to your much greater happiness.'

'Oh, but I am happy, I am very happy indeed!'

'Are you?'

'Oh yes!'

'Confined on a ship, unable to put the smallest scheme into being, unable to help others or occupy yourself, are you happy?'

It was her turn to remain silent.

'You see,' he said, leaning towards her, 'as I see it, the progressive world, our world, is necessarily divided into two classes – those who take and use and enjoy the best of what there is, and those who wish for something better and try to create it. Your brother belongs to the former class, I to the latter. We need each other to secure the balance of our lives and we must each appreciate that. I do not wish to talk about this theory in general now, for we have not the time, and I hope in the months to come, there may be more time, but I would like to plant in you the seed of an idea about my feelings in one particular. I believe, you see, that things should be better in all areas of our world, in education, in medicine, in universal prosperity, in employment – oh, in so much. But I feel, among all those large issues, that things should also be better for women.'

Sarah's voice was astounded. *'Better!'*

'Better,' he said calmly.

She spread her hands in a gesture of amazement. 'Yes, I see that they should be better for poor forgotten women like Mrs Evans on the ship, the ones begging in Scutari, but better for – for –'

'For you. And your sister. And for all the gently born women who have nothing to do, just as you have had nothing to do for six weeks but sit in your ship and sew.'

'But what else could I do?' she cried.

'That is precisely what I mean. Society will not let you do anything. The class that uses the best of what there is, is a class of men who like women to be idle, dependent, available for amusement. But I see in you little frustrations. I observed you on the way to Malta, in Malta, here. I heard you were almost imprisoned on your ship and I knew you were chafing at your idleness – '

Sarah turned towards him.

'Then why did you not come?'

He shrugged.

'I was not sure that you would welcome me and I knew your brother would not. Never fear, I have not been idle. I would like to see the soldier's lot improved as well as yours and I have been gathering evidence in bushels and despatching it home. But I have thought of you, often, and of how much happier you would be with an occupation.'

'Suggest what I might do! Teach?'

'Ah!' Robert smiled at her. 'Teaching! A perfect example for me. Women all over England entrust their children to governesses to do what they themselves are incapable of doing. But although a governess must have every gift and accomplishment to fulfil that sacred duty, she must not demean the boy she teaches by marrying him! Whereas he *may* marry an ungifted, unaccomplished woman in the hallowed state of prosperous idleness!'

'Then you agree it would be hopeless for me to teach?'

'Far from it. The opposite in fact. If women of your station begin to occupy themselves, in teaching for instance, it will acquire respectability and status and bring thousands of women to satisfaction and happiness. Do you not see how impossible it now is for a woman to use her wits profitably or to gain any moral satisfaction from life whatsoever?'

Sarah said, 'What is it you want me to do? What do you want of me?'

He took her hands in his.

'Nothing, dear Miss Drummond. Please do not look so troubled, I have an irritating habit of crusading and I cannot resist fertile soil. I want nothing of you – at least, nothing yet, and even then, not in this way. No, I simply want you to feel

56

yourself more fulfilled, even if it means gainsaying your brother sometimes. I teased you once that you could do nothing but washing, like the soldiers' wives, but it was only mockery. I want you to insist upon doing what interests you, what absorbs your mind, what makes you feel at the end of a day that it was a day well spent. Now come, enough preaching. Grant me one more quadrille to show me you forgive me for hammering on at you and then I must go back to Scutari and return my borrowed plumes.'

Sarah rose slowly, still looking deeply abstracted.

'Do – do you think it wrong then, if women marry and are entirely guided by their husbands?'

Robert laughed.

'Wrong? Certainly not! But if *you* marry, do your best to choose a husband from the second of my classes, not the first.' He took her hand and drew it within his arm. 'Think, Sarah, of the possibilities of a union where each party was striving to create something better, both for each other and the world. Is that not a splendid prospect?'

The cholera has come. We had heard of it among the French and prayed it would steal no further but three days ago it struck the Light Division and men are dying in their hundreds. It can kill in hours. Edgar has forbidden us to leave the tent. I suppose I must see in that some sort of victory, for he was all for sending us back to the *Hercules* which is moored in Varna harbour, and Blanche pleaded and begged to be taken there, but I *will* not go. I had to fight so hard for a tent in the cavalry lines here so that at least we might be part of camp life and might see and be seen, and I *cannot* give it up. I should have known, I think, that Edgar would not let me help with the sick, even among the officers, but it is well nigh intolerable to sit here in a cloud of flies in my burning canvas cone and hear the groans of pain and misery.

The heat is abominable. I have taken off all my petticoats to Blanche's horror, and am simply in a brown holland gown, a gown tail and linen drawers. She is still dressed for Mount Street, dear girl, though her new plaid is quite worn with use and far too thick for this boiling sun. She is grown so thin, though no less pretty, and I pray and pray that this new demon of resolution in me will let me behave less ruthlessly to her. I cannot seem to stop, I cannot. We had only biscuits and brandy yesterday for dinner, for something yet again has gone wrong with the supplies and there seemed nothing else to be had, and Blanche wept and scolded at me, for Edgar had told her how much more comfortable we should be upon the *Hercules* and I did not feel moved by her tears *one bit*. What is become of me? I used not to be able to bear to see her smile eclipsed, let alone a tear, and here I am like a grim-faced tyrant forcing her to endure what she hates that I may feel some participatory pleasure in what goes on.

I have not seen Robert in four days. My constant fear is that he has fallen ill and is without help. If he does not come to the tent in two more days, I shall go and seek him and Edgar must simply bear my disobedience. He told me he thought the cholera would come, for although this valley is like paradise to look at, it is low and damp and full of noxious mists. He says the soldiers are bored and wretched with the heat, both here and down at Varna, and they drink themselves stupid and eat quantities of ripe fruit and great cucumbers grown in filthy beds and therefore their bodies can have no resistance to infection. The peach brandy and some violent spirit called arrack are dangerously cheap. He says it is terrible to see them senseless in the blazing sun, swarming with flies, and believes it is the sheer monotony of hanging about waiting for a sight of the Russians that makes them behave so madly.

I long for a sight of him. He was so delighted to see us in the camp and so admiring of my efforts to turn our little tent into something resembling comfort. He is formal with Blanche, I wish I could detect more warmth in his manner to her. I know she simply thinks him a boor. She is seated at the flap doorway of our tent now, upon a camp stool, and there are three or four officers there.

I can see M. de la Haye among them. He has been constantly these last few days and always seems to find some pretty thing to bring Blanche, some roses or ribbons or little antique treasure he says he finds in the Varna bazaars. It is quite a ride from the French camp – above nine miles – but he never seems daunted and there is no doubt that he can talk just the kind of nonsense Blanche likes. He is very formal with me but I always feel his formality is masking a good deal of mockery. He calls me *'La belle dame formidable'* and to my despair I always seem to blush when he says it.

It is so much more satisfying to be where everyone else is, though not one hundredth part as satisfying as it would be if only I were allowed to go among those poor wretched sick men. Robert said all the water must be boiled, so I boil great quantities every day on a fire I and our little maid have built outside the tent, and all I wanted to do was take this cleaned water to the sufferers. I promised I would touch them as little as possible, that I would wash the moment I returned, that I would take every possible precaution, but Edgar says no.

Edgar permits us to walk the length of our own line, but only escorted, and no further. It is hardly amusing. The white cones of the tents stretch like tidy mountain peaks as far as you can see, and there is not a tree in sight. The country beyond is beautiful, though, from what we saw as we rode up from

Varna, with plenty of wood and water and meadows hopping with frogs. I saw storks and two green and yellow orioles, quite beautiful, and an eagle and several woodpeckers.

The ants are terrible, huge and red, and the water of the nearby streams is said to be full of leeches and all manner of slimy nastiness, but we have not been allowed there. I personally think the flies are the worst. They seem to have jaws like nutcrackers and bite quite fiercely. Sometimes at night I can hear the poor horses screaming, they are so maddened by them. Edgar says pits have been dug for them and wet bandages have been put across their eyes but the flies still bite and draw blood at every sting. It makes me almost glad to think our poor horses who died at sea have at least not this to endure.

I made a loaf today! We have no table so I had to knead it on the ground and I fear the result will be a mixture of barley and sand and red ants. An officer took it off to a field kitchen to bake and I eagerly await its return. The food is very poor, stringy old chickens mostly, and stale eggs and sour milk. I am grown quite used to it but Blanche still can hardly eat. I try to save her the breast of every bird. Robert showed me a story in his newspaper written in London which describes the comforts of the British Army and how it lives on pâté de foie gras and champagne, which made me quite angry but he merely laughed and told me he had sent the truth home in his reports only a week ago. I wish he would come.

Lord Cardigan himself has come several times to visit Blanche. It makes Edgar tremble when he comes. He is handsome in a proud, angry way and has the longest legs I ever saw – though I believe Robert's are longer – and has sent men out to find the Russians on patrols from which they stagger back more dead than alive. A hundred horses died on one patrol alone and he would not let the men take their greatcoats for the chill nights. Robert told me he does not live in camp but has a beautiful yacht moored in the harbour. Edgar said that was because he suffered from bronchial weakness which made Robert laugh.

I do not think there is a man working harder than Edgar and whenever I feel I could scream with desire to leave the tent, I remember the gratitude with which he comes back to us each night and eats whatever funny thing I have managed to find.

He came here with only enough shirts for a few months since we thought we should be home by April, and I have made a few good shirts out of the pieces of several. There does not seem to be enough of anything and the country yields nothing but these old hens and fruit. I should like to ask Edgar if the commissariat is at fault and did not bring enough, but it does not seem just to question him when he is so tired and busy. Robert looked as if he knew a good deal but glanced at Edgar and would tell me nothing.

The officers seem to be leaving. I shall be glad to stop for my hand aches and in any case I promised Blanche that I would try to mend her cream silk. When she will wear it I cannot conceive, but it seems to comfort her to have it by, even though it must be crushed away to save space. Our little maid manages to sleep in a corner only big enough for a dog and does her best to keep up with our washing and plain sewing.

I wonder how long we will remain here?

# *Five*

Robert Chiltern did not succumb to cholera, but how he escaped, he did not know. He had been allotted a tent down by the horse lines, in disagreeable proximity to the regiment's slaughter house, and past his doorway flowed a stream of unimaginably repulsive refuse. He turned his tent around so that its opening faced in the opposite direction. Lord Cardigan, riding through the camp and observing this minute flaw in the symmetry of the Light Division, ordered it turned back. So Robert stifled with his tent flaps fastened, writing by night in the flickering gloom afforded by fires and lamps and was out for as much of the blazing day as was possible.

He had bought himself a pony from a passing Turk. It had been used to pulling an araba and was at first reluctant to accommodate a rider. What had happened to his own horse in the dreadful journey up the Black Sea from Scutari he could not discover, but either it had perished on the seventeen-hour crossing and been tossed overboard or else someone whose mount had suffered that very fate, had appropriated it. He did not blame them. He paid the Turk only a fraction of the huge sum of piastres demanded and was grateful for his shaggy purchase, from whose back he could almost touch the ground with his feet. He used it to ride round the great cavalry camp, and also urged it the twenty miles down to Varna to the camps there, and the filthy harbour and the hospital.

'You cannot blame the British soldiers for hating the Turks,' he said to Sarah.

She was sewing as usual. A careless heap of shirts lay on the baked ground beside her, the white cloth liberally speckled with ants, like red pepper, and she was piecing and patching with a skill Robert could only admire. She bit off a thread.

'Why? I thought they were supposed to be brave in battle.'

'We haven't actually had a battle, you know. Five months

hanging about and dying and not a shot fired. They hate the Turks because they are unbelievably idle and filthy and we have to inherit their squalor. The hospital down there – ' he waved a hand in the direction of Varna, 'can kill off a healthy man with a slight wound in hours, of dysentery or cholera. It used to be a Turkish barracks. The smell is abominable. I counted thirty-five empty arabas waiting to carry away the dead – '

'Don't,' Sarah said suddenly. Blanche's face, framed in a long soft tangle of pale hair, had appeared in the tent doorway. She ignored Robert.

'Are all those shirts Edgar's?'

'No. I've done a collection along this line. One lucky man still has three whole ones but most have only one or two. I don't think the laundry ladies are very gentle in their methods.'

'I didn't know you could make shirts,' Blanche said. 'Why do you? Why doesn't Mary do it?'

Sarah gestured to a bent stitching figure in a triangle of shade cast by the neighbouring tent.

'She is.'

Blanche looked briefly at Robert, stretched out along the dried bare earth.

'How long shall you be, Sarah?'

'As long as this pile takes me.'

Blanche gave a moan of anger and despair and wrenched the tent flap across the opening. Sarah said nothing but her lips were set.

'Are you allowed to ride with me?'

She looked up for a moment. His eyes were not teasing.

'Not today. I do want to finish these, and there is my water round.'

Robert sat up.

'Your what?'

'Water round. Most of the sick were being given nothing but spirit to drink or filthy water from those slimy streams. Edgar – I, thought it best not to go myself to take boiled water to the men, but I have a team of regimental wives who go, night and morning, and they bring me news of the worst cases. I can try to persuade Edgar to have them all put together so as to reduce infection and make nursing easier but I cannot be sure they are.'

Robert said softly, 'Admirable!'

She looked a little self-conscious.

'No. It is only one step up a mountain. I don't even know it does any good. I only know that it does *me* good and I am afraid that is very wrong.'

'Wrong? *Wrong?* Did you not listen to one word I said to you at the ambassador's ball?'

'Oh yes,' she said gravely, 'I listened. I have remembered every word. When I say I feel I am in the wrong, I mean that in pursuing a course that is right for me, I am doing wrong to others. Edgar does not like my new attitudes, he wishes to protect me from all that is unpleasant, and in my determination to be at least a little useful, he sees a wilfulness he interprets as lack of love.'

She glanced up. A small troop of soldiers' wives was coming straggling up the lines. They wore a strange assortment of their own petticoats, cast off pieces of uniform and the tawdry glitter of cheap bazaar jewellery and they carried a dented collection of cans.

'Your handmaidens, Miss Drummond.'

'I am beginning to fear that they spend the pittance I give them for this service on drink.'

Robert laughed.

'You are learning so fast.'

'I am quite changed,' she said simply. She laid aside her sewing and rose. At the side of the tent in the scant shade it afforded stood several huge stone jars and from these she ladled water into the billy cans with as much care as if it had been liquid gold.

'How has it been today, Mrs Evans?'

The woman addressed looked considerably tidier and cleaner than she had when she had beseeched Sarah for help aboard the ship. Not content with begging Colonel Lowe to let her stay with her husband's regiment, Sarah had found her various pieces of clothing, including a large white apron which Mrs Evans wore as a mark of her new respectability. She had been darting admonishing glances at her more disreputable looking companions as they came up the lines, and now favoured them with a look of pure superiority before stepping forward to answer Sarah's question.

'Bad, miss. Eighteen gone since reveille, miss. T'farrier's gone down with it now, miss, and there's hardly a soul fit to stand to doctor the horses.'

'Eighteen!' Sarah said in despair.

A woman at the back of the group sniffed loudly.

'An' I dunno as water 'elps much.'

'Then what do you suggest would help?' Sarah asked sharply.

'Arrack and cucumbers?'

'I'll tell you the only thing that could help,' Blanche's voice broke in suddenly from the tent doorway, 'and that is to go home! To leave this horrible place at once and never come back!'

'Oh, Blanche,' Sarah said in deepest reproach.

'I don't care!' Blanche stepped out of the tent into the blinding heat. She was hatless and wore her only thin dress, a gown of the palest blue muslin impossible to keep fresh without a proper laundry and which drooped about her now like faded petals. She had scooped her hair up behind her head and bound it with a blue ribbon, and to Robert, rising slowly from the ground, her appearance had the same disturbingly intimate air that she had had that day so long ago now, sick upon the *Hercules*. She turned her strange, lovely, fretful face upon him.

'I don't care any more, Mr Chiltern! I don't care what Sarah thinks of me, or these women! Why should I stay? It is hateful here, hateful, and I am sick of the heat and the boredom, sick of it!'

Sarah put down her billy-can and came to her sister.

'Go inside, Blanche.'

Blanche glared at her.

'Why should I? Why are you always telling me what to do? We are only here in this awful tent to please you so why should I do what you say as well?'

Sarah's lips were trembling.

'Please, Blanche. You are making a spectacle of yourself. I promise to talk it all over when they have gone, but go inside now, please do.'

Abruptly, Blanche's defiance melted and she slipped back into the tent. Sarah stood for a while gazing after her, then she straightened her shoulders and looked towards Robert.

'You see now perhaps why I say I am wrong. I never made

65

anyone unhappy before and now I make the two dearest to me on earth unhappy.'

Robert moved behind her to take the next empty can from a waiting woman and began to fill it from a jar.

'Why should their reaction to you be your fault?'

The women pressed closer in interest. Sarah spoke as if they were not there.

'It is my fault. I am the one who is changed.'

'It is their fault. They are the ones who have not changed.'

He straightened up and looked at her. His glance made her look down in confusion as if she wished that the triumph of practicality over vanity had not resulted in the brown holland frock. She smiled a little awkwardly.

'I shall accompany your minions on their errands of mercy, Miss Drummond. Do you have any particular instructions for me?'

'Oh no,' she said. 'You know more than I in any case. I can only do it at arm's length. I have never seen a man with cholera.'

One of the women snorted slightly. Robert came quite close to Sarah and bent so that he could speak for her ear alone.

'Moral victories are only won step by step. You have made a magnificent beginning.' He looked round at the group of women. 'Right. Shoulder your burdens, and prepare to step out.' He turned back to Sarah, 'I will be back tomorrow to tell you what I find. There are rumours we may even be leaving Devna soon, perhaps to cross to the Crimean Peninsula. Before that happens I shall obtain permission for you to ride with me so that I may show you what a delightful place this really is.'

Behind his back a blue shadow flitted from the tent. Sarah saw her from the corner of her eye and held her breath, waiting for an outburst. But there was none. Blanche merely seemed to wish to exchange a few words with Mrs Evans, who nodded and smiled and seemed to slip something into her pocket. Then Blanche ran back again and Robert herded his motley troop away down the lines, leaving Sarah standing watching him as if it would be her last sight of him for years.

'Sarah!'

She turned reluctantly.

'Sarah, will you forgive me? I am so sorry to be so pettish

and tiresome and to speak so in front of those women. It is just that I hate the discomfort here and I am frightened of falling sick and sometimes I cannot bear it a moment more.'

Blanche had smoothed her hair and bathed her face. She was standing in the tent doorway wearing such a pretty air of supplication and remorse that Sarah's heart was melted. She put her arms about her sister and kissed her warmly.

'We shall say no more about it. I quite understand you, you know, even though I think you would be happier if you did not expect this funny life to be exactly as it is at home.'

'You are not to preach. I have said I am sorry and you must be content with that. Now I am going to mend my plaid to show you how well I mean to do, and tonight we shall try to persuade Edgar to let us ride out a little.'

Sarah went back to the shirts. The pile of completed ones was still depressingly small by comparison with the heap of pieces. Still, it was something. At the end of the day she could point to three or four men who now possessed whole shirts instead of the rags and tatters they had been reduced to before. She looked up abruptly, remembering something.

'Blanche! Why did you speak to Mrs Evans?'

Blanche settled herself carefully upon her camp stool before replying.

'I thought she might do some sewing for us too. She looks quite a decent clean woman and I really don't see why you should prick your fingers all day when there are others to do it.'

'Oh, Blanche!' Sarah was delighted. 'Oh, Blanche, how sweet you are! Did you give her money?'

Blanche nodded.

'Of course. But only a little. She is to be my responsibility, Sarah, mine entirely. I shall pay her when she shows me what she has done. It is to be nothing to do with you.'

Sarah came quickly over and kissed her cheek.

'I have done you a grave wrong in speaking to you so sharply.'

Blanche smiled up at her and did not speak.

A letter awaited Robert in the stifling heat of his tent. He found it after a long and discouraging tour among the sick, discouraging both because they were so miserable and so many, and also

67

because their manifest astonishment at the sight of drinkable water was plain evidence that Sarah's orders were not being carried out. Questioning revealed that the water was commonly used for laundry since it saved dreary and back-breaking trudges to the streams that ran through the valley, and the common opinion seemed to be that no one in their right minds would drink water when liquor was available. There was no remorse for duping Sarah, or for the unscrupulous taking of her money, and Robert, aware that the regiment's wives were driven to their hard attitudes by their non-existence in the eyes of the military authorities, returned to his tent in an uncharacteristically dejected frame of mind. He knew he should have to tell Sarah that her scheme had failed, and he dreaded the blow to her spirits and hopes. It was made all the worse by having seen how welcome something as simple as water was. He had tramped from tent to tent amid the stench and flies to find men quite helpless with fever and pain, almost all of them desperate for water. Most of them seemed to be nursed by men nearly as weak and wretched as themselves who had hailed Robert's coming with a heart-rending thankfulness. He had seen so much these last three months that had made him angry, so much incompetence, mismanagement and cruelty, but this afternoon had been deeply, thoroughly discouraging and Robert lowered himself into his camp chair in the gloomiest of spirits.

The letter had been propped up against his candlestick, an old wine bottle into whose neck he had jammed whatever candles he could find. He had been without a servant now since leaving Scutari, and found it was in many ways preferable since he then had no one to consider but himself. He did, it was true, have to provide for himself, but the soldiers around him were generous with their erratic supplies, and he fared no worse than they did. It occurred to him occasionally to wonder if any of those who decreed the staple diet of salt pork had ever eaten it as relentlessly as the soldiers did. It had become almost unrelieved as a diet in the last month and was no help to thirst in the August heat.

He picked up the letter without interest. It was from Hope. Hope wrote most weeks offering suggestions and giving directions, most of which Robert ignored since Hope had failed to use his imagination with any of them. He had come across

William Russell four days ago in Varna, and had heard, not without resentment, what support and encouragement and lack of interference he was receiving from his own editor. Russell had been unsympathetic.

'What, will you have everything? Delane's done all in his power and yet I'm still not allowed to pitch a tent inside the lines, and there you are snugly tucked in and safe from robbery!'

He had shared some French brandy with Robert, and they had settled down to mutual fury and despair over the handling of the campaign. When Robert had left, Russell had put a heavy hand on his shoulder and thrust his great bearded face close.

'Don't give up. Tell 'em the truth. Your editor's not here to see for himself after all. You'll have to convert him as well as your readers.'

Sighing now, Robert picked up the letter and tore it open. It contained his last two despatches with sections heavily underscored and a sheet of Hope's own large hand. Robert sat up. He had never had a single word queried before. He glanced down his own writing and saw where Hope's pen had struck.

The Duke of Wellington must be turning in his grave to see such flagrant mismanagement of men. We possess no commanders, with a few notable but unheeded exceptions, who have any experience beyond that of sticking pins in maps. The little business of feeding, nursing and occupying men is quite beneath their notice. Food ran short for the first week of August; the solution to cholera is to herd men into buildings unfit for pigs.

Lower down, red ink glowed angrily again.

And do we know where the Russians are? We do not. And do we know how many there are? We do not. And how long have we now had to discover these elementary facts? Nigh on four months. And who is the better organized army in all this muddle? The French. And are the Turks worth saving? Ask any British private soldier. They are *not*.

Robert read no further. He turned instead to Hope's letter and read with despair that these passages Robert had written with such passion displayed the British army in a light that undermined the morale of the British people and therefore were not acceptable. Hope had written :

I must put down the violence of your views and the emotionalism of your observations to inexperience. The readership of this paper does not wish to hear that the crusade they supported so staunchly is bungled and not worth the candle. May I remind you Lord Raglan served a lifetime's apprenticeship with the Duke of Wellington and therefore must be allowed to know his business better than you do. You must also remember that your attachment to the army rests solely upon your not giving offence or being obstructive, and I have, in your own interests, edited out such passages as I have marked from your dispatches prior to publication. I attribute your lapses to the tiring conditions of the campaign since your work up to now has been much acclaimed. It would be a pity should your recall become necessary.

Robert struck the ammunition box that served him as a table, and swore.

'So I may not write the truth but merely what serves *The Clarion*!'

How dared Hope talk of inexperience, sitting comfortably in London in clean linen with the prospect of an excellent dinner before him! How dare he suggest that Robert should subdue the truth in order to placate an authority that refused to see things as they were! It could not be done. Unplanned, Robert had embarked upon his own crusade to show the British public what lives the soldiers who fought for them lived, and for no one was he going to abandon that, in all its stark reality. He got up and beat the air in fury.

Outside in the dusk, someone called his name. In the mounting clatter of food being prepared all about him, it was impossible to recognize the voice. Shouting to wait one moment, Robert lit his candle and went to the tent flap. Edgar Drummond stood out there, his cap under his arm, wearing an expression of great resolution.

'Drummond!'

'I left a letter for you. I left it on the box. Did you find it?'

Robert's face darkened again.

'I did.'

'May I come in?'

Robert held the flap aside for Edgar to pass in. He fidgeted for a moment, laid his cap down, took it up again, and seemed uncertain how to begin. His uniform was immaculate, closely buttoned to the throat despite the Secretary for War's decree that uniform in camp might be relaxed in the heat of the Bulgarian summer. Robert wore his shirt open and no jacket, and the sight of this informality seemed to contribute to Edgar's unease.

'Sit down, Drummond.'

Edgar took the camp chair. Robert sat on the edge of the ammunition box and looked down on him.

'I have – have something to say. I brought your letter here myself, as I said. I – I believe I know what was in it.'

'Did you open it?'

Edgar looked horrified.

'Indeed not. I know for – for other reasons. I took the liberty of writing to your editor myself, since your campaign to expose the shortcomings of the commissariat were making our work intolerable.'

'You wrote!'

'Yes. I wrote. It is very much on my conscience that I did not tell you of my intention, and that is why I am here now. I wished to explain how difficult you make things for administrators and how I was thus compelled to act to try and prevent you making things worse. You have no conception of the troubles under which we labour.'

Robert picked up the papers and brandished them.

'My editor does not complain chiefly about my campaign, as you call it, against the commissariat. He cannot have heeded you. He does not care for my comments on our commanding officers.'

'He did heed me. I asked him not to be too specific.'

'Ah, *did* you? Not too specific. And did you also ask for my recall?'

Robert had stood up. Looking bravely up at him Edgar said, 'I did not ask for it. I asked for it to be hinted at should you not be more constructive in your reporting. I feel most keenly that I should have told you of my letter. My conscience is not at all easy that I have acted rightly. That is why I have come.'

Robert folded up his length on to the edge of his camp bed.

His knees and Edgar's almost touched in the tiny space of the tent.

'If you are angry, Chiltern, I should understand. I have not acted honourably.'

'I am not angry. I may be surprised, but not angry. You say your work is beset by troubles which I aggravate. May I suggest that if you thought of men rather than the rule book not only would those troubles evaporate, but so would my criticisms. The solution lies with yourself.'

'I have superiors.'

'So have I. And I intend to ignore him. I advise you to do the same.'

Edgar sighed heavily. 'It is not possible.'

'Then it is not possible that I should remain dumb. It is very – good of you to confess to me and it explains Hope's sudden severity. But why do you think the British people even wish to remain in happy ignorance of the truth?'

'They do not understand the difficulties.'

'Drummond, I do not understand *you*. Why in heaven's name should my attacks on the commissariat affect you? You are a cavalry paymaster, are you not? What on earth has the inefficiency of the supply troops to do with you?'

Edgar twisted his cap round in his hands.

'The regiment's quartermaster died of cholera in Malta, cholera presumably brought from England. The matter was kept as private as possible to avoid alarm, and I offered, since Colonel Lowe has been so good to me in finding me a commission in this regiment, to adopt some of the administrative duties left unfilled.'

'You astound me,' Robert said.

Edgar did not look up.

'I imagine you mean that the office of quartermaster is always filled from the ranks. I have not assumed all responsibilities, just the more major ones, so that it shall not be generally known I am any more than paymaster.'

Robert got up carefully in the small space in the centre of his tent that allowed him to stand at full height, and shook himself as if to startle his wits into clearer understanding.

'None of this appears relevant to me, Drummond. I am not attacking *you*, in the unofficial post of part-time quartermaster or whatever you are, but the whole administration, civilian and military, of this wretched army. I cannot see that I am any threat to you at all.'

'I object on two counts. The first is on behalf of the military administration of whose difficulties you have no conception, and the second is that Colonel Lowe knows full well of the connection between you and my family, and will very soon assume that the model for the inefficiency of which you write is myself. To disappoint him after all his goodness to me would be unthinkable. I owe my career to him.'

'And you would not care for him to take it away?'

Edgar inclined his head.

'But,' Robert pursued, 'you do not care if your action takes mine away?'

'It does not mean to you what the army means to me.'

Robert was at last growing angry.

'It does not?'

'No,' said Edgar, 'it does not. You have no respect for authority, no understanding of honour, no admiration for perseverance. You laugh at what is ordered and dignified.'

'You misunderstand me absolutely.'

Edgar now rose. There was hardly room in the tent for both of them, chest to chest in the stifling dark heat of the evening, the candle throwing jumping shadows up into their faces.

'You will not write to Frederick Hope again, Drummond.'

'I suppose in return I can hope for no moderation in your reports?'

'I will write what I find. Just as I always have.'

Edgar endeavoured to bow, but found it impossible, and sidled towards the tent flap, his head bent in token.

'In recompense for writing behind my back,' Robert said, 'will you grant me the favour of taking your sisters up the valley on horseback? I promised to show them how pretty it can be.'

Edgar said nothing for a while. He knew Sarah at least was chafing for some liberty and that Blanche was fatigued with monotony, but he had so far been adamant in refusing all requests to escort his sisters out of camp. The possible dangers were too great. The dangers of Robert Chiltern seemed even greater.

'I had rather escort them *with* your permission.'

The man was impossible. Edgar felt himself quite helpless. He shrugged, unseen in the darkness, and attempted to say that it would not be convenient.

'I take your mutterings as an affirmative, Drummond, and I bid you good night.'

Edgar looked up to speak, but the tent flap had been drawn across, and all he could do was to gaze, with impotent desperation, at the tall black shadow jaggedly imprinted upon the canvas.

A sense of having been subtly worsted kept Edgar from sleep that night. He lay in the heavy blackness which whined with mosquitoes, and wrestled with the recollection of his interview with Robert. It had seemed to him when he wrote to Frederick Hope that his reasons were entirely clear and unquestionably justified; in the light of this evening's conversation his conscience was no longer comfortable with what he had done. He still found Robert alarming and in some obscure way a threat – in fact talking to him always seemed to increase these vague fears – but there was an undeniable reasonableness it what he had said tonight. Edgar and his logic could not dodge it. It was difficult to conceive how a career as a commercial scribbler could in any way approach the stature of the army, but there was no doubt Robert saw it as of equal significance to himself.

Lying trimly and without stirring in his narrow bed, Edgar sighed heavily. Flickering shadows to his left showed that his sisters were also sleepless and had lit their lamp. For an instant the luxury of confiding in Sarah beckoned Edgar, but he banished it sternly. She was a woman, she could not possibly conceive the depth of the situation, and furthermore she was his sister and it was his duty to protect her from what was disagreeable, not burden her with it. Besides, there was something in her attitude to Robert Chiltern that might make her less than a wholehearted supporter of her brother and that was not to be countenanced.

A scream rose from the horse lines, followed by a second and then a burst of shouting. The flies were terrible at night and chose all the most vulnerable places of the poor beasts to bite. A mosquito had stung Edgar maddeningly upon the jaw, but he would not raise his hand from his side to satisfy the barely controllable urge to scratch. He set his teeth and ploughed back again to his exchange with Robert, although that had much the same effect upon his brain as mosquitoes had on his body.

There was no doubt, Edgar forced himself to reflect, that his power was very small. High words to Robert on his influence with Colonel Lowe had very little foundation in fact – indeed, Robert seemed to be in the colonel's company as much as anyone and there appeared to be no attempt to discourage him. James Lowe had an unfashionable reputation for humanity which Edgar supposed must find some answering chord in Robert's curious passion for inessentials, and perhaps – Edgar did not like to think of this but drove himself onward – the colonel would refuse to have Robert sent home even if a direct request were made.

Dawn came with a brief breath of cooler air and the camp woke muttering to another familiar day. Edgar took elaborate trouble over the precise details of his appearance to disguise the marks of fatigue from his sleepless night and joined his sisters for breakfast.

Sarah put a wing of cold chicken before him and a piece of greyish bread.

'You look exhausted, Edgar. It was an unbearable night, wasn't it? Look – I have scratched my arm almost raw.'

Edgar fingered the hard hot lump on his jaw.

'You should not scratch them.'

'I don't see why not,' Blanche said irritably. 'They itch just as much whether you do or not.'

Edgar picked up his lump of bread, tore a corner from it with difficulty and replaced the rest on his plate. Sarah watched him with pity and amusement.

'I'm afraid I need more practice.'

'Practice?'

'I made that loaf. It's the second one. The first was full of baked ants –'

'Don't!' Blanche said.

' – so I threw it away. This one is cleaner but heavier. Perhaps it would do as ammunition.'

Edgar and Blanche regarded her without smiling.

'I wish you wouldn't be so *cheerful*,' Blanche said savagely.

'Is there no bread to be had, Sarah? It is hardly right you should make it yourself.'

'Oh!' Sarah said in exasperation. 'Do you really want me to sit here and do nothing, nothing, nothing in this boiling heat, day after day after day? Cannot I even make *bread*?'

'*I* sit here all day. I hate it.'

'Blanche does,' Edgar said. 'Look at Blanche's hands. Look at yours.'

Sarah was reddening.

'I sometimes think you have no imagination at all. What do hands matter? We aren't in Mount Street –'

Edgar stood up.

'Standards always matter. When the framework of life becomes – altered, it is all the more imperative to cling to the order and standards that are the backbone of ordinary life.'

'Moral standards, yes,' Sarah argued, squinting up at him against the sunlight, 'but not clothes or food or – or *hands*.'

'This,' Edgar said in a tone of deep offence, 'is fruitless.'

He stooped and picked up his scarcely tasted breakfast, balancing the tin plate with exaggerated care on the edge of the table.

'I will see you this evening.'

Blanche groaned.

'Oh think, think, all this awful, endless day to get through before this evening –'

With compressed lips Edgar surveyed them both, one flushed with rebellion, the other pallid with bored fatigue. It was his custom to kiss them when he left in the morning but this morning he could not see how such a gesture could be appropriate. However, it was his habit and he was their brother, so he stooped and brushed their foreheads with hot dry lips, and then left the tent without a word.


Colonel Lowe and his staff had left his quarters when Edgar reached them. George Nash and Dick Carson were lounging outside, picking their teeth and sharing a flask of brandy, and neither looked up when Edgar approached. He was forced to ask where the commanding officer had gone.

George Nash yawned cavernously.

'Cardigan sent for him. We're to move.'

'Move!'

Carson stood up. He was well over six feet, broad-shouldered and narrow hipped, and his clothes fitted him like a second skin. He glanced down at Edgar briefly and devastatingly.

'We're to cross to the Crimea.'

George Nash slumped lower in his camp chair. His long legs in impeccable expensive boots prevented Edgar from taking any steps forward.

'Lots of splendid organization for you to get your teeth into, Drummond.'

Edgar swallowed.

'Did – did Colonel Lowe leave any message for me?'

The two exchanged glances.

'No.'

'Why should he?'

'I thought – if we are to move –'

'We aren't going *today*, Drummond. Not this *minute*. More's the pity, mind you. Many more days of this and I shall grow roots.'

Edgar stepped awkwardly around George Nash's boots and seated himself neatly on a vacant stool.

'Do you know nothing more?'

Dick Carson yawned.

'Nothing. How's your sister, Drummond? The pretty one?'

'The blonde, I'll bet,' George Nash said with the first spark of animation. 'The blonde's my taste.'

Dick Carson pulled a face. 'I've no opinion on blondes. Blondes won't wear. No, it's the dark one I've my eye on though even she's getting too thin for my liking –'

Edgar gave an exclamation of outrage.

'These are my *sisters* you are speaking of!'

George Nash eyed him with amusement.

'Who else d'you suppose we were speaking of?'

'But in such terms, so familiarly, I resent your impertinence deeply –'

Dick Carson took a single slow stride and loomed over Edgar.

'*Resent*, Drummond?'

Edgar attempted to rise but Carson was too close to allow him space.

77

George Nash said, 'Come off it, Dick, let him alone. What do you say to a hand of whist?'

'Excellent notion! Join us, Drummond?'

'Colonel Lowe strongly disapproves of gambling –'

'Oh, pooh pooh, Drummond. Colonel Lowe don't disapprove of anything. In any case he's not here to approve or disapprove. Will you make a pair?'

Edgar shifted a little.

'Don't be a prig, Drummond.'

'Come *on*, Drummond –'

'Such an old woman –'

'Very well,' Edgar said stiffly.

George Nash took a handful of gold from his pocket and tossed it lightly.

'Who'll you partner?'

Edgar eyed the sovereigns apprehensively.

'I – I am not sure who to ask.'

'Whitby. Ask Whitby.'

'No. No thank you. Not Whitby.'

'The writer chap then. Chiltern. He's a capital player. Ready to lay it on too.'

'No.' Edgar said with resolution.

George Nash sighed and tipped his hat over his eyes against the sun.

'We don't need to play with you, you know, Drummond. Plenty of fellows willing and able –'

Dick Carson, still standing, shouted out suddenly, 'Hey, Talbot! Harry! We need a fourth for whist. Be a good fellow!'

Harry Talbot was no taller than Edgar but so sleekly self-possessed that his lack of inches passed without notice. He had brilliant blue eyes, a faultless moustache and small predatory white teeth.

'Am I to partner – *Drummond*?'

'Indeed.'

'Well,' said Harry Talbot, leaning on his stick and grinning down at Edgar, 'what a wonderful piece of luck, what really good fortune. We'll clean up, won't we, Drummond, what with your flair and dash and my steadiness. What are we playing for?'

'Guinea a point?'

Edgar gasped and tried to stifle it.

'Shirt buttons, Drummond!'

'You must be *chinking* with gold, Drummond,' Harry Talbot said, still grinning. 'Simply chinking. I haven't seen you spend a halfpenny, not one. And with your good little sisters stitching away at your linen so devotedly and baking your bread and smoothing your path and keeping you from naughty deeds such as drinking and gambling, your pockets must be positively leaden. It's my duty, dear boy, my absolute duty, to lighten the load and make it easier for you to rush about doing all the useful things you do that keep us all so wonderfully supplied. I never saw so much salt pork in all my life. I can't imagine where you found it all. If I hadn't had the foresight to bring a little hamper or two I should be snorting myself by now and be just right for bacon.'

'Cut it out, Talbot,' Dick Carson said amiably.

Harry Talbot drew a camp stool up beside Edgar and sat down in a confiding attitude.

'Drummond, tell me, do you see yourself as really useful workaday bacon or a more superior, though necessarily idler, sort of ham?'

'I did not wish to play whist in the first place,' Edgar said stiffly, regarding Harry Talbot with unease, 'and I have no wish at all to partner you.'

Harry Talbot smiled widely.

'Nor I you, Drummond, I do assure you. Not the smallest wish. Can you imagine two men less well assorted? But we cannot disappoint Carson and Nash, now can we? That would not be officer-like, now would it, Drummond? Hussars never shrink from anything, do they Drummond, duty or pleasure. So stiffen your spine, dear boy, and submit to the privilege of partnering me.'

The sun was now beating down between the tents on to the baked earth between the lines. It was not mid-morning yet, but the heat was already beginning to bounce fiercely off every surface, off cloth and metal, wood and leather, and in an hour or so, sitting between the lines of tents would resemble sitting in an oven. An ammunition box had been brought by a soldier and placed among the camp stools, and George Nash was throwing neat curves of cards across its surface while he waited.

79

Edgar ran the tip of a finger inside the high stiff collar of his jacket.

'If we are to play, may we not begin?'

'Capital, sir! What a blaze of enthusiasm!'

Dick Carson and George Nash had pulled stools close to the box. They now seated themselves as comfortably astride as if they had been in the saddle and settled to the business of dealing cards. Harry Talbot watched them, his chin propped on his stick, and Edgar watched all three and was very uneasy. He was not a good player, he had not the smallest amount of gambling spirit, and his fellow players filled him with awe and despair. He picked up his cards and sighed.

'Forward, partner,' Harry Talbot said.

They lost the first hand as both Harry and Edgar had known they would do. Harry Talbot said nothing. Edgar stared down at the top of the ammunition box and felt the sweat of discomposure mingling with the now familiar hot dampness that resulted from wearing broadcloth in broiling sun. A small thudding pain was beginning above his right eye, knocking like a little gong in the blackness. A voice said pleasantly above him, 'I'm glad to be able to offer you all a more constructive occupation than cards soon,' and there was a sudden tumble and commotion around him as the other three got to their feet.

Instinctively Edgar followed suit and found himself face to face with his commanding officer and some tall figure whom he could not, in his horrified confusion, put a name to. Colonel Lowe regarded him good-humouredly.

'I didn't know you had a taste for whist, Drummond.'

The pain above Edgar's eye developed into a steady thrumming across the whole of the top of his skull. He felt his brain quite stupefied and was conscious of his mouth working without a word being audible.

'I don't know about taste, sir,' Harry Talbot said easily, 'but he certainly hasn't much aptitude.'

'Well, Drummond?' Colonel Lowe said.

The tall figure beside James Lowe leaned forward and revealed itself to be Robert Chiltern.

'He was standing in for me, sir.'

A breath of relief escaped unbidden from Edgar's lips. Out

of the tail of his eye he saw George Nash and Harry Talbot exchange grins.

'Really,' James Lowe said.

'I was bound to a game sir. It was only wishing to discover all I might about the move to the Crimea that kept me away. They were short of a fourth. Drummond never plays!'

James Lowe smiled at him, then swung round to the others.

'Carson? Nash?'

Dick Carson smiled back.

'We're always glad of Chiltern, sir. He's a capital player. Wins too much for my liking, of course.'

'Of course.'

Harry Talbot said, 'I've rarely been so relieved to see anyone, Chiltern. Many more hands with our noble paymaster as partner and I should be shirtless. Difficult to feel he really enjoyed it, somehow.'

Edgar gazed straight ahead. Relief and humiliation surged and struggled within him, and he could feel several steady trickles of sweat sliding down his cheeks and neck into the collar band of his jacket. He said jerkily, 'Are we to move, then, sir?'

'Probably, Drummond. Next week perhaps.'

Exclamations of pleasure broke from the others.

'Capital, sir!' Harry Talbot said. 'No news has ever been more welcome! May we then dare to assume that someone has actually seen a Russian?'

Colonel Lowe appeared to be suppressing a smile.

'I think all we can assume is that there is a better chance of seeing one on the Crimean Peninsula than here. There is a huge Russian battery at Sebastopol in the Crimea, so presumably the odd Russian is attached to it.'

'Do you have any orders for me, sir?' Edgar said woodenly.

'None at present. I wish I had. I wish I had orders for all of you. I am well aware of how heavily time hangs, and although I would not actually forbid gambling, I could wish you could all spend your time more profitably. It is hardly an example to the men on whom boredom weighs more painfully than on you. I don't like to see your standards slackening merely because you are idle. You all have horses. Use them. It's hardly a picnic for them here either. There is no need to wear full uniform in this heat in camp, Drummond, but on the other hand, Nash, I don't care to see you looking as if you had just got out of bed. We will assume there will be another week at Varna. It is going to be a disciplined and constructive week. It begins now.'

In silence the five men watched him walk away. Dick Carson stooped and picked up the cards, George Nash shouted at a nearby soldier to remove the box and stools and then moved to link his arm in Harry Talbot's.

'The horse lines then, Talbot?'

Harry grinned up at him.

'At the double. Drummond, will you favour us with your company or would you prefer to ask Chiltern to be your stand-in?'

Edgar said nothing. He continued to stare after Colonel Lowe and did not move a muscle until he heard Carson and Nash and Talbot stumble off laughing and knew that he was alone with Robert.

'That was hardly necessary, Chiltern.'

Robert shrugged.

'As you wish.'

Edgar spun round, his face full of anger.

'Do not condescend to me, Chiltern! I am a soldier, a member of the army, I have orders, *orders* to be here! I will not be treated by you, a mere – camp follower, only tolerated by the – the extraordinary generosity of the colonel, with such mockery, such contempt. You have no business here, no authority. I will not stand for it, for your – your attitude, ingratiating yourself with the colonel, toadying to my fellow officers, it is intolerable, *intolerable*.'

Robert was breathing fast.

'If I stay,' he said furiously, 'I shall hit you – ' and he turned on his heel and strode away. Six paces off, he stopped and looked back. Edgar was just where he had left him, fists clenched at his side, chin high.

'Oh come, Drummond, don't let's quarrel. Such a small thing and no harm done.'

Interested faces appeared around the tents at the sound of Robert's call. Edgar observed them and resolved to say no more. Robert came back a few paces and held out his hand.

'Come, Drummond, don't be an ass.'

Edgar stood like a rock.

'There's no way of pleasing you, is there? Standing up to you, standing up for you, they're both wrong. Well, I shall go and visit your sisters and have my feelings soothed. It is as well that some at least of the Drummonds know how to be gracious.'

When he had gone, several soldiers remained among the nearby tents to see what Edgar would do. He was standing still rigid in the blazing sun, staring before him, just as he had done since the colonel had come upon them all ten minutes before. After a while they grew tired of him, the spectacle of his motionlessness became monotonous rather than impressive, so they dawdled off and left him, alone and upright between the tents.

# Six

In the final week of August, orders came at last to strike camp and move down to Varna, prior to crossing to the Crimean Peninsula. Edgar, about some official business, went off immediately to Varna, promising he would be back to escort his sisters down to the harbour and instructing them not to leave the lines. He had been gone but an hour when Robert Chiltern was with them, accompanied by George Nash and a quartet of horses.

'The expedition into the interior, Miss Drummond!'

Sarah rose delightedly from her stool.

'But, Mr Chiltern, Edgar is but just gone!'

'And I am but just come. He has not refused me the pleasure of taking you riding and as we are here but a night or two more, I must take my chance while I can. Captain Nash has come to see that things are proper, you will observe.'

He sounded as he had not sounded for days. He had hardly been to see them in two weeks and when he came had seemed so dangerously full of some suppressed emotion that it had been impossible to ask him the reason. Edgar had been silent too, though it was not evident whether it was for emotional or occupational reasons. It was noticeable that they took care to avoid each other.

Socially, they had been much gayer weeks; two reviews of cavalry, several magnificently makeshift dinner parties and the furtive entertainment, which Edgar would not allow them to join, of going into the camp of the Rifle Brigade to watch Lady Erroll and her white Arab being painted in oils. During all this, Sarah had persisted with her mending. The water round had stopped, of course, after Robert's reluctant disclosure of its fate, and if it had not been for the occasional appearance of Mrs Evans and her transactions with Blanche, transactions Blanche conducted with childlike secrecy, they would hardly have seen another woman.

But now, for an hour or two, there was the heady chance of liberty! Blanche of course had not only her habit with her but a plumed hat which had survived somehow since its purchase in Bond Street six months before. The men stood outside in the sunshine and fidgeted, and Sarah did everything in her power to hurry. She need not have troubled. Blanche was a full half-hour about her preparations and emerged at last to a burst of applause from onlookers who had gathered to witness their departure.

The road out of camp was white with soft thick dust. On either side the country rolled away in gentle green ripples to the sides of the wide valley, studded with plushy clumps of trees and bushes. Sarah, riding beside George Nash whom she had met a few nights previously at Lord Cardigan's tent, the only tent to have the shade of trees in the camp, observed that she could hardly believe that this peaceful and English-seeming pasture could have proved so dangerous.

'We've lost twelve thousand since we came,' George Nash said.

Sarah turned a look of horror upon him.

'How can you say such a thing so calmly?'

'How else am I to say it? With such numbers dying every day one becomes numb. It will be better in the Crimea, I hope. At least one can get to grips with the Russians at last.'

Sarah looked ahead. Robert and Blanche were now riding side by side. As they had all left camp, Robert had led the way with the other three behind him, but now he seemed to have dropped back so that he was level with Blanche.

'Shall we trot?'

George Nash smiled obligingly.

'As you say, Miss Drummond.'

It was a mistake. As the hooves of their horses struck the roadway, soft choking clouds of dust rose about them and filmed their eyes and lips. Urging her pony sideways on to the grass at the side of the track, Sarah found herself separated from the others by the suffocating cloud she had raised, and had to canter to catch up. Blanche turned as she joined them.

'Why, Sarah, you are quite covered!'

For a moment, Sarah seemed about to speak, but closed her lips and contented herself with the vigorous application of her handkerchief. Robert was pointing with his whip.

'Shall we cut up there, George? There's a lovely little pool and shade about a mile over that shoulder. I've been there several times when the savage breast needed soothing.'

George Nash was eyeing Blanche with open admiration.

'Ain't too far for the ladies?'

'Far!'

He turned to Sarah.

'You've been pretty well kept prisoner, Miss Drummond. Thought you might be out of practice.'

'Then we shall have to prove you wrong,' Blanche said coolly, and turned her pony's head towards the shoulder Robert had indicated, rising green and smooth out of the meadowland. The men were by her side in a moment, cantering over the dry grass, Sarah following them alone.

Once over the shoulder, which proved only a shallow inverted basin of land, the country was even more lovely. A little valley lay before them through which a stream ran so brightly that it did not seem possible it should be guilty of the foulness she had heard attributed to all the local water. The land was dotted with outcrops of rock and graceful groups of trees. Robert dropped back beside Sarah.

'There! Is it not delightful?'

'I never doubted it, you know.'

He laughed. She looked at him with some trepidation, as if uncertain as to whether today's spirits were false or genuine after the peculiarity of his mood recently. He leaned across and smiled at her for a moment.

'I believe I have been a boor.'

She started to tremble very slightly.

'I – I could see you had something on your mind.'

'They were cutting my reports, Miss Drummond. Every despatch I sent back was edited. I wrote today to say I would not work under such conditions.'

'But you should not! You might lose your post! How can you be light-hearted when you may have cut off your own chances so finally?'

'There are other, perhaps better, occupations.'

George Nash and Blanche were trotting down into the valley. Sarah made as if to follow them, but Robert put his hand on her pony's bridle.

'Spare me a moment. Do you disapprove of politics?'

Sarah turned to him in amazement.

'Politics? I – I know nothing of them. My father is a Whig and so is Edgar, but why should you ask me?'

'It may be what the future holds for me. I should be sorry if you felt you could not speak to a new Tory.'

'I should always feel I could speak to you.'

He smiled.

'I had hoped so. I have been growling in my tent like a bear with a sore head since – these last weeks. It is hard to bear the indignity of having my reports mistreated by men who do not know one end of a bayonet from the other. It is even worse to contemplate that it is not merely newspaper editors who suffer from such ignorance, but Parliament. I do not believe that ministers are ill-disposed towards the common soldier, but their sheer ignorance of war is beyond belief. I begin to think, Miss Drummond, that Parliament, now it lacks Sir Robert Peel, could well do with voices such as mine.'

Sarah said with diffidence, 'Is – is this all part of your scheme? Is this part of your wish for a better world?'

'Fate may have it so but fate will have to send me some money, I fear. I should need at least five thousand pounds to have a hope of being elected, and if I were to attempt to stand in my father's place when he wishes to stand down – and if he can bring himself to sanction my views – I should have a dyed-in-the-wool Whig electorate to convince. But that is all in the future, and I mean to do my damnedest for the British soldier before I move on to anything else. I do not believe their commanders see them as Christian men with a soul each, but merely as a morass which inconveniently must be clothed and fed and watered. Come, stop me. I am preaching again. Shall we join your sister?'

Sarah trotted down the gentle slope beside him, seeming much preoccupied. Occasionally, she would glance at her own worn clothing, then down at Blanche's elegance in the valley below, then, with some perplexity, at Robert. His appearance by now resembled that of a civilized brigand, and he wore his strangely assorted clothes with the easy indifference he seemed to feel for most material things. He had pushed his cap to the back of his head and was humming as he rode beside her, abstracted again in his own thoughts.

The pool was indeed lovely. It lay below a jutting crag over which the water poured in a brilliant cascade, encircled by trees and cushions of bright moss. They watered and tethered the horses and Sarah said she would like to rest a little.

'Farther than you thought, eh?' George Nash said.

'A little,' she lied politely.

Blanche settled herself on a rock and he immediately stretched himself at her feet. Robert had wandered away to lean against a tree and gaze, and although she looked after him as if she would have dearly liked to follow him, Sarah restrained herself and mounted the crag above the waterfall to find a secluded retreat. She sat down by a tree and took off her hat, leaning her head back against the trunk and listening to the relentless splash of the water hurling itself down into the pool. The sky between the trees was very blue, the sun hot. It was the first natural shade she had sat in for a month, the first time she had heard running water for much longer, the first chance to escape the confines of the curious life Edgar had brought her to. He would be so distressed that they had left the camp, so displeased that they had allowed Robert to escort them. Robert had obviously chosen George Nash as escort since he had horses and was perfectly unobjectionable, but his presence would not rule out Edgar's disapproval of the whole arrangement. Sarah sighed and closed her eyes.

Perhaps it was only minutes later that she opened them. The sun seemed as high and bright as ever. She scrambled to her feet, shook out her skirts, picked up her hat, and descended the crag with care. By the pool George Nash lay stretched asleep; except for the four horses, he was alone. She stooped over him briefly to see if he would wake, but he was sleeping as soundly as a child, one arm flung across his forehead, his head cushioned in the thick grass. Sarah went to the edge of the group of trees and looked out, but the land lay still and empty in the sunlight. She thought of calling out, but it seemed unnecessary to waken the sleeper. She took her gloves and laid them by his head as a token she was not far away, and then set off to follow the stream as it ran away from the pool along the edge of the trees, glittering in the sun-speckled shadows.

It was something of a little adventure. She had not been alone like this all the time she had been away – indeed, she was hardly ever alone at home except those rare afternoons at Oakley when the idle, silent house had oppressed her too much to stay indoors one minute more. The thought of walking alone in empty Bulgaria, even only for a few minutes, had the exhilaration of the forbidden about it. Stepping quietly in and out of the shadows by the edge of the water, Sarah smiled to herself.

She rounded a corner and found that the stream left the trees and began to flow downhill through a meadow. Perhaps thirty yards below her Robert Chiltern was standing, bareheaded, his back to her. She was about to call out to him when something in his attitude, something profoundly preoccupied, caused her to check her call in her throat. Then she saw that beyond him Blanche was kneeling on the river bank, stretching down towards something Sarah could not see. She too was hatless, Sarah could see the grey feathers in the grass, and her pale curls had tumbled round her shoulders. Sarah could not move. She stood and looked at the still, silent figures in the quiet green landscape and could not call or stir a step.

At last Blanche got up, slowly, cradling in her palm some frail pink blossom. She began to walk towards Robert, slowly still, holding the flower and gazing down at it. There was something dreamlike in her movements, she seemed to drift and float through the long summer grasses, her bleached head bent over the pink petals of the flower. Robert did not move. He stayed there, watching, legs slightly apart, and she came on towards him in the silence, not looking but seeming to know the way. As she reached him he leaned forward a little, and plucked the flower out of her hands, hurling it into the stream. She gave a little cry and her hands went up, and Sarah saw him catch her to him and her arms go round his neck as he bent over her. They stayed like that for minutes, clinging, pressed together, and neither looked up to see Sarah stumbling in panic back along the edge of the trees.

For two weeks now I have longed to write, to be alone, to disburden myself of some of this weight of misery. But all has been bustle and muddle as we struck camp at Devna and moved down to Varna to embark. Now we have crossed to the Crimean Peninsula to be drenched by night and roasted by day, and I have given in to Edgar and am shut up in the ship once more.

I did not mean to give in. I cannot help myself. I feel quite forsaken. I think I did not know how much I loved him until I saw him give his love to Blanche but I know it now and my heart quite sickens within me at the useless weight of it. I have prayed, night after night I have prayed, but I think God has turned his face from me for my wilful behaviour before that dreadful day. In wishing to help myself I had neglected those I should serve, and I must be punished. But it is hard, very hard. Everything is now sour and bitter to me, even Edgar's affection is meaningless because it is not the love I want. I strove to please, to be what Robert thought I might be, and was beginning to see what satisfaction I might feel when the cup was dashed from my lips.

The one aim I have now is that no one shall know how I am stricken. Robert is quite dazed with happiness, Blanche as contented as a kitten, so they are not likely, either of them, to be observant of any pain on my part. Edgar is very distressed that Blanche should have chosen a man he regards as unsuitable and he is very angry with Robert. He has persuaded Colonel Lowe that Robert should not be allowed to draw provisions with the regiment, nor to have a tent or the protection of camping in the lines. I have no doubt that Robert will manage very well on his own but I am horrified that Edgar should be so vengeful. He has forbidden any question of marriage until the winter is over and our parents have been consulted. Marriage! What shall I do when Robert is quite taken from me by marriage? Can I bear to be nothing to him then? I will not stay by and play the hypocrite when they are married, professing calm affection when my heart is wrung with jealousy and forbidden love. But I must stay now, I *must*. I must force myself through this campaign and perhaps my feelings will be tempered in the fire and come out fine and strong.

They are anything but fine and strong now. Sometimes they make me writhe and twist, I am in such pain. I do not know how I act to Blanche so calmly yet how could I do otherwise since she has not the first idea of doing me a wrong? We did not speak very much of Robert before – I did not dare to lest my feelings should betray me – and I thought she bore an intense dislike for him. I have heard it said that the more violent passions are very akin one to another, and thus I suppose it only needed the smallest push from fate for her hatred to be transformed to love. She speaks little of it still but she wears an expression of such complete satisfaction that I can tell how entirely she rejoices in his love.

As for him, I am thankful work has occupied him so absolutely since we landed. I have hardly seen him. When I think of how he spoke to me but a single hour before I saw him with Blanche that day, I could cry aloud, at the incomprehensible injustice of it all. Had he thought of Blanche before? Was he as thunderstruck as I was? No, he had thought of it. He had contemplated her with love ever since we left England and I was no more than a useful decoy. He talked to me and sought me out to mask his true feelings. I am a poor silly fool not to have seen it before. I forgive him, of course I do. I cannot withhold any benign feeling from him, least of all forgiveness. Does he speak to Blanche as he did to me? Does he tell her of his aspirations and hopes, his grand designs and extraordinary sympathies? They have only been together but three times in the past two weeks, and I always contrived to be as far away as I could, even if it were only the other end of the ship, and as much occupied as I could be.

Occupation! What am I to do now? I am quite back where I began, stuck in a ship's cabin, with nothing to show for the last month's freedom except pricked fingers and a broken heart. Edgar says if there is any fighting we may watch it, but what solace he supposes that may be, I cannot conceive. When I think of all the wretched men out there without proper shelter on these soaking nights and having to walk about all day while their wet clothes steam dry upon them, I could scream with despair at the incompetence of the authorities. Two nights ago we had a terrible storm and I could not sleep for the tossing of the ship and sorrow for the soldiers – and for my miserable self. For some reason the tents that had been landed were sent back to the ships, and the men had nothing but their greatcoats. . . .

Robert too, I suppose. I imagine he is on shore with them. I should not torture myself with imagining his state of mind, but I cannot help myself. I cannot understand his behaviour. I want to go home, yet I could not bear to. I long to see him but shrink from it. I wish I was out there with the soldiers, so full of bodily misery that the heart's soreness would have no place. I wish, I *wish* . . .

# *Seven*

That September was fine and warm. Early autumn, the most reliably lovely of the Crimean seasons, brought blue skies full of larks and ripened the grapes in the vineyards. Everyone's spirits rose with the sun; cholera hopefully had been left on the western shore of the Black Sea and, with it, boredom and the unrelieved superfluity of salt pork. Sarah and Blanche were rowed ashore each morning from the *Hercules* in a paddle-box boat, and carried through the surf by half-naked sailors during which procedure they could not but observe that the majority of the sailors were entirely naked. Once ashore, they were greeted by officers of the regiment, some in dress uniforms now washed almost clean of colour by the nightly downpours, and given ponies to carry them into camp. Edgar, worn down it seemed, appeared hardly to care whether they obeyed him or not. He accompanied them into camp each morning, saw that they were in the care of someone reliable, and then departed about heaven-knew-what business, wearing his usual air of uneasy preoccupation.

On the third morning of this pattern, the unavoidable happened. Sarah was seated by the colonel's tent while Captain Nash and several others drew a map of the Crimean Peninsula for her in the smooth mud at her feet. Some three feet away, Blanche, graceful in her grey plumed hat, was recounting her exchange with Lord Cardigan who had spoken to them as they rode up from the beach that morning.

'So I said, "I hope, my lord, that this bay is named Calamita for no good reason," and he said, "We hope the Russians will have every reason to think it rightly named, Miss Drummond," and then I said that I doubted there *were* any Russians and he said – '

She broke off abruptly with a look of irritation. When her voice ceased, Sarah looked up from the meandering lines of the

93

Crimean rivers which seemed to cross its western half like watery ribs and saw that Robert was approaching. Beside him trotted Mrs Evans, which accounted for the annoyance in Blanche's gaze. She was still dressed in her clean white apron even after the nights she must have spent with nothing for cover. Besides her apron she wore a dark stiff skirt, an old uniform jacket and her habitual expression of self-satisfaction.

Robert looked exhausted but happy. His dark hair was tousled, his boots muddy, he seemed longer and thinner than ever, but his smile and eyes were buoyant and his step elastic. He came over to Blanche as if there were no one else present. As he bent towards her, Sarah resumed an intent study of the mud at her feet.

'Where did you say the Russians were?'

'Here, Miss Drummond. South-westerly corner. Place called Sebastopol. We shall drive them down to that tight little corner and besiege them into submission.'

'There – there seem a good many rivers to cross before we get there.'

'Four of them. The Alma first. I say, Miss Drummond, you should not be out in the sun like this! You've gone pale as a ghost.'

'It's nothing – nothing – I expect it was having so little time for breakfast. It will pass – please – do go on –'

An unfamiliar stick moved on to the map and pointed at a spot on the southern edge of Calamita Bay.

'That's where I have spent the last few nights. I was lucky enough to share the dry space under a cart for two of them, and to find a kindly colonel with a bit of biscuit to spare. Are you not going to say how glad you are to see me, Miss Drummond?'

'In – indeed I am, Mr Chiltern. I am sorry you have been so uncomfortable.'

'Oh that! What is a little bodily discomfort when the rest of one is rejoicing? Now, have these gold-braided nincompoops told you what we are to do next?'

Five sticks descended simultaneously upon the map. Sarah looked away for a moment and observed that Blanche was still earnestly consulting with Mrs Evans. The latter looked as if she were about to object to the instructions Blanche was giving her, perhaps protesting that if battle really was at last imminent, then plain sewing for ladies could hardly be expected to take priority. She sat up straighter in order to see more clearly. Blanche had given Mrs Evans a folded paper of some sort, a white triangle and Mrs Evans had tucked it carefully away under the white apron.

'I fear we have bored Miss Drummond. Her attention appears to have wandered.'

'I – I am sorry to be such a poor pupil.'

'Sarah never could abide geography,' Blanche said, sweeping over to them. 'She dreamed through every lesson but history and poetry. You would find it far more profitable to instruct me.'

Sarah rose and silently offered Blanche her stool. It was instantly taken and the circle closed round once more. Mrs Evans was still standing where Blanche had left her, as if her conversation with Blanche entitled her to participate further. Sarah beckoned to her to come near.

'Did my sister give you a note?'

'Oh, ma'am, I couldn't say to be sure, indeed I couldn't.'

'To whom are you to deliver it?'

Mrs Evans said rapidly, ' 'Tis only a list, ma'am, a list for sewing. There's a deal to be done and Miss Blanche wishes to look her best, ma'am.'

'I see.' She sounded unconvinced. 'I hope any work you do for my sister does not prevent you from fulfilling any useful tasks you might perform for the men.'

'No indeed, no, ma'am. I'm only too glad to help out, ma'am. If you'll excuse me, ma'am –'

She bobbed briefly and trotted away among the tents. Robert appeared at Sarah's elbow, with disconcerting suddenness.

'And what have you found for yourself to do now?'

'I – I am most surprised that you should ask.'

'Why? I am as interested as I ever was.'

'Then I must disappoint you. I have found nothing to do. We come into camp every morning and return to the ship every evening. That is all.'

There was a short pause. Sarah stared woodenly before her at the gap between tents through which Mrs Evans had disappeared and Robert scrutinized her profile.

'You have abandoned my notions, then?'

'For the moment, perhaps.'

'I have offended you?'

'Oh – oh no.'

'I had hoped we might become closer friends than ever now. Can that not be?'

Sarah turned to him.

'To suppose that,' she said furiously, 'only serves to show what a very poor student of human nature you are.'

Then she walked briskly back to the group around Blanche. Robert stood looking after her for some moments, then he crammed his battered forage cap back on to his dishevelled head and strode away among the tents.

Reveille sounded at three the next morning. Sarah heard it, faint and thin, lying sleepless in her narrow berth on the *Hercules*. Robert felt it had been sounded directly above him as he lay rolled in his groatcoat under a hedge, his head pillowed on his knapsack which contained his notebooks and a small flask of rum. When he opened his eyes, it was on to blackness, but as his sight grew more accustomed he could see a dim red glow to the right, which meant that the French, as usual, were ahead of them all, and up and breakfasting.

He struggled stiffly to his feet, shook himself, picked up his knapsack, patted the pocket which contained a lock of white-gold hair wrapped in paper and set off in search of breakfast. There was a good deal of muttering and grumbling around as men tried to light fires with damp wood, but after some cajoling Robert managed to secure a stale egg from an infantry sergeant and a lump of biscuit from a private whose dysentery prevented him from eating anything. Armed with these, Robert elbowed his way as close to a fire as he could and crouched beside it to eat. The men made way for him good humouredly, acknowledging his preparedness to live life as ruggedly as they did. In companionable silence he chewed and swallowed his unpalatable breakfast, then he straightened up, thanked them for their brief hospitality and set off, notebook in hand to survey the army as it started off south in pursuit of the Russians.

There was plenty to watch. For six hours there was struggling and cursing, shouts and orders, and it was not until nine o'clock that the remaining twenty-six thousand men of the British Army stepped out, resplendent in scarlet and gold with the sun glittering on the tips of their bayonets. There were twelve miles to march to the Alma, the first of the four rivers between the allied camp and Sebastopol and it was behind the Alma that the Russians were waiting.

Robert tried to obtain a pony, but it was hopeless, and in order to remain with the chief body of the army he was forced to fall in beside the Twenty-Third and march along with them. As he tramped, he could hear the impatient drums of the French ahead, beating out their exasperation at British confusion, and far into the distance he could just perceive plumes of black and white smoke.

'What is the smoke ahead?' he shouted at the nearest man.

'Ruskies are burnin' the countryside! Bin doin' it for days so's we shan't get a morsel!'

'Then they know we're coming!'

The soldier nodded. The man behind him seemed suddenly to crumple and stumble, falling sideways out of rank into the suffocating dust of the road. Robert quickly dropped back and pulled him away from the stamp of passing feet. He put a hand on his forehead and felt the scalding skin. Cholera still, then. It had crossed with them, and waited during those rain-soaked nights and sweat-soaked days and now with the fatigue of marching in burning sun on an unfed stomach, it was striking viciously. An araba came up beside Robert, already half filled with sufferers.

'Takin' 'em to the rear!' the driver shouted.

Robert stooped and put his hands beneath the soldier's shoulders; the cloth of his coat was dark with sweat. Between them, he and the driver heaved the man into the araba, where he lay as he was tumbled, as inert and helpless as a rag doll. The cart rumbled on, and Robert joined the ranks again to tramp onwards in the heat, his knapsack jolting on his back, his mouth and throat cracked with dust and dryness, one hand in his pocket around the little paper packet.

After an hour they stopped. Lord Raglan and his staff came riding through the advance columns, cheered thunderously by the troops as they passed. Robert sat on the ground, head bent, and scribbled furiously. He had personally counted thirty-two men carried to the rear since they set off, many of whom he was sure, were too weakened to carry the burden of their knapsacks and weapons, not to mention the weight of a brass shako. All around him were shouts for water. He wanted water himself so badly he dared not let himself dwell upon it, but he at least had had something to drink but a few hours before, and some of these men had seen no water in days.

At eight that morning the *Hercules* began to steam slowly southward down the coast, following the army as it tramped towards Sebastopol. Sarah had risen at six, white with sleeplessness, and had bathed her face and dressed and gone on deck, to strain her eyes eastward to where she knew the army was encamped. Robert had by now slept rough on the edge of whatever regiment would tolerate him for fourteen nights, and was now presumably part of that faint clattering that betokened an army about to move. She remained there almost two hours, loth to go below again and lost in sad reverie, until she heard the deep thudding of the engines start far below her, and saw that the coastline was beginning to move imperceptibly past.

Their little maid appeared to call her to breakfast. Blanche was sitting before the small table in their cabin with a broken roll in front of her and an expression of impatience on her face.

'I thought we were to go ashore.'

'The army is on the move. I heard reveille called long before dawn. The ship is actually moving so you will not be forced to go ashore today.'

'But I want to!'

'You cannot leave a moving ship.'

'When will it stop?' Blanche demanded.

'I imagine when the army does.'

'But that might be too la –' Blanche stopped and picked up a morsel of crust. 'Is the French army gone too?'

'The French army? Why should you care? I imagine they are all gone together.'

'I particularly wanted to go ashore.'

Sarah poured herself some tea with studied care.

'You must reconcile yourself to not being able to.'

'What shall we do all day?'

'What we do on every other day.'

'I am sick of this ship!'

'And I,' said Sarah, rising and flinging down her napkin, 'am sick of your endless complaints!'

Blanche preserved an injured silence. The sun began to filter into their cabin, touching the polished wood and brass and Blanche's carefully ordered hair. Sarah stood by the porthole, gazing at the coastline across the strip of sea, her face set and hard.

The door opened and Edgar appeared, his hands as usual full of papers.

'Why may we not go ashore?' Blanche asked.

Edgar sighed, and seated himself in Sarah's empty place.

'My dear Blanche, I thought you did not care for the shore.'

'I – I have learned to like it. Anything is better than suffocating in here.'

Absently, Edgar took up a roll Sarah had picked up but not tasted. He broke it and began to put pieces of crust into his mouth.

'We shall not stop until the army stops, my dear.'

'May I go ashore then?'

'If you must. It is thought there will be an engagement with the Russians before long and Lord Raglan has most kindly said that you may watch with members of his staff.'

Some colour had crept into Blanche's cheeks.

'May I send a message on shore?'

'To Mr Chiltern? No, you may not. Have I not made my feelings perfectly plain already as to the unsuitability of any such union? I do not wish you to encourage him.'

Blanche shrugged and glanced at Sarah. With visible difficutly, Sarah said, 'I think you are unreasonably hard, Edgar.'

'I expected you at least to see how unsatisfactory Mr Chiltern is as a suitor for Blanche. It mystifies me that you should champion him.'

'It may mean a good deal to him to hear from Blanche,' Sarah said, gazing rigidly out at the slipping coastline. 'After all, he has precious few comforts now.'

Edgar sighed and dropped the remaining morsels of roll. He stood up.

'I must go. I believe, Blanche, that you may write this once but I am adamant that Chiltern should not be encouraged.

This will be the only communication. I will send someone to you to take it for delivery.'

Sarah slipped round the table and caught Edgar by the shoulders.

'You are kind and good, indeed you are. We are nothing but a trouble to you and I know we often try you sorely.'

He kissed her forehead. 'On the contrary, your presence is a great consolation to me.'

Sarah regarded him thoughtfully for a moment or two.

'Do you remember once stealing Mamma's peaches to give to some poor governess we had? And how we were caught at it by Aunt Price and I was shut up in the dining room until nightfall?'

Edgar smiled faintly. 'I ate bread-and-water for three days afterwards. I remember that. Blanche, do you recall it?'

Blanche was sitting lost in a happy abstraction. She looked up as Edgar spoke.

'Yes,' she said, 'I remember it. But I cannot think why we didn't eat the peaches ourselves.'

As the afternoon wore on, sporadic gunfire could be heard from the shore. Both sisters sped up on deck and gazed earnestly shorewards but nothing could be seen except small plumes of smoke here and there in the still September air. Blanche had seemed much calmer since she had written her note, and had taken great pains not to let Sarah see as she addressed it, presumably so as not not to distress a sister with no acknowledged lover to attend to. One of the ship's officers had come to collect the note, just as Edgar had promised, and had assured Blanche that it would be taken on shore the moment the boat was moored and delivered that night. A glad relief spread over Blanche's face at such assurances, a relief she seemed at no pains whatever to hide.

'We have stopped!'

Sarah craned over the deck rail. A small figure was signalling from the shore.

'I suppose the army has halted. Perhaps that really was a battle that we heard. Look, oh look, a boat is going out!'

Blanche leaned over with her. A small dinghy was leaving the side of the *Hercules*, rowed by a single sailor while two others sat at bows and stern.

'There goes my letter,' Blanche said with satisfaction.

Sarah turned away from the rail.

'So they must have found the Russians, then.'

'I have seen my first encounter,' Robert wrote that night by the light of a candle begged from an infantry officer. 'We found the Russians waiting for us at the Bouljanak, a little stream which our soldiers fell upon as if the waters were running gold. There was a detachment of Cossacks, a determined and professional looking bunch despite the smallness of their sturdy horses and the roughness of their appearance, and they fired round shot in among our cavalry with admirable accuracy. Our artillery answered them, and after a short while they retired, but not before I had seen two cavalrymen riding coolly to the rear to have their wounds dressed, one damaged so badly that his foot hung by a mere strip of skin, yet he was laughing and joking with his comrade. We have come ten miles today and I feel as if I had walked a hundred. Tomorrow there will be little marching, but there is small doubt of the bloody business to be done.'

I cannot sleep tonight, not a wink. I have never been so distracted with worry in my life and there is nothing I can do under darkness so I am resolved to write in a vain endeavour to occupy myself and somehow to pass the time till daybreak and perhaps, oh please God, perhaps some news.

Blanche is gone. Where I do not know, nor with whom. To say I am agitated is to understate my condition a thousand times for I am on fire with anxiety and apprehension. I must control myself, I must, for what use will I be when day breaks and there is something to be done?

Oh, Blanche, Blanche, where are you? We rose together this morning just as usual, the sun glittering on the water after the milky autumn haze had gone, and we breakfasted quite amicably and then Edgar came and said there was likely to be an engagement that day for the Russians were waiting for us beyond the River Alma, and we might go and join Lord Raglan's staff as promised. I did not take much heed of what Blanche was doing as she dressed, though I was surprised she did not think it safe to leave her trinkets on board. I protested that our things had always been safe and she declared that times of war made people behave curiously and she did not want to risk it. I thought no more of it, fool that I am.

We were rowed ashore, and there waiting for us – no, for Blanche – was Robert. He looked so tired and hollow-eyed, but wonderfully handsome still, and he was leading two ponies for us, a chestnut and a little grey. Blanche chose the grey – oh where has it taken her now? Robert greeted us so smilingly and teased Blanche that he had not heard from her, and she blushed and stammered so that it was pretty to see her. I explained how the note must have gone astray, and Robert declared that as he had spent the night out in the open among the ranks of the Twenty-Third, he must indeed have been hard to find. He told us how sick the soldiers are, how desperate for proper food and sleep. Edgar came up then and took charge of us and Robert kissed Blanche's hand in farewell and I was forced to look away.

We rode a long way, it seemed, perhaps an hour or more, and the heat became very dreadful. We kept passing soldiers fallen by the wayside, convulsed with fever, and at each one, I longed to dismount and help, but Edgar made us ride on and there was nothing for it but to obey. I wanted so badly to know where Robert was, and what he would do if battle began, but Blanche did not mention him and therefore I could not. We passed some trampled vineyards full of French soldiers cramming their cheeks and pockets with grapes and Blanche seemed much interested in them. Why, oh why? Is that something of the secret of her going?

We came at last to Lord Raglan, who sat on his horse on a rise of higher ground above a swamp. He greeted us most charmingly and pointed out what an excellent view we should have of the fighting and the river below us. I began to feel that I did not at all wish to see the fighting, that I wished above all to know where Robert was, and besides that to go back to where all those poor sick creatures were lying and dying.

From where we sat on our horses, I could see the River Alma winding below us, and beyond it a wide sweep of higher ground which seemed fairly to bristle with Russians and Russian guns. I turned to Blanche, fearing that it had been a mistake to let her come, and saw that she was indeed white-faced but that her eyes shone with excitement and she was smiling. I said to her, 'You need not look,' and she replied, 'I shan't for long.' Oh if only I had known then what she planned, if only I had known and stopped her!

When the bugles sounded the advance, I thought for a moment I should faint at the knowledge of what was to come. But what did come was far worse than anything I ever saw, and fainting would have been a puny response to such courage and such bloodshed. The Russian guns began to belch forth flames and smoke and great black balls that came bouncing and thudding through the ranks and left so many screaming or still. I believe it was above an hour and a half we sat and watched them fall, and so intent was I upon the terrible spectacle before me that I never thought to look round. Oh God, that I had looked! Just one glance and I might have seen her go!

But I never looked, I never saw. I kept gazing at the smoke-filled inferno before me and sometimes the smoke would clear for a moment and I could see the horror quite clearly, and then another boom would thud out and I could only hear the pain it caused. A Frenchman came galloping up at last and saluted Lord Raglan and gave him a message. I know now that it was a declaration from the French that they would have to fall back if the British did not advance further. Lord Raglan turned to me and said that he and his staff would ride on down across the river, but that we were to stay where we were with the escort he left for us. And still I did not look back, not one glance! I remember thinking I saw a grey muzzle close by my pony's flank, but I never checked to see who it might be. . . .

I saw the soldiers begin to march down towards the river, some of them going through the vineyards and emerging with bunches of grapes held between their teeth. I saw them all go on down to the river and begin to cross it, wading waist deep in the river with their rifles held above their heads, some of them even stopping to drink as they pushed through the water. And all the while they struggled onwards, the Russian guns never stopped but thundered on at them without a pause until the water was quite choked with red coats and red blood. My eyes were smarting with smoke and tears, but still I never thought to look behind me, not once.

I could not believe they could still advance, but they did, on and on that red flood poured, battling up the slopes towards the Russians for every inch of ground. I think I must have cried aloud quite often, for the officers beside me kept looking across and smiling. In the end we were all cheering as if our hearts would burst, and when we saw the Brigade of Guards fall upon the Russians like lions and drive them back in hopeless retreat we were all weeping and cheering like madmen. . . . Oh yes, the battle was won, but what of all those poor broken bodies down the hillside before me, or drifting in the river? And what of Blanche?

When I turned at last, I found her gone. Perhaps four hours I had sat in my saddle and never turned once. I shall blame myself to my dying day that I never thought to turn, for I know that when he is not by, Edgar instinctively trusts Blanche to my care. And I have failed him. And her. And Robert. Why did she go? Was she so wretchedly unhappy that she could bear it no longer?

Thinking of what she could not bear, how is Robert bearing his pain tonight? For if she has run away, she has run away from him as much as anyone. The moment I raised the alarm of her going, I sent to find him, and he came flying up but minutes later, having been in the thick of things all that afternoon, his face chalk white but for a scarlet smear where a piece of shot had grazed his cheek. I was in such a state of turmoil I told him everything in as bald a way as I could, and I could see he could not at first comprehend what I was saying. And then at last he drew out of his pocket a little folded paper, and took from that a yellow curl and kissed it, and if at that moment I could have given her back to him I would, I *would*.

Then Edgar came and I had to confess the terrible story once more and he said I must go back to the ship at once, and I begged to stay but he was adamant and by now I was shaking so violently I doubted I could sit my horse much longer. He began to consult with the others around, and with Robert, and I was forced to leave them there and trail down that blood-stained track where we had ridden together but six hours before. Captain Nash took me back, and others whom I hardly noticed, and we rode in silence while my heart and conscience gave me such pain as I hope never to know again. They tried to cheer me at the last as I was carried to the paddle boat, and to say that nobody could slip away unseen in such a populous place as a battlefield, that Edgar would surely return with news before nightfall, and that it would only redouble his anxieties if he knew *both* his sisters were wandering abroad and lost. I tried to thank them for their kindness but could not speak.

Mary has brought me a little wine but I cannot drink it. I have tried so hard to pray but I do not think God hears me now. Oh why does Edgar not come? Every minute I wait to hear the splash of oars – the night is cold but I have left the porthole open so that I might hear the first sign of his coming. Every minute he does not come seems like an hour to me, and I must sit here surrounded by Blanche's dresses, Blanche's hats, Blanche's pretty things and not know what is become of Blanche herself. I have just looked in the glass and I am grown an old hag in just a few short hours. My eyes are gritted with exhaustion but I dare not close them for always behind my lids I see Blanche's face and the ruddy glare of battle. Please God may I never again spend such a night as this.

# Eight

It was not until the sun was high the following morning that they returned, Edgar and Robert together, temporarily united in their loss. They had spent the night in a fruitless and frustrating search around a battlefield choked with wounded among men whose preoccupation with life and death was bound to take precedence over the fate of the merely missing. Colonel Lowe, a man who had seen years of active service in India, possessed of a humane and compassionate character rare among cavalry officers, deputed several of his staff to accompany Edgar in his quest, and promised as much help as he could muster when daylight came.

When it came it revealed a scene of absolute desolation, acres of hillside thick with blanketed bodies and echoing to cries for help and water. It was not possible to take a single step without grinding underfoot fragments of shell and shot, firelocks, caps and helmets, bullets and swords. The air was rank with the smell of spent powder and blood and a September mist hung dank and heavy over it all. The mist matched the prevailing spirit as all elation at the triumph of victory was swept away at the realization of the price paid for it.

At daybreak Lord Raglan was apprised of Blanche's disappearance and at once the search became something coherent. Only one man among the escort he had left with Sarah and Blanche the previous day had actually observed Blanche riding away and as the man she was with appeared to be in British uniform he had merely supposed her to have sickened of the sight before her and to have asked to be taken away. As, he said, her sister had raised no objection to her going and the battle before them was at its height, he now, with the deepest regret, admitted he had thought no more of the matter until Miss Drummond had raised the alarm.

It seemed an impasse. No one else could be found who recalled seeing Blanche the day before, nor could any trace be discovered of the officer in British uniform who had been seen to escort her from the heights. Gradually the mist began to thin, and a golden September sun rose out of its swathes into a clear, pale sky. As it did so, as if illuminated by its rays, a strange and extraordinary piece of evidence came to light.

Some British soldiers, combing the heights south of the Alma which the Russians had occupied, in search of plunder, were returning towards the allied lines. They crossed the river northwards again to the point on the river's banks that the Zouaves had occupied the day before and were skirting the blackened ruins of a burnt-out village on the shores when a shout went up. There, in an orchard of plums and apples curiously untrampled, lay a picnic basket, an expensive wicker basket containing the remains of a cold chicken, some peaches, two bottles of champagne – and a lady's petticoat. The men gathered round in amazement. There was no question of what should be done with the wine and fruit, but the petticoat . . . It was evidently expensive, its ruffles adorned with exquisite drawn thread work and flower heads embroidered in blue silk. The wag among the soldiers bent forward and speared it on the point of his bayonet, and then signalling to his comrades to shoulder the basket, he tramped off, singing, towards his own lines, the petticoat flying indecently behind him like some frivolous flag.

At last they came for Sarah. Edgar came with the two fellow officers who had supported him throughout the night, and he and Sarah met in a miserable silence that was evidence of how little progress he had made since he saw her last.

'It is my doing,' Edgar said, 'I should never have brought her to a place where she would be so unhappy.'

Sarah shook her head.

'Oh no. It is mine. I have been so unfeeling to her. I have made everything so hard for her to bear.'

On the shore members of Lord Raglan's staff awaited them with a horse for Sarah. That ride back to the battlefield was hardly to be borne : in every way so unlike the precise ride she had made but a day before, with Blanche beside her in her grey hat, her grey habit with its swallow-tailed coat, laughing and pointing things out, and knowing all the time what she had in her heart to do that day.

Lord Raglan welcomed her with the solicitude generally given to invalids.

'Forgive my – appearance, my lord. It has been a distressing night, and I have not taken off my clothes.'

He brushed her apology aside.

'There is no need, my dear Miss Drummond, no need at all. I cannot express to you my intense sorrow and anxiety over what has taken place. Indeed, I hold myself somewhat to blame since it was I who encouraged you to follow us. I want you now to recount to us in every detail how your day passed yesterday, and as quickly as you can, since time is of the utmost importance.'

It sounded a bald and, for her part, negligent story. She looked straight ahead as she recounted it, and saw Robert among Lord Raglan's staff, standing there straight and tense, hanging upon every syllable she uttered in case it might unlock the mystery of Blanche's disappearance, and indeed, of the state of her heart. There was it seemed, so little to say. The only elements about the day before which had been unusual had been Blanche's hurry to get ashore and her taking her few jewels with her, and both these were now explained by her flight. Neither fact threw any light on why she had gone, or with whom, or where.

Lord Raglan was touched upon his shoulder. An infantry officer stood behind him holding something white and most unsoldierly. There was a low exchange between them, and then Lord Raglan turned to Sarah.

'Some men of the Forty-First discovered a picnic basket down by the river early this morning, and with it was a lady's petticoat ! I do not for one moment suppose that – '

Sarah sprang forward, seizing the garment from the officer's hands.

'Oh yes ! Oh yes, it is Blanche's ! This is hers ! I should know it anywhere ! She had it mended but a few – '

She stopped and stared down at the crumpled, muddied bundle of frills in her hands.

'My lord. Would you be good enough to ask my brother to find the wife of Trooper Evans?'

Mrs Evans was without her apron. She had spent a comfortable night with her husband after a day she had much enjoyed, watching the battle as if it were a spectator sport, unworried by any impending tragedy since the cavalry, whose number included Trooper Evans, had never been called upon. She had risen at dawn, prepared a breakfast of rum and biscuit for her husband, and had then washed her apron in water intended for the horses, and hung it upon a convenient hedge to dry in the ripening sunlight. It was rumoured that when the day's work of burying the dead, both Russian and British, was done, they would be moving south once more towards Sebastopol. Mrs Evans had struck a bargain with the driver of a supply wagon that he would allow her to ride in his wagon when the army marched if she would put her extremely competent needle to good use upon his disintegrating uniform. To fill in the time before the army's departure, Mrs Evans resolved to go down on to the battlefield, and see what she might retrieve that would be of use or of value. Having secured her damp apron by tying its strings around some twigs in the hedge, and commanding two other regimental wives, who were doing some rudimentary laundry nearby, to keep an eye upon it, she set off. She had not gone above a hundred yards before she met Captain Drummond. Captain Drummond and Miss Sarah Drummond were two people she most particularly wished to avoid, but the captain had several of the commander-in-chief's staff with him and looked so grim and purposeful that thoughts of flight were out of the question. Her hands went down instinctively to smooth her apron and her heart gave a little plummet of dismay to find that the garment, her badge of respectability, was absent. She bobbed a small curtsey in recompense.

'Good day to you, sir.'

Edgar did not reply. Instead he motioned to two of the men who accompanied him, and Mrs Evans found that they were instantly by her side, and not in a way that suggested even the smallest gallantry. Her arms were taken hold of. She looked up at Edgar, mounted beside her, and said with a brave attempt at indignation, 'What is up, sir? I do protest, sir, 'deed I do! A respectable body like me, sir –'

'I advise you, Mrs Evans, to save your breath. There will be ample opportunity for you to speak before Lord Raglan. Make haste, please, for there is not a moment to lose.'

Stumbling between her escorts, Mrs Evans was led through the camp, acutely conscious of the spectacle she made and mortified to observe the number of regimental wives who seemed to have gathered expressly for the purpose of goading her on her undignified way. Tripping in the ruts, almost all her energies were concentrated upon the difficulty of going as fast as her escort compelled her, and upon seeming not to mind the laughable picture she presented, and it was not until she was brought to a sudden halt and commanded to curtsey to the commander-in-chief that she had energy to spare for the predicament she was in.

She dared not raise her eyes above the buttons on Lord Raglan's dark blue coat. She was only dimly conscious of what he was saying in her panic and it was not until his voice gave way to the more urgent and familiar one of Colonel Lowe that she realized a reply was required of her.

'I repeat, Mrs Evans, were you in the habit of receiving mending and plain sewing to do for Miss Blanche Drummond?'

Mrs Evans tried to look boldly at the colonel, but failed signally. Her head dropped again and she muttered her assent.

'Then I imagine this garment is familiar to you?'

A crumpled parcel of frills was thrust beneath her nose.

'I couldn't say, I'm sure, sir. Could be anybody's, sir. Miss Blanche wasn't one to let her things get in such a state, sir. To be sure –'

'This petticoat, Mrs Evans, was found near a picnic basket down by the river this morning. We do not need your proof of its ownership, Miss Sarah Drummond has established that it is her sister's already, and that you recently mended it. Evasion of the truth, Mrs Evans, will do your own cause nothing but harm. Miss Blanche Drummond is missing, as I am sure you are well aware, and we require from you an explanation as swiftly as you can.'

The man on her right jerked her arm as if to hasten her. Mrs Evans shot him a reproving glance and spoke boldly to the colonel.

'I don't see why I should know, sir, I'm but a plain woman who did a bit of sewing now and again to oblige, sir, hardly the person Miss Blanche would take into her confidence now, sir – '

'She gave you letters!' Sarah cried out. 'I saw her, once or twice she gave you letters and on one of those occasions at least you were at pains to hide the destination!'

There was a short pause, during which Mrs Evans directed all her efforts into an elaborate attempt to look unconcerned. Colonel Lowe stooped slightly so that his tanned, finely lined face was but inches from her own.

'There will be no more prevarication, Mrs Evans. If you do not at once admit all you know, you will be taken down to Calamita Bay at once and you will be put upon a transport ship which will take you down to Constantinople and thence to London with the greatest possible speed.'

Mrs Evans shut her eyes. It was only by the greatest good fortune and scheming that she had managed to come as far with the army already, since the complement of wives with 'her' regiment had now dwindled to a mere three. Trooper Evans was proud of her ability to contrive things for him, and she had acquired a status among the soldiers that would be hard to exchange for the certainty of raw poverty in England. It was, she reasoned in rapid panic, Trooper Evans to whom she owed her first loyalty, not any whimsical miss and her intrigues. She opened her eyes again.

'She's gone with a Frenchman, miss. A Mr Dellahay or some such name. I've been takin' letters all summer, miss, carryin' them to the edge of camp, miss, and giving them over to a French soldier what's been there to meet me.'

She paused for a moment and observed, not without a small satisfaction, that the faces round her were riveted to her every word. Miss Drummond was as white as snow, ready to faint she looked but for her eyes which could have burned holes in paper that fierce that were they –

'Go on, Mrs Evans.'

'It seems this Mr Dellahay knew how Miss Blanche was hatin' the life and he wasn't carin' for it much either, all this hangin' about and no action – '

'I imagine you gleaned such information from the letters as they passed through your hands?'

'Only a glimpse 'ere and there, sir, when they weren't folded too careful. Mr Dellahay said he'd take Miss Blanche away if she cared to go, and they could go to some friend of 'is in Constantinople, sir, and then he'd take her to Paris and make her Madame Dellahay, sir. He said he'd do it under cover of the first action there was since everyone would be too busy to notice them slippin' off, and 'e told her all the plans in advance so's she'd be ready like, and then she sent 'im a letter to say they'd been asked to watch the fightin' at the Alma from 'is lordship's position, and 'e come up to get 'er disguised, and said 'e'd bring a disguise for her so as she could slip away easy.'

Mrs Evans paused for breath and to retrieve the customary refinements of her speech when addressing ladies and gentlemen.

'Where is she gone in Constantinople?'

It was a new voice, a deep voice quite cracked with some kind of strain. Mrs Evans looked up against the sunlight with difficulty and saw the tall silhouette of the newspaper man between her and the sky. He'd been sweet on Miss Blanche, she knew, and Miss Blanche had laughed quite openly with the Frenchman about him, poor fellow. Trooper Evans said he was a regular soldier for all he was a gentleman and lived as rough as any of them and was writing home to the newspapers every day to tell them in England how the poor soldiers fared. It seemed a shame that silly girl had used him so ill, a pitiful shame. Mrs Evans squinted into the sunlight and spoke in softer tones.

'It was a county, sir, a County Rambert or some such name. He's lived among the Turks all his life, sir, with little boys to wait on 'im and cushions to loll on, sir, and not a mortal thing to do but write poetry and listen to music and look at the stars all night, sir. He'd offered Mr Dellahay his hospitality back in the spring, sir, said 'e'd be only too glad to 'elp – help, sir.'

The men around her exchanged glances. She saw Colonel Lowe bend towards Lord Raglan and heard him say something incomprehensible about a hedonist of the worst kind, and then both men looked towards Edgar who was pulling on his gloves with the air of a man bent on immediate action.

'With your permission, sir, I shall go at once.'

Lord Raglan put a hand on his shoulder.

'There is a yacht at your disposal, dear boy, which will make the shortest work possible of the three hundred miles to Constantinople. Messages will go to the ambassador immediately by the electric telegraph, and he will be asked to watch all vessels coming into the harbour. They have but a day's start on you. You may rest assured that the greatest care will be taken of Miss Sarah Drummond in your absence since I am sure you agree a desperate chase across the Black Sea would be hardly fitting occupation for her.'

Edgar bowed and thanked him. Pausing only to salute his colonel, he turned and was about to depart down the avenue which had opened up for him among the press of men, towards his waiting horse, when Robert barred his way.

'I shall come with you, Drummond.'

Edgar looked straight ahead.

'Thank you, Chiltern, but it will not be necessary. My servant will accompany me and I shall get on quite swiftly with him alone.'

Robert's exhausted face twisted with fury.

'Damn it, man, I *shall* come! I have as much right or more as you, and you have none to stop me! You can –'

His arm was caught. Looking down with an impatient exclamation, he saw Sarah there, her face drawn with fatigue but her eyes still blazing with energy.

'Do not go, Mr Chiltern, I beg you do not go.'

'Ah, so you would join the family conspiracy to keep me away from your sister as an unfitting suitor? I thought you at least smiled upon us!'

'It is not that, Mr Chiltern. It is quite the reverse. Oh, Robert, do not go, do not for your own good, to spare yourself more pain, do not go!'

He looked down at her more quietly.

'You think she would not come back for – for me?'

Sarah nodded.

'Do not go. It is the only chance!'

Robert continued to look down at her upturned face for some moments, during which Edgar fidgeted to be gone, then he said softly to Sarah, 'So be it.'

She gave a little sigh and turned to her brother.

'Godspeed, dearest Edgar. I know you are in too much hurry to wish to be detained by anything, but I would remind you how intolerable it will be for me to be here, idle, while you are gone, not knowing if you are successful. Please, Edgar, I beg you, will you let me try to do something, some small thing, to help the wounded while you are gone? I would promise to be prudent, but I think I shall be quite torn in pieces by anxiety while you are gone and I should like so much to help. I know you agree with Lord Raglan that I should not accompany you, but perhaps you might relent in the other matter, perhaps even Lord Raglan might think it possible – '

She stopped abruptly. After her flood of words the air seemed dramatically silent and empty. Edgar glanced up, away from her, towards Lord Raglan, and then he leaned forward and kissed her cheek.

'You must be patient, Sarah,' he said. 'The matter is unthinkable,' and then he turned and sprang into the saddle and was gone down the hillside to the sea.

We have ruined this place. I say we because I now feel a seasoned camp follower and must identify myself with the army, and we, the British Army, have destroyed Balaclava. When we sailed into Balaclava harbour a week ago I thought I had never seen a place so lovely, a little pool of water, almost land-locked, with the mountains all round reflected in it, and round the shore the prettiest little houses imaginable with roofs of green tiles and charming terraced gardens and orchards stretching up the slopes behind them. Roses everywhere still, late roses, and honeysuckle and vines and neat rows of pumpkins and tomatoes. Oh, it was a fairy-tale place!

Now it is quite ruined. Twenty-five thousand men have trampled all over it of whom the larger proportion have dysentery, and the little pretty harbour is choked with ships and the water is full of filth and smells abominable. The gardens are all battered down and the houses overrun with soldiers and there are heaps of rubbish everywhere. Lord Raglan ordered the Greek inhabitants of the place to go when we came, and I thought him very hard to do so, but now I am thankful they did not have to see the destruction of their little paradise.

I am still waiting for Edgar. I tried to pass the last few days in painting Balaclava before its charm was quite gone, but it was a futile, silly occupation, and I find that my mind is only diverted from its preoccupation by conversation or writing. So I am writing again. The telegraph brought word that he had reached Constantinople but a few days ago but the message said no more. I am grown so used to the knot of anxiety in my heart that I scarcely recall how tranquillity felt.

I have discovered so much since Edgar left, such sad things. There is no doubt that Blanche's apparent fondness for Robert was no more than a feint, a screen behind which she could plot more freely. I have seen him but a few times, but it seems to me that Robert knows it well himself, for he is so silent and grim and will hardly be enticed away from among the soldiers for a moment, as if only by flinging himself into his work can he forget even for a little while. I suppose it is best I should not see him for I should not know how to comfort him, and I should have my own pain to contend with as well as his – my doubled pain at losing him as well as losing Blanche. For she is lost to me too, for she kept those secrets from me, all those miseries and the schemes they drove her to, kept them all from me who has known her inmost thoughts all her life. But perhaps I have not, perhaps I never have. Perhaps I have had this selfish blindness that would not pity her always here, always part of me. . . .

I have thought and thought until my head was whirling as to why she should choose M. de la Haye, but I do not know. I simply do not know. I cannot think that his promises of comfort and pleasure were enough to lure her. I can only think he offered much more. He had it all so excellently planned, the monster, for at the Alma only a small company of Turks was between his Zouaves and the sea, and thus he was in a prime position to slip away. They found all Blanche's other clothes, rolled up and crammed among the loose stones of the orchard wall, and I cannot contemplate without savage fury the kind of man who would plot such a thing, plan such a wicked, cruel, unthinking thing. I can see him in my mind's eye, standing laughing at our innocence in that orchard with champagne in his hand, promising Blanche that she need not hurry, that they had plenty of time to make good their escape, that he had thought of everything! Oh, I am grinding my teeth in fury as I write!

It must, I suppose, be some consolation that our parents do not know. Lord Raglan has impressed upon all who do know that no word is to be sent home for the moment, and Mrs Evans has been sent to work upon one of the hospital transport ships going up and down to Scutari until such time as Colonel Lowe decides what next shall be done with her. I almost envy her. Colonel Lowe has come constantly to me, and shown the most singular and touching attention, and when I begged him to think of some task I might perform to beguile these dreadful yawning days, and mentioned nursing, he told me I did not know what I asked. He says he is much perturbed about the state of the hospital ships himself, for they are impossible to keep clean and wounds fester terribly on those long crowded journeys down to Scutari. The ambulance wagons Lord Raglan asked for in May still have not come and I share Colonel

Lowe's feelings that the arrangements that the French have made for their sick and wounded put ours to shame.

I am frustrated beyond anything to sit here in my cabin and wait and wait and wait. The army is moving on to besiege Sebastopol which now lies to the north-west of us, for we sailed past the harbour mouth of the city last week on our way to this charming and devastated place. Colonel Lowe says it hardly deserves the name of siege for the allied forces are so grouped that the Russians have easy access in and out on the northern and eastern approaches of the town, but he admits that his opinion is not often heeded as there seems to be some stigma attached to military experience gained in India rather than Europe.

I find great comfort in talking to him, for he has much admiration for Robert. The commanders are finding the newspaper correspondents less and less welcome because the picture that is emerging in their reports at home does not reflect well upon our administration or our generals. Robert once said to me that the only commanders in the cavalry who had the humility to listen to others as well as a degree of their own experience were Colonel Scarlett of the Heavy Brigade and Colonel Lowe of our regiment. I repeated this to Colonel Lowe who seemed much flattered. He said it was a pity Robert had spurned the army for he not only has intelligence and courage but has a way with men that is truly impressive. I do not know who occupies my thoughts most, Robert or Blanche. I know who occupies my heart and a weary, painful burden it is to me, watching and waiting and longing and fearing to see him.

If I should hear he had fallen ill, nothing on earth should keep me here. Colonel Lowe says our army is cut in half by sickness and I daily dread to hear Robert has the cholera. I should go to him at once, I should not care what Edgar might say, I could not endure to stay –

# Nine

To Edgar's dismay, the yacht that had kindly been put at his disposal was not one of the new and swift steam yachts. It was a three-masted schooner of some hundred tons, but all the same would achieve a speed of eight or nine knots an hour which was at least twice the speed of the old brigs used as hospital ships which wallowed their way so sickeningly south to Scutari. Those were hulks indeed; *The Heron* was an elegantly appointed vessel, extremely comfortable and competently crewed, and if he had been in a better frame of mind, Edgar would have revelled in the week it took them to reach Constantinople. For the first time since the spring he had good food properly prepared, clean linen in quantity and somewhere comfortable and dry to sleep, but none of these things could divert him from the terrible anxieties that made every day of ceaseless pacing on the deck seem like a month.

Two days before the end of September *The Heron* glided into the harbour at Constantinople. The skyline of domes and minarets and towers looked just as romantic as it had done in April; the water, seething with rubbish, just as repellent. Turks and Greeks in baggy trousers and torn voluminous shirts trod barefoot in the filth of the quayside and among them, immaculate in the ambassador's livery, stood a messenger from the embassy.

Edgar stepped towards him carefully.

'Captain Drummond?'

Edgar inclined his head. The emissary bowed and presented a letter.

'The ambassador wishes to say that you are most welcome at the embassy during your time in Constantinople. I am to be your guide if you so wish and for as long as you wish it.'

Edgar felt that the invitation was almost royal. He murmured his acceptance of both offers and turned away to open his letter.

Lord Raglan had been as good as his word. A telegraphed message had reached the ambassador, the harbour had been closely watched, and only that morning a gentleman and a lady, answering very much to the description of Miss Drummond and the Frenchman, had landed from a small yacht and been hurried away in a closed carriage. The carriage had been followed and its destination noted. As it was known *The Heron* was but half a day behind, the ambassador had thought it more delicate to leave the task of actually retrieving Miss Drummond to her brother. The messenger he sent knew Constantinople well and would guide Edgar to the address he sought. Both Edgar and his sister would be warmly welcome at the embassy that evening. The ambassador concluded by warning Captain Drummond that the quarter of the city he was bound for was old, entirely Turkish, and to be treated with great circumspection.

Edgar folded the letter and slipped it into his pocket.

'Shall we go?'

A carriage was waiting, the ambassador's arms emblazoned on the panels. A small crowd had gathered round it, which made no attempt to fall back so that Edgar might climb in but rather pressed curiously closer. He was thankful when the door closed behind him and he set off, with his impassive and formal escort, away from the waterfront.

The sun was beginning to set, throwing a rosy translucence into the sky and long purple shadows across the narrow streets. An early autumn chill was falling with the dusk and as the carriage plunged into the dark labyrinth of squalid lanes behind the harbour, Edgar could see the golden and scarlet glow of lamps and braziers through doorways and grilles. The ambassador's man leant forward and pushed up the carriage window against the powerful stench that rose from the gutters of these alleys.

'Have we far to go?' Edgar asked.

His companion shook his head.

'Not far in distance, Captain Drummond, but the old quarter is not easily penetrated and thus we cannot make swift progress.'

They were indeed going slowly enough for screaming little ragged boys to climb on to the footplates and hang upon the doorhandles, howling, until pushed off by others wanting a turn. The narrow-fronted houses pressed in on either side, towering up in a welter of shutters and balconies, all of them seething with the bold black-eyed people whose open inquisitiveness Edgar found so offensive. There were, of course, no women to be seen, though a parcel of black robes could sometimes be glimpsed deep in an interior, but those insolent men and boys, chewing and smoking, in their tawdry rags of robes and turbans and ballooning trousers, were lounging in every corner of the crammed and stinking district.

Edgar leaned back in his corner and attempted to concentrate his thoughts upon the task ahead of him. It struck him that during all those hours pacing upon *The Heron* he had somehow assumed that the ambassador would have intercepted Blanche on her arrival, and that his own job would be that of stern recrimination – the sternness proportionate to Blanche's undoubted repentance – followed by forgiveness and consolation. The deep anxiety he had felt was because – though his mind squirmed away from framing it too precisely – he feared that Blanche might have been seduced on the journey south, for if she had been sufficiently hysterical and irrational to run away like the heroine of some third-rate melodrama there seemed little chance she would have proved herself strong-minded enough to resist a man who had already persuaded her to so much.

Edgar had worried endlessly as to how he should ascertain this fact – he dreaded the merest thought of a confession, although he desired very much to see Blanche submissive – and acutely as to what he should do with her once the awful truth was known to him and thus became his responsibility. That she should be sent home was indubitably right, but whether he should ask for compassionate leave to escort her himself, or inflict the burden of her upon Sarah he could not decide. In either case, his father would blame him and he would be seen, as indeed he keenly felt he had, to have failed in his duty of protecting his two beloved sisters.

It all seemed a great deal more lurid and unmanageable having to drive deep into this rotting warren of the old city to face the inevitable scene rather than having it as he had imagined, in one of the handsome, Europeanized rooms at the embassy. Twilight was thickening fast, the alleys were growing ever darker and the cries and shouts outside the closed windows of the carriage became sinister rather than merely irritating.

Abruptly, all signs of humanity vanished. The emissary leaned forward and lowered the window at Edgar's side and he craned out. They were in a straight narrow passage, bound by high walls on either side over which some thick foliage was spilling raggedly. As his eyes became accustomed to the gloom, Edgar could make out that ahead of them a great studded door was let into the right-hand wall, and before this they stopped at last.

'Where are we?'

'This is an old palace, Captain Drummond. It has been inhabited these forty years or so by Comte Rambert, a Frenchman whose parents fled here from Paris at the time of the Revolution. It is here that your sister was brought.'

Edgar put his hand out to open the door.

'Is the count known to the ambassador?'

'Hardly, sir. He is a man of private and eccentric habits. He does not mingle with the European residents of Constantinople.'

'Will you wait for me here?'

The emissary cleared his throat.

'Do you not wish me to accompany you inside, Captain Drummond?'

Edgar opened the door.

'No,' he said, 'I wish to go quite alone.'

He was let in through a postern into a small vaulted room lit only by a flame burning in a globe of red glass suspended on a long brass chain from the shadowy heights of the roof. It seemed to be some kind of guardroom, for several figures in turbans and wide breeches and bare feet sat cross-legged around the walls, on the floor, with rifles balanced across their knees. None of them, not even the bearded old man who had opened the postern, gave the slightest acknowledgement of Edgar's presence.

'I am Captain Drummond of the —th Hussars,' he said. His voice sounded thin and foolish.

Nobody answered. The old man shuffled across the tiled floor and opened a farther door, and through it Edgar could see a line of columns stretching away into the dimness, and more vaulting and more glass lamps, some red, some blue.

He said, 'I wish to see your master. Take me to him.'

The old man continued to hold the door open, gazing wearily before him.

'Does nobody speak English?' Edgar demanded.

It seemed that nobody spoke at all, let alone English. With an exclamation of indignation Edgar stepped quickly across the room and through the door the old man held, and heard it closed immediately behind him. He felt the beginnings of a small wish that he had allowed the ambassador's man to come with him and quelled it at once.

Before him a colonnade marched away, enclosing to his right hand a paved courtyard in whose centre a still tank of water reflected the first small stars. The pillars were striped around in twists of cream and burgundy stone, and above the capitals, spiralled like turbans, the roof rose in great arched ribs to a central spine of carved and gilded wood. From the glowing blots of rose and sapphire light around the courtyard, Edgar could see that the jewel-like lamps went all around the colonnade, but none of them gave sufficient light to see if there were any doorways anywhere, any obvious route that he should take. It was all dim, silent, empty and alarming.

Resolutely, Edgar set out under the line of lamps straight before him, his feet ringing out disconcertingly on the coloured tiles of the floor. Before he could even reach the end, and set out upon the second side of the square, huge double doors, hitherto concealed by the gloom, were flung open, revealing a cavern of rich light within, and a tall man in a turban.

Edgar stopped, and put his hand on his sword. He was perhaps ten paces from the doorway, and against the darkness could make out nothing of the man on the threshold.

'Captain Drummond?' the man said pleasantly. His English was clear but accented. 'Will you not come in? We have been expecting you.'

Edgar remained where he was.

'Expecting me?' he said warily.

'Naturally. We saw you disembark safely from *The Heron* and have been expecting you every moment. It is not an easy house to find. Will you not come in?'

He turned and called something into the room behind him,

and a boy with a lamp swinging from his hand came running out and seized Edgar with his free one.

'Come, come, Captain Drummond! It is only our wish to make you welcome.'

Unwillingly, Edgar was pulled over the threshold into a huge high room lit with pierced brass lanterns fixed to the walls, and quite devoid of furniture apart from magnificent carpets and a few divans covered in rugs. Once inside, he detached his hand firmly from the boy's.

'Do – do I address the Count Rambert?'

The man smiled. He was tall and thin, dark-skinned and dressed in a wine-coloured robe sashed in copper gauze. His gaze travelled lightly over Edgar's scarlet and white.

'Indeed no, sir. I am merely his secretary. But he awaits your coming with great impatience.'

Edgar longed to ask if Blanche was with him but forbore to put that most delicate of questions to anyone but the count himself.

'If you will follow me?'

The secretary turned and began to cross the great room softly on his slippered feet. Edgar followed him loudly in his boots. They went through a maze of chambers, all dimly lit, all tall and shadowy, and with each one there was a little more furniture, carved chairs, cabinets, ancient weapons arranged like fans and fish skeletons on the walls, sofas and piles of cushions, alcoves, low tables, stools. As they went onward too, Edgar became aware of a thin piping sound and of a smell, a sweetish, slightly sickly smell, heavy and indolent.

At last they came to a high dark door, beside which torches burned in iron brackets. The secretary turned and smiled once more at Edgar.

'The count expects you, Captain Drummond. His welcome will be shared by Monsieur de la Haye, and your sister, Miss Blanche Drummond.'

The door swung inward, and the piping rose to a thin clear thread of music, and the soft sweet smell came out in a cloud like incense. The room seemed at once dark and glowing, as full of objects as the previous ones had been empty, and on a kind of dais at the far end was a tumble of rugs and cushions and an old man in a gold and russet gown, and a young one in the outrageous uniform of the Zouaves – and Blanche. They were, it seemed, quite unaware of his entry, and they were all laughing.

Edgar stepped forward.

'Blanche!'

Her face went quite pale at the sight of him, and she jumped to her feet, clenching her fists.

'How dare you come here, Edgar? How dare you?'

Below her the two men continued to loll. The old one held out a languid hand to Edgar, a hand so heavy with jewels that the fingers were hardly visible.

'*Alors, le galant capitaine!* Welcome, *mon brave.* Come in and be comfortable, come in!'

Edgar hardly heard him. He gazed, stricken, at Blanche's furious white face.

'I – am come to help you –'

'I am not going back!' Blanche shouted. 'Never! You shall not take me back!'

Henri de la Haye let his head fall back on the cushions behind him, and laughed. The count propped himself upon one elbow.

'Come, come, *mes enfants*, no quarrelling. Henri has only brought me this pretty child two hours ago, and now you come, Monsieur Edgar, and make her angry –'

'She should not be here, Count. She should be with me, as is proper. I am come to take her back to my protection.'

Henri de la Haye turned a face full of laughter towards Edgar.

'Protection, monsieur? *Protection?* Never in all my life have I found it so easy to extract a lady from – protection. We had a picnic, even, while you played your battle games, did we not, Blanche? We drank champagne, my fine friend, we dressed your sister as the most charming little drummer boy –'

'Come,' Edgar said loudly, and held his hand out to Blanche. Blanche stamped.

'Go away, Edgar, go away! I am not coming with you, not ever. I am going to Paris with Henri. We are to be married!'

Another burst of laughter forced Henri de la Haye back on the cushions. Edgar sprang forward, his face darkening with outrage.

'You blackguard! You conscienceless villain! To dare to lay a finger upon my sister –'

'Come, come! This will never do!' The count exerted himself sufficiently to beckon to some unseen person in the corner. 'You need a pipe, my friend, for your *colère*, and a cushion for your limbs. When you are settled, we may go on.'

Edgar suddenly found himself surrounded by boys, small black-haired boys, with moon-pale faces and huge dark eyes, dressed in absurd and theatrical robes. Like Gulliver, he was laid hold of, and then drawn irresistibly down on to a pile of cushions at Henri de la Haye's side, stiff and inflexible in his uniform and heavily impeded by his sword. Henri de la Haye leaned towards him.

'I promise you, *mon vieux*, that I never do things in discomfort when I might do them in comfort. What pleasure could there be for us in that terrible little ship, thrown about like two coins in a pocket? No, I said to myself, wait, wait until the city, where my good friend will provide us with everything that is comfortable. And look how it is, are we not comfortable? *Assoie-toi*, Blanche, it is unpleasant to have you standing over us.'

Relief and fury held Edgar's tongue a prisoner.

'I am going to Paris with Henri!' Blanche repeated, remaining on her feet.

A hookah was brought and placed at Edgar's side, and a small hand held out the mouthpiece. He waved it away. It was absurd, lying there like some dog on a rug, while the odious Frenchman laughed and that depraved old man drew on his pipe and Blanche stood there and stamped.

'You are coming back with me to the embassy, Blanche, and there will be no argument.'

Blanche burst into tears. She put her right hand over her eyes, and held out her left, quite naked of any rings, to Henri de la Haye.

'Henri! Henri! Stop him! Say I am coming to Paris. Say it, say it! Say I shall be your wife! Tell him it is true!'

The count took his pipe from his mouth and surveyed her with detached amusement. Then he turned his hooded gaze upon Henri de la Haye who had flung his arms behind his head in order to lounge back more comfortably.

'Tell him, Henri, *tell* him!'

'*Chérie*, you must go with your brother tonight –'

'No!' she screamed.

'I insist. There is no place for you here. We have had a time together *bien amusant, n'est ce pas*? I thought we should have more time, but here comes your big, brave brother and away goes my little friend.' He shrugged. 'But it was an excellent adventure, was it not? And I do begin to regret that the ship was not a little, just a little more comfortable.'

At the same moment that Blanche fell, weeping and shouting, to her knees, Edgar leapt to his feet.

'I did not know the world held so black and base a villain! Come, Blanche, there will be no more delaying, not one moment more!'

The door opened behind them, and the secretary entered.

'May I show you out, Captain Drummond?'

Blanche lunged forward and caught at Henri's ankles.

'No! No! You promised to marry me, you promised, you promised! Don't send me away, I can't bear it, I cannot –'

Count Rambert raised his hand.

'The noise is insupportable. What a barbaric race these Anglais are.'

From the passage outside came three or four figures. In a moment Edgar was being propelled helplessly back through the maze of rooms he had crossed but half an hour before, and behind him, sobbing and gasping, her arms firmly held, came Blanche. He strained his ears to hear what she was saying so brokenly as they were hurried along, longing to hear his name, Sarah's name, any token of repentance, but all she was saying over and over again, was, 'Paris, oh Paris, oh *Paris*!'

She said nothing to him all the long ride back to the embassy. If Edgar had not thought the reaction too trifling for such a momentous business, he would have said she was sulking. The emissary got upon the box and left them to each other, but their solitude availed Edgar nothing. She pulled up the hood of her cloak and turned her face from him and would not open her lips.

At the embassy, things were no better. She refused to respond to the comfort, the familiarity, even the note the ambassador

sent to her-room. She withdrew into it with the maid provided
for her use, and would not say one word to Edgar, not even to
wish him good night. Disinclined for food or company, and
thoroughly disheartened by the whole over-dramatic and undignified episode, Edgar took himself to bed, to toss and worry
upon it until the dawn came stealing up the Bosphorus.

Eight o'clock brought a message from the ambassador bidding
Captain Drummond and his sister to breakfast. It was not a
summons even Blanche could refuse. An hour later, pale and
heavy-eyed, and still wearing the violet silk gown she had worn
yesterday, she presented herself for Edgar to escort downstairs.

'I trust you slept well?'

She tossed her head crossly.

'Does it look it?'

'Your nerves are much unstrung by the terrible strain you
have been under.'

'If you mean having to sit in a tent for five months you are
quite right. If you mean the last ten days with Henri, you are
quite wrong. My nerves were entirely in order until you came
stamping in last evening, upsetting everything, spoiling my
plans – '

'We will talk of this when you are calmer.'

She took her arm away from his.

'We will not talk of it at *all*.'

The ambassador and his wife received them with great
splendour. There were but the four of them at breakfast, in a
room large enough to accommodate four hundred with wide
windows overlooking the Bosphorus, and superb French furniture. Blanche became all at once quite gracious and received
compliments upon her safety after her adventure and expres-
sions of anxiety as to her health after her ordeal, with smiles
and words of thanks. When they were seated, and she had
refused everything pressed upon her but tea and toast, the
ambassador turned towards Edgar.

'And perhaps my staff may be of assistance in securing Miss
Drummond and her sister a comfortable passage home?'

Blanche put her cup down and turned to him with the most
artless of smiles.

127

'How good you are, Sir John, but it will not be necessary to trouble your staff. I am not going home.'

Edgar's head came up from his plate with a jerk.

'My dear –'

Blanche looked with another charming smile at her hostess.

'I am going to Paris, you see. We shall leave immediately, I think, and be there almost the moment the season is in full swing.'

The ambassador's wife, uncertain of anything much beyond the fact that she had two strangers to breakfast, smiled back.

'Delightful! I dote upon Paris! I go every spring for gowns and nowhere are there prettier hats. Charming!'

Blanche's face lit up with pleasure.

'I have never had a Paris gown in my life! Can you believe it? I cannot wait to be upon the journey. Thank goodness it is only a matter of days before we set out.'

Helplessly Edgar gazed at her with all the sternness he could muster. The ambassador looked up from his devilled kidneys.

'You must curb your impatience a little longer, Miss Drummond, I fear. It will take your sister above a week to reach Constantinople, perhaps a fortnight –'

'Oh!' Blanche said airily, 'I am not going to Paris with my sister. Monsieur de la Haye took me away from those terrible battlefields, and now he will take me to Paris. He has promised me such treats! I do believe Paris must be the most exciting place on earth –'

'Blanche!' Edgar said with vehemence. 'Come, come, my dear. No more of this.' He turned to his hostess. 'Forgive us, please, Lady Stratford. My sister is quite exhausted with her trials and hardly knows what she is saying.'

A pink spot had begun to burn feverishily in each of Blanche's cheeks. She stared back at Edgar with a bright false smile.

'On the contrary, Edgar, I am perfectly clear, and if you will be so good as to lend me your carriage, Lady Stratford, for a few hours this morning, I may make all my arrangements and thus will need to trouble you no further.'

Edgar gripped the edge of the table.

'Enough, Blanche!'

'My dear Miss Drummond,' the ambassador said smoothly, 'you cannot really suppose we should let you cast yourself away upon such a man as Henri de la Haye? His association with Count Rambert is quite enough to condemn him, entirely apart from his infamous conduct towards you. He has not even his profession now, for he is disgraced as a deserter. He could not go back to Paris if he wished to. He dare not.'

'He does not care!' Blanche cried passionately. 'He says the world is wide!'

'It will have to be very wide to conceal him, my dear, very wide indeed. There is no question of your having anything more to do with him, none at all. Is that not so, Captain Drummond?'

Edgar nodded. Blanche began to scream. Lady Stratford rose swiftly and guided her from the room, sobbing hysterically. Edgar sat immovably in his place and stared out at the morning sunlight on the sea.

'You must be firm, Captain Drummond, very firm. Her head has been filled with foolish notions. Unless you are to have a very wearying time until her elder sister can join her, you must be very firm.'

'Yes, sir.'

'Do you intend to ask Lord Raglan for leave to accompany them home?'

'I had rather not, sir.'

'Then who shall escort them, Captain Drummond?'

Edgar was silent.

After a pause, the ambassador said with some impatience, 'It is as well you are under my roof, Captain Drummond, for I believe I may be able to help you.'

Edgar's gaze shifted at last.

'I should be grateful, sir.'

The ambassador rose and began to pace slowly up and down before the window.

'There are plenty of people to take advantage of the war, Captain Drummond, and certain London shipping companies are hardly backward in doing so. I am informed that several of them are running . . . paid *holidays* to this area, and this of course means that a number of English people are in and out of Constantinople quite ceaselessly. I have of course met none of these . . . tourists myself, but my staff can perhaps find you some respectable family under whose protection your sisters can safely travel home. I believe it costs about five pounds a head for the privilege of using a seat of war as a playground.'

Struggling with the indignity both of this plan and of his own inability for initiative, Edgar said nothing.

'Do you wish me to proceed in the matter?' the ambassador said coldly, 'or do you have a better notion of your own?'

Edgar sprang to his feet.

'No, sir. No, I do not. I should be – grateful for your help, sir.'

The ambassador surveyed him for a moment.

'In that case, Captain Drummond, I shall send a message back to Lord Raglan desiring him to urge your sister to make all speed in coming down to Constantinople. I would advise you, once again, to be firm, very firm, in all your dealings with Miss Blanche Drummond.'

He signalled to the footmen who waited by the double doors leading to the ante-room. In perfect unison they grasped the door handles and pulled the doors open. Breakfast was over.

Blanche gave Edgar very little chance to be firm in the days which followed. Reluctant to take any further help from the ambassador, Edgar found lodgings for them both in a house nearby and installed them there with surprisingly little fuss from his sister. She merely complained of a violent headache and asked to go straight to bed upon arrival. Thereafter, she kept the doors of her sitting room and bedroom locked, and declared, in a note brought to him that first morning, that she simply wished to be left undisturbed and alone. Edgar had no idea how to attempt to reason with her.

For two or three days he did nothing in any direction. He despatched a letter to Sarah in an attempt to relieve his feelings at Blanche's reception of him, and felt only, when it was gone, that it had contained passages that were both unworthy and unmanly.

'I could wish, dearest sister', he had written, 'that it had been proper to let you come. I freely confess it, though not for one moment do I regret my decision to leave you safely where you are. But only you could fathom what is in Blanche's heart, I think, though I am I must confess, cut to pieces that she no longer seems to regard me as once she did.'

That done, he paced along the shore of the Bosphorus, below the elegant and splendid houses of the rich Europeans, and teased and worried at his problem until his mind was quite raw. The worst of it all was that the problem which had seemed so enormous and consequential aboard *The Heron* had, at his actually touching it, dwindled into a small and sordid intrigue, fraught with Blanche's hysteria and his own incompetence.

Almost a week after his arrival, some small development broke into the monotony of his despair. News came from the Crimea that Sarah would leave and come down to Constantinople the moment Edgar and *The Heron* returned. The yacht would be made ready as quickly as possible and had been offered for Sarah's use on the first stage of her journey home.

This was half way satisfactory. Edgar was profoundly relieved that Sarah had raised no objection to going home, but he could have wished she had not determined to wait for *The Heron* but had managed to secure another offer of a yacht that might bring her down immediately. Her plan would mean that she could not possibly reach Constantinople until the very end of October, at the earliest, and the problem of what to do with Blanche in those empty weeks was a weighty one.

The ambassador came to his rescue. One of the embassy secretaries had been detailed by him to discover a suitable escort for the Misses Drummond back to England, and now produced a solid, respectable family called Bagshot as likely candidates. They came from Clifton, Mr Bagshot had a business closely involved with the fitting out of ships for the navy, and there was a large, cheerful daughter of Blanche's own age. Mr Bagshot was summoned to Edgar's lodgings, showed himself to be entirely reliable and very sympathetic to Edgar's dilemma, and declared that as he was taking his family home in the first week of November, nothing would please him more than to escort Blanche and Sarah as well.

That afternoon, Edgar presented himself at the Bagshots' hotel to meet the mother and daughter. Both were ample, amiable and quite as sympathetic as Mr Bagshot had been. So encouraged was Edgar by their kind reception of him, that he ventured to broach his new problem to them.

'My added difficulty is this, Mrs Bagshot. I have to return to the Crimean peninsula in order that my sister Sarah may use the yacht I have with me at present in Constantinople. It means there will be an interval of at least three weeks between my departure and my sister's arrival. I am quite undecided as to what would be best for Blanche in my absence.'

Mrs Bagshot leaned forward and patted his hand.

'There's no difficulty to that, as I can see, Captain Drummond. We shall have her here with us and we shall all get to know each other so that on the journey home we shall indeed be like a family. The day you leave, your sister shall come to us.'

In the gratitude and relief that swept over him at this offer, Edgar felt that his path now lay straight before him. It was only on his journey back to his lodgings that he remembered he had yet to break the news to Blanche.

To his amazement, her sitting-room door was actually ajar as he passed, and she called to him when she heard his step.

He found her sitting in a perfect welter of finery. Silks and furs and gold chains and trinkets lay scattered about on the sofa around her, and she was sitting in their midst looking almost restored to her usual looks.

'Blanche! My dear! What is all this?'

'Is it not charming, Edgar? Lady Stratford sent me the cleverest dressmaker in all Constantinople, and I'm to have a travelling dress made of this, and the dark green silk to replace my poor worn out old plaid, and the pink for the opéra to go with those darling rose quartz earrings, and a wizard of a shoemaker will come in the morning to measure –'

'But where is it all come from? I thought you had hardly left your bed in a week.'

Blanche picked up an ostrich plume and ran it through her fingers.

'Oh, don't look so stuffy and disapproving, Edgar! You have had time enough and more to stop being such a damper of fun. Where does it all come from? Where do you suppose, Henri, of course!'

Edgar gazed at her in horror.

'I don't know what it takes to convince you, Edgar. I *told* you that Henri will take me to Paris! I told you he is going to marry me! And here is the proof! Every day these lovely things have been coming, I cannot tell you what a relief it is to see pretty things again – '

'Have you written to Monsieur de la Haye?'

Blanche took no notice of his tone.

'Of course I have. I wrote the first moment I could and I have written every day since. What did you expect?'

Edgar groaned aloud and seated himself on the nearest chair.

'Blanche, you must listen to me.'

'Only if you are going to be amusing. Look at this pretty watch. Isn't it charming? You must admit that he has the best of taste. And these amethysts! Even Mamma's are not half so large or dark – '

'Blanche, I have spent the day with a family called Bagshot. They are here on some sort of excursion and are very respectable and worthy. They have a daughter of your age and they are going back to England at the beginning of November. Until Sarah comes they have offered to shelter you at their hotel, and then they will take both you and Sarah home with them. Mr Bagshot has even offered to take you both back to Oakley Park himself. Blanche, you are *not* going to Paris. You are going *home*.'

Blanche looked up from the length of silk she was playing with and smiled.

'Nonsense, Edgar. I don't need the vulgar Bagshots. I am going to Paris to marry Henri.'

Edgar got up and stood over her, his fists clenched.

'You are *not*!' he shouted. 'Even if I were to countenance it, Monsieur de la Haye has no intention whatever of marrying you! These baubles are merely his farewell! Can you not see? He is giving you dresses and jewels to release himself from whatever pie-crust promise he made you!'

Blanche went white.

'That's not true, it's not, it's not!'

Edgar calmed himself a little.

'It is perfectly true. He would be the first to admit it.'

Blanche looked around her at the scattered silks and jewels.

'You are quite wrong, Edgar, quite wrong. If he were standing here among all this evidence of his attachment to me, he would laugh in your face.'

Edgar drew a deep, unsteady breath.

'I will get him here. Tomorrow morning I will get him here and I will ask him point blank what his intentions are. Then you will see once and for all that he is a blackguard.'

'On the contrary, you will see that he wishes most ardently to marry me and you will have to content yourself with waving me off to Paris.'

Edgar came and knelt by her.

'If he comes,' he said, 'and I am right, Blanche, will you abide by me and allow the Bagshots to take you home?'

Blanche laughed in his face and snapped her fingers.

'Of course!' she said.

'I am serious. I am reduced to the abominable expedient of asking Monsieur de la Haye what his intentions are before your face. Do you understand that?'

'Oh perfectly!'

Edgar drew out his pocket book, and tore out a blank leaf.

'Tomorrow's date is October 5th. I shall write here "I, Blanche Drummond, promise to obey my brother in the event of Henri de la Haye proving himself unwilling to marry me." Now sign please, Blanche.'

Blanche took his pencil and wrote with a flourish.

'Tomorrow I shall give that scrap of paper to Henri to light his cigar!'

# *Ten*

The Crimean winter had begun. Men were out for twelve hours at a time now in the newly dug trenches around Sebastopol under inky skies that deluged them with rain, and ceaselessly whipped them with merciless winds. There was no shelter to go back to at the end of it either but leaking tents where the inevitable salt pork and stale biscuit awaited them. Thirty British transport ships were wrecked in the gales that screamed across the Black Sea and one of them plunged to the bottom with her full cargo of forty thousand pairs of boots. From the *Hercules,* moored in the comparative calm of the innermost waters of Balaclava harbour, Sarah watched the awful grey waves swell and heave and smash ships like toys against the great cliffs of the harbour mouth, and imagined Edgar struggling towards her through those churning seas.

From the heights above the port, Robert was watching also. Colonel Lowe had given most welcome evidence of his sympathy by allowing him the use of a small hut of the type reserved only for officers. Huts for the whole army had been requested but as yet had not arrived, but poor rough little dwelling as it was, with nothing within but a camp bed and folding table and stool, it was a sanctuary when compared with a tent, and Robert shared it with as many as could be accommodated.

He had heard no more from London, and chose to interpret the silence as his victory. The ferocity and volume of his reports had not abated in the smallest degree and as more and more evidence came to light of the confusion and chaos of the administration, his own sense of a personal campaign to be fought for the lot of the British soldier gained momentum. Writing furiously by the smoking light of his lantern, in the hut crammed with the weary and sodden men seeking the small comfort of his tiny fire, he continued to bombard *The Clarion's* readers with his anger and despair.

The plain fact is that there is no shortage of food or clothing or stores in Balaclava, but they lie rotting and sodden in the harbour because there is no way of getting them to the heights twelve hours' march away where our main encampments are. There is not enough forage to feed the pack animals, which in turn prevents more animals being brought in to help, and the noble beasts of the cavalry are reduced to eating each others' manes and tails. A labour force of Turks has been brought in to make new roads, but the ground is too hard to dig, and they die in such numbers that our men waste a good deal of their time in burying them. How patient our men are, how silently they bear their sufferings, ankle deep in mud, wet to the skin, rewarded only with green coffee beans they have no means of roasting.

He had a sensation that Colonel Lowe gave his reports tacit approval. He had often seen the colonel with back copies of the newspaper, and had caught more than once his kindly and sympathetic comments to the men, evidence that he shared Robert's feelings in large measure. He took to coming to Robert's hut quite frequently, ostensibly to hearten those sheltering there off duty, but it seemed also that he wished his presence to sanction Robert's opinions.

One evening during the second week of October, he came to Robert bearing a letter. He had been that afternoon upon the *Hercules* and found Miss Drummond in a considerable state of agitation. At this announcement, Robert threw down his pen, and the occupants of the hut withdrew to the wild night outside in tactful silence.

'You have not seen Miss Drummond yourself lately, Robert?'

Robert stood up.

'No, sir. I have not. Not since the day after the Alma. I abided by her advice and have stayed here endeavouring to obliterate memories of what I cannot have.'

'I think,' Colonel Lowe said gently, 'you are a little hard on her. She is there on that ship, shut up as she was bidden, and there is not a lady left among the British at the moment besides herself and Mrs Duberly, and Mrs Duberly is a great horsewoman and out riding most days. Lady Errol has gone home with her husband after he was wounded. I believe Miss Drummond is lonely. There is no one left to call upon her. She has

136

much to bear, and I think she particularly rejoices in your company.'

Robert stared at the ceiling for some moments, his arms folded across his chest. When he spoke he did not look at the colonel, but continued to look firmly at the unplaned planks inches from his head.

'And I rejoiced in hers until everything was – changed. I cannot explain my feelings except that I know there has always been the seeds of something explosive in me. I had hoped I could always channel it, harness it. I am working at that even now.' He stopped and turned to the colonel with a smile. 'You are both patient and understanding, sir. You said you had a letter for me?'

Sarah had written only briefly. She had received a letter from Edgar and would write the contents in full for Robert if he chose. If on the other hand he preferred to hear of Blanche at first hand, she would be pleased to see him on the *Hercules.*

'You should go to her, Robert.'

'Is she much distressed?'

'She has been informed that she is to go home.'

Robert turned away.

'It is the best thing for her, sir.'

'She would disagree with you, violently. She is a girl of immense moral energy and feels it is wrong for her to go. I think she would like to explain to you herself and hear your opinion. Your honest opinion.'

'My honest opinion is that she could do a great deal of good if she were only allowed to. It is nonsense to protect her like some precious bloom as if she had not the fibre to withstand unpleasantness. She has seen enough horrors now with her own eyes, and imprisoning her only makes her sense of futility more burdensome.'

Colonel Lowe smiled and put a hand on his shoulder.

'Her words exactly, Robert.'

'Then I shall certainly go and applaud her. I suppose – ' He stopped. 'I imagine there is no news of – another kind?'

Colonel Lowe shook his head.

'Both sisters are to return to England. Sarah is to sail down to Constantinople. Blanche has refused to return to the Crimea.'

Robert gave a little sigh, followed by a faint smile. He held out his hand.

'Thank you for coming, sir.'


Wrapped in Edgar's cloak, Sarah stood on the deck of the *Hercules* and watched him come. He was rowed out to her through the choppy grey waves, and it often happened that the boat disappeared in a trough of water and looked alarmingly as if it had capsized. Then abruptly it emerged from its tussle with Balaclava harbour, and lay tranquilly beneath the towering bulk of the *Hercules* and Robert stood up, and looked up to see her craning figure and took off his cap to wave a greeting.

She returned to the cabin to welcome him. Days before she had begged Mary to stow away all Blanche's possessions since they haunted her so, and was now glad of this piece of fortuitous foresight. Denuded of the capes and hats and parasols, the cabin had lost a good deal of charm and gained a good deal of character, furnished now only with Sarah's writing materials and books and sketches and her sole remaining bonnet.

Robert had to stoop to enter. She held out her hand to him, and he kissed it and pressed it before taking his own away.

'I am so glad to see you, Mr Chiltern. I was very willing to send you a copy of all the information I have myself at the moment but I so much prefer to hand it to you in person.'

'You seem admirably composed, Miss Drummond.'

'I have had little else to occupy myself with,' she said sharply.

'I am truly sorry for that. I am, indeed, Sarah.'

She inclined her head but did not look at him. Edgar's letter to her lay upon the table and she pushed it towards Robert.

'Please read this. Then you will know as much as I do.'

He looked much moved.

'I am profoundly grateful that you permit me to do so.'

She did not watch him while he read, but gazed out of the porthole towards that exhaustingly familiar view of the battered village on the shore. The waterfront was the usual jumble of sacks and figures and droop-headed animals, and a thin grey rain had begun to fall, like needles, into the darker sea. Little flecks of foam appeared on the water's surface and the clouds began to tear and shred overhead in the gathering wind.

'When do you go down to Constantinople?' Robert said behind her.

'I am awaiting Edgar's return. I can only suppose he is having a terrible journey in these seas and that it is taking far longer than it should. I do not want to go, Robert,' she said with sudden energy. 'I cannot tell you how I would welcome a really good reason to stay, but I can offer none beyond my *wish* to stay, and that I cannot justify, even to myself.'

Robert pushed the letter away from him and came to stand by her.

'Is it that you do not wish to go home?'

She nodded.

'If I go home, I feel it will be like going back into a box and the lid will close on me and I can only move about within the box's prescribed limits. It isn't that I have achieved very much in the last few months, but I have seen wider horizons, I have seen what I might do – if it were only permissible or suitable or whatever the objection is – and I think the box would stifle me.'

He smiled at her.

'I think so too. May I tell you of something remarkable that I have heard of? A certain Miss Nightingale, a Miss Florence Nightingale, whose family have apparently done everything in their power to quell the spirit of enterprise in her, has managed to persuade the authorities to let her come out and look after the soldiers in the hospital in Scutari. She has raised a body of thirty-eight nurses and they are on their way at this very moment.'

Sarah was listening intently.

'You say she defied her family?'

'I believe so. Her mother and sister particularly I am told and she has, in the past, been much admired for her looks and her drawing room accomplishments – ' He paused, smiling down at Sarah after his emphatic and teasing delivery of the last words.

'Is – is the hospital at Scutari very dreadful?'

'I am told it beggars description. They die at a rate of forty-two in every hundred. I gather also that Doctor Hall who is the principal medical officer out here has informed Parliament that the army is a thousand beds surplus to requirements at the moment. His report apparently and unbelievably said that "every man is provided with all that is necessary for his comfort and accommodation." There *are* no beds at Scutari. The men are lying on the floor which is rotten and covered with filth. Forgive me – ' he stopped abruptly, 'I did not come here to bombard you again.'

'What did you come for?'

There was silence for a moment then he said in a low voice.

'I came to see you, and – you know the other reason.'

Looking out of the porthole again she said, 'You now know as much as I do. I have lost Blanche quite as much as you have as I clearly did not know, as I believed I did, what she was really like. Edgar is, as you see, bringing me a letter from her and perhaps that will illuminate me a little more. I do not want to go to Constantinople. I do not want to have to take Blanche home. You will think me hard and merciless but I am cut to pieces at her actions, she has estranged herself, she clearly neither wanted nor needed me as I depended upon her doing. I do not want to do what Edgar wants me to do so in a sense I am become separate from him also and I am now alone. So are you, but you are more used to it than I am, it is easier, in this world, for a man to be alone. It is not convenient for a woman – ' she bit her lip and could not go on.

He seized both her hands.

'Oh God, Sarah, that things had not turned out this way! I am so much to blame. If only, if only – '

'No!' she almost shouted, tearing her hands free, 'Don't speak like that! What's done is done, just as I am changed and cannot or would not for all the world, be as I was before. It's no good regretting, no good at all. You must accept what has happened and you must lock it in the past and bury it there, *bury* it. Blanche is over and done with.'

'For you too?'

'Not if she really wants me, really needs me. But she cannot simply have me as a convenience, I am grown past that.'

Silence fell abruptly between them. Robert looked down at her all the time and saw the spots of colour burning in her cheeks.

'Sarah, is there anything I can do for you?'

'I think not, but thank you. Tell me, is the siege to be long drawn out? Is it thought Sebastopol will fall by Christmas?'

'It is. I very much hope so, for winters here are said to be terrible.'

They looked out together upon the sea which was now whipped into grey wildness.

'There are sacks of clothing out there on the shore which are used as stepping stones in the mud because no one can get them to the camps, and some of the men on the heights are already in rags. They are so good, those men, Sarah, so good, so uncomplaining.'

'I can believe it,' she said softly.

He sighed and turned away from the view. Smiling down at her he said, 'I shall try to do as you bid me. God bless you, Sarah – and may you achieve your heart's desire.'

She did not look at him, but when he took her hand, she pressed his warmly, and then heard his steps cross the cabin, and the door close behind him, and all the time she gazed out resolutely upon the wintry sea.

Constantinople
October 5th

My dearest Sarah –

You cannot imagine how unhappy I am! Everyone is so cross and disagreeable, Edgar most of all, and they treat me as Aunt Price used to, as if I were a silly child, and no one will let me know my own mind.

If Edgar had not come bustling down like some old governess, I should be in Paris by this time and the season in Paris is at its height just now and I should have been there for Christmas. But Edgar has spoiled everything and I do believe has persuaded Henri to let me go, for Henri never spoke to me the way he has today before Edgar came. It is true that I was more impatient than Henri to be gone to Paris, but I have such a hatred of Constantinople and this awful country and I could not wait to be where things were gay and delightful and the talk was not endlessly of sickness and war.

You must come down to me. I am quite ill with unhappiness and I need you here to comfort me. No one else will do. Edgar has driven Henri away and has proffered in his place a dreadful bourgeois family with a stout father and a stouter mother, and a frumpy daughter with a passion for the most unsuitable and vulgar garments imaginable. They are here on a sightseeing tour, if you can imagine anything so laughable, and we are to go home with them as soon as you can get down to us.

It will be a tedious journey, you may depend upon it, but we shall be home at least by Christmas, thank God, and perhaps I may begin to forget the nightmare it has all been since we left home. I sometimes wake in the night screaming for fear I am still in that dreadful tent or that terrible ship, and that the air is full of flies and evil smells and then I call out for you and you are not there and I cry myself sick with misery. Oh, Sarah, I am so unhappy!

Make all the haste you can. Henri bought me some very pretty silk before Edgar sent him away, and we shall amuse ourselves having it made up. At least Constantinople is one small step nearer civilization and I have had some new bonnets made and a grey travelling dress I meant to wear to Paris, but I do not think I can bear to wear it now since I am too bitterly disappointed so much as to glance at it. Perhaps I shall give it to the frumpy Miss Bagshot even though she could not squeeze her solid flesh into it.

I have nothing to do now, nothing at all. I am to be removed to an hotel with the Bagshots this afternoon and I know Edgar has set a watch to stop me from communicating with Henri. He made Henri say such cruel, wicked things to me today, you would not believe a brother could be so hard. He says I must give back all the pretty things Henri has lavished on me, he has no more feeling than a stone!

I shall look every day for you. Set out the moment you receive this, do not delay an hour.

Your unhappy sister,
Blanche Drummond

In five days I am to go. *The Heron* is being lent to me and I
have no choice but to accept it and go. I can hardly bear to
leave, but my main reason for staying must be to be near Robert
and what a senseless, pointless wish *that* is, since it gives me as
much pain as pleasure and I think means little to him.

I still long and long to be of some use here. I would regard
a duty here to be heaven sent it would be so welcome. My mind
keeps revolving upon Miss Nightingale, and I tell myself that
if she could brave such opposition as she has, then so could I,
but she does not have my family troubles, she is not torn with
love and loyalty as I am. If only a great hand would come
through these black clouds and point to me, while a voice
called out 'Sarah Drummond, such and such is your duty', I
could shake off all these doubts and difficulties, but I feel that
as things are, I cannot see *clearly* what to do!

Edgar has come back quite done up. He was dreadfully sick
at sea, and has spent several days here in the cabin with me to
recover, he is so weak. He kept talking of Blanche as a child
and speaking of her gaiety and her independence and blaming
himself that those qualities in her have become fretfulness and
impatience with difficulties. She gave him so much pain in
Constantinople with her bitter reception of him and almost
shook him in his conviction he was doing the right thing, so
resentful was she. He has gone on shore the last few days and
yesterday asked me to go with him. I nearly wept with relief!

It was a terrible expedition. The harbour stinks abominably,
and the waterfront, when we tried to land, was so choked with
the rotting carcases of animals, and decaying foodstuffs, and
flour spilling out of sacks in great damp lumps and human filth
that I wished I had pattens like the girls of Northamptonshire
wear in winter. All the soldiers about look so wretched and ill-
clothed and ill-fed and I saw poor howling men being dragged
along through the rubbish to the hospital ship moored in the
harbour. I felt quite savaged with pity, so overwhelmed with it
that when I got back to the *Hercules*, I seized Blanche's letter
and tore it into tiny shreds.

How can I pity *her* when men must suffer like they do here

in the mud and filth and cold and wet? I could hardly believe her letter. No word of explanation, no regrets at our intolerable anxiety, no gratitude for Edgar's care, no thought for Robert, or for me. Nothing, nothing but a string of self-pitying complaints. I wept and raged when I read it until I quite frightened poor little Mary, but I feel as if my beloved sister has been torn away and some petulant peevish stranger put there in her place who expects me to love her as once I did Blanche.

I know it cannot be altogether her fault. I know these last seven months have subjected her to wicked hardships, but she has made no attempt to bear them. I saw those men yesterday – and I shall go on shore again today with my extra shawl and I shall give it to the first poor ragged fellow I see – and they smiled at me and spoke bravely, and never one raised his fist at my warm clothes and plump cheeks (they are not so plump as they were but they are not grey and hollow like most of the soldiers). She sits in Constantinople and talks of dresses and trinkets and the ugliness of Miss Bagshot as if they were matters of moment and men drag their poor sick bodies through the days here, some of them barefoot but for rags.

How am I to bear the journey home? What shall I speak to her about? I am to be in daily communion with people who chose to come to the east as a holiday and who know nothing of the drudgery and hopelessness and waste of precious life which goes on here, and I shall seem priggish and stiff to Blanche for I cannot, *cannot* sympathize with her or condone what she has done or even understand, let alone accept, the pain she has caused us all. And when we get to England –

I can hardly make myself think of it. We will be escorted to Mount Street and we will walk up that gloomy staircase past those thundery pictures and we will sit like luggage, in the drawing room, until the trunks have been put into Papa's carriage, and then we will descend the staircase again and climb into the carriage and the door will bang upon us and the lid of my box will be locked over my head. Then we will jolt away to Northamptonshire and I will feel the sides of the box pressing in on me and I shall want to scream at the sight of Blanche's mounting satisfaction. When we get to Oakley I shall have to explain and explain and explain and because of my box and my position as only a woman, Papa will not really take me seriously and will think I am overwrought and probably send me to Europe for the rest of the winter and I shall have to go still wearing my box – Mamma, at least, will hardly have the energy to be interested, which is something to be thankful for.

And every night I will lie in my familiar bed and I will think of my bunk here, and the soldiers in rags in the mud and snow, and Edgar too and Robert – oh Robert, *Robert* . . . I do not think I shall ever sleep once I am home, I do not see how I *can*. I shall just be an empty husk moving about the house and my heart and mind will be throbbing and crying out in the wilderness where I cannot follow them.

It is like looking at eternity, but without the comfort of paradise to watch it from. I see a long, long dreary tunnel and down it I must walk, day after endless day, on my round of drawing rooms and dining rooms and carriages and shrubberies and church and insupportable pointlessness.

I must school myself. This is self-indulgent and destructive. What use do I imagine I have here? None at all, nothing to do but dream to myself what I might do, and live in hope and dread of seeing Robert. Apart from the little solace I am to Edgar – which I feel grows smaller every day – I am no use here at all, I am just one more mouth to feed, one more complication in all arrangements, one more body to be accounted for. I am best out of it, it is best for everyone else that I go. I should not have come, I should have stayed asleep and contented in England, I should not have let myself be swayed by other people's opinion of what I could do if I would –

Oh Sarah, Sarah, how can you write so, how *can* you? Would you go back one minute, deaden one nerve, stifle one feeling? If you cannot be thankful that you are alive to so much, however it costs you, then you do not deserve to be alive. Writing is making you foolish, you are indulging yourself. Put down your pen and make yourself ready to go ashore. You have five days left and you must not disgrace yourself on any one of them. You will greet Edgar smilingly, you will ask that kind and noble colonel if there are any little commissions you can perform for him in Constantinople or indeed in London, you will send a sisterly and sensible note of farewell to Robert. You will begin this new phase of life, Sarah Drummond, as you *have* to go on with it.

# Eleven

In the early afternoon of 24 October, Colonel James Lowe left the cavalry camp to ride down the South Valley to Balaclava, to bid Miss Drummond farewell. He was, as usual, thankful to leave the camp for even a little while since the ceaseless bombardment of the siege guns battering Sebastopol was more exhausting than the physical privations of his everyday life. Mouldy biscuit had by now become so familiar that he could not recall the taste of fresh, and as for salmon or pheasant or beef, they were fantasies which haunted his dreams as insubstantially as if he had never known them in real life. The damp blankets in which he rolled himself at night had become bearable with familiarity, as had become the necessity to shave in icy water and the, initially profoundly distressing, scarcity of clean linen. His sleep, when not haunted maddeningly with the memories of banquets, was often poignantly filled with images left over from the North West Frontier, images that seemed to have forgotten the savage winters slicing down the Khyber Pass from Kabul, and only brought to his dreams the charms of Peshawar and Jellalabad, the groves and banks and sunlit courtyards, warm and full of the smells of charcoal and jasmine. He would waken from these poetic pictures to the thudding reality of the Crimea, and would silently admonish himself for his evident need to escape, even in sleep.

He had mixed feelings about Sarah's imminent departure. Edgar had not been the kind of junior officer he had ever experienced before, with his grim devotion to the rule book and convention, combined with such rigid moral uprightness and comparative physical frailty, and James Lowe was at first inclined to feel that his sisters, both owning identical, unmistakable blue Drummond eyes, were birds of the same feather. It was not until the episode at the Alma, when the younger and more obviously fascinating sister had attempted to elope with an officer of the Zouaves, that he had looked at the elder Miss Drummond with any especial interest, but she had seemed to him then to be so peculiarly frustrated by her own powerlessness to help that his attention was caught.

He remembered particularly her cry to her brother as he rode away that day, begging that she might at least be allowed to nurse a little if she must be left behind, in order to assuage her own intense anxiety as well as to be of some use to the community she found herself in. It was also remarkable that Robert Chiltern, a man for whom Colonel Lowe felt mounting admiration and liking, was prepared to accept her advice not to set off in pursuit of Blanche Drummond himself. Impressed by both these points, James Lowe had called upon her in her cabin on the *Hercules* two days after the Alma, and had found a girl agitated not, as might be conventionally expected, simply over the shocking episode involving her sister, but also over issues with much wider implications. They had talked together a good deal in the days following and he had learned much about her and how much she felt she owed to Robert's enlightening views. Indeed, if Robert had not committed himself so publicly to the younger sister, Colonel Lowe might have been strongly, and enviously, suspicious that Sarah entertained hopes for him herself.

He was going to miss her. There was no doubt of it. He found that there had been many things he could confide in her, many personal things, such as his painful knowledge that being an 'Indian' officer, however good, however experienced, would always be held against him in the British Army. She seemed to understand, with comforting acuteness, what it was like to be frustrated in the pursuit of some goal by the convention of general opinion. 'Indian' officers were below the salt as far as the hierarchy of the British Army went, and ever would remain so. James Lowe had wished often that he had obtained a commission in the Heavy Brigade rather than the Light, for it was commanded by Colonel James Scarlett, a man who possessed the sterling virtues of modesty and excellent sense. He knew where he lacked experience and was prepared to ask for help, he had even appointed an 'Indian' officer to his staff. Sarah had been sympathetic in a way that made James Lowe feel she understood his position personally.

147

On the other hand, however, he was as a gallant and protective man relieved to see her go. She always looked neat and attractive to him, but he was aware that she almost always wore the same gown now, and that his standards had become lopsided having seen no lady but her and Mrs Duberly in months (Mrs Duberly had taken to heavy boots and some cast-off cut-down officer's trousers under her gown tail for riding . . .). Colonel Lowe felt that circumstanced as she was, it was perhaps better Sarah did not stay. He would have been the first to encourage her in any enterprise but sadly, it was not his authority she looked to. He thought of her back in London, with a new bonnet and pelisse and muff, taking the family carriage along Jermyn Street to make the few small purchases for him she had offered to do, and he felt sad and satisfied all at once.

She was packing when he knocked. She looked as if she had not slept much the night before, her eyes smudged with fatigue, but her hair was braided up as neatly as ever.

'Is not this a farce, Colonel Lowe? I have quite literally worn through most of what I brought, and what is whole and warm I have given away. I cannot tell you how much I wished I was a man yesterday when I was scattering garments along the quayside, for most of my things are quite useless to men. Will you look? I had three trunks quite full, and two hat boxes, and now I can hardly fill half of one trunk and I am reduced to a single bonnet.'

Colonel Lowe perched himself on the edge of the table.

'I do hope you have not been over-generous, Miss Drummond. I hope you have left yourself enough to be comfortable on the way home. It will be winter in England too, remember.'

She coloured a little and bent over her open trunk.

'A very different winter.'

'Yes, I am thankful to say, for your sake!'

She said something indistinct into the trunk.

'I beg your pardon?'

She turned a flushed face towards him.

'I am embarrassed to think of being comfortable when all of you are so – so wretched. It is worse because I do not *want* to be comfortable – ' She stopped and bit her lip. He waited, surveying her profile until she resumed in a brisker tone, 'Forgive me, Colonel Lowe, I meant to be self-pitying no more. Please scold me for my ingratitude, it is what I deserve. Now come. Major Mason of the Inniskillings has sent a bottle of champagne as a parting present, and as I am sure it must be nearly his last, it would choke me to drink it, so I insist you take at least a little.'

She was talking far more and far faster than was customary. She ran about the cabin finding glasses and a corkscrew and a towel to use as a napkin, chattering all the time in a most uncharacteristic manner, and pausing in her flight now and then to cast another book or sheaf of papers pell-mell into the trunk to lie among a number of articles whose white frilliness precluded Colonel Lowe from looking at them too intently. He pulled the cork efficiently and poured the wine into glasses, holding one out to her and smiling.

'No, no, indeed, Colonel, I shall not. I have had callers all day to bid me farewell and I shall give the second glass to the next one who comes. Please drink yourself, please do. You have been so good to me, so kind, so –'

He took both her hands in one of his and held them firmly, then pressed the wineglass lightly to her mouth.

'Drink, my dear Miss Drummond. Just a little. It will do you good, and in any case, I cannot bear to drink alone. It would be an insult to Major Mason not to taste it yourself.'

She shut her eyes and gulped, like an obedient child taking medicine. He found that he did not in any way wish to release the hands he held so he retained his grip firmly and raised the wineglass again.

'Once more.'

Again she swallowed. Then she opened her eyes and smiled at him, and her look was brilliant with tears. He let her hands go then and stepped back to pick up his own glass and raise it to her.

'*Bon voyage*, Miss Drummond, and many thanks to you for the delightful hours we have spent together.'

She inclined her head.

'As soon as Sebastopol falls,' he said encouragingly, 'we shall all be home. Perhaps we shall meet again in the spring and all this will be as far behind us as a dream.'

'I do not – want to forget it.'

'You won't. It is not in your nature to do so. But the sharper edges will soften. Now then. You are so kind as to do a few things for me in London. Is there any small thing I can do for you here, any messages for instance?'

She turned away and bent over her bunk, feeling beneath the pillow with one hand. Then she straightened up and held out a note to him.

'I have used you as messenger too often, Colonel Lowe, but would you take this last letter to Robert Chiltern? I feel the Drummonds have used him ill and I should not like to go without a word to him.'

'It will be a pleasure.'

A knock sounded on the door. Colonel Lowe said, 'One moment!' and then he took Sarah's hand in his and pressed it.

'I shall miss you sorely but I am very thankful to think you will be safe and comfortable once more. The seas are calmer now and the journey down the Black Sea should be much better than your poor brother had. Would you write to me from Constantinople, write and tell me you are safe and well?'

'Oh yes!' she said eagerly, 'I will write from every port, from England, often, I shall be so glad to. So glad to – to be in touch!'

'Godspeed,' he said, and let her hand go.

Two officers of the regiment were chatting outside. They stiffened to attention as Colonel Lowe came out.

'There is some excellent champagne in there,' he said to them. 'But you must spoonfeed Miss Drummond with some. She will not drink it without help and she needs it. It's an order.'

They smiled back at him.

'At once, sir.'

Colonel Lowe did not deliver Sarah's letter in person. When he returned to the cavalry camp dusk was settling dampily among the tents, and the news was that the Russians, who had steadily been building up a force around Sebastopol, had reached a staggering total of twenty-five thousand men, infantry, cavalry and guns. The camp, which seemed to have become inured to the siege in recent days, was humming with a new sort of expectancy. The news of the size of the Russian force had been brought by a Turkish spy to Sir Colin Campbell of the Highland Brigade, who had written urgently to Lord Raglan. It was known that Lord Lucan and General Airey had been informed, but not that any of the commanders had decided to take action. Colonel Lowe's staff were beside themselves with impatience.

'We'll be caught with our breeches down, sir, and the Russians will have us for breakfast!'

Colonel Lowe stroked his chin.

'There was a false report of just this sort three days ago, if you remember, and a large percentage of the cavalry division spent all night at their horses' heads to no purpose. I imagine that none of you, wish to repeat that bitterly cold and pointless exercise? However, we must take some precautions. Have all the rations been issued for this evening?'

'Such as they are, sir. Short again on most things, poor devils.'

'And yourselves?'

'Much the same, sir.'

James Lowe sighed.

'I've a case of claret left. You are all to have it but only in quantities that are heartening, rather than stupefying. I feel this may be a night to warrant a little encouragement. Captain Carson, would you be so good as to take this note to Mr Chiltern, the journalist, as quickly as you can?'

Robert was writing furiously by the light of a tallow candle which smelt appallingly rancid. He had returned to his hut after dark to find the welcome present of a heap of broken-up beer crates besides his hearth, which did a great deal to atone for the fact that he had gone hungry since the night before and even now had no sustenance to look forward to except the piece of salt meat he had restrained himself from eating the previous evening. He had been given swallows of rum at intervals during the day by generous soldiers but these had only acted as a temporary anaesthetic to his pangs of hunger.

He had spent the day down at Balaclava. He had first gone down with the thought of seeing Sarah to say good-bye, but he had felt strangely loth to do so, as if he were cutting short some lifeline, and had in any case become so involved with the embarkation of invalids and the landing of returned men from Scutari that he had left it too late to persuade anyone to take him out to the *Hercules*. Five hundred men, passed fit for service, had returned from the hospital at Scutari, and as they straggled past him out of Balaclava and up the hills to the encampments, Robert saw many of them falling with exhaustion and weakness into the mud at the roadside. Depressed and angered anew by this spectacle, Robert had hurried back to his hut in the gathering darkness, and only when he was half-way up the stiff pull to the heights did he remember Sarah. He stopped for a moment in his angry rush, and spun round, to gaze down at the blackness of Balaclava harbour below him, and saw the dim bobbing lights of the anchored ships. She was down there, packing in her cabin, and he had not been to wish her godspeed. Stricken suddenly, Robert cursed himself, then he blew a kiss out into the black cold night air above the harbour, and resumed his homeward tramp.

He was writing with such fierce concentration that he did not at first hear Dick Carson knock. The beer crates were crackling like pistol shots as they burned, being both damp and full of knots, and as yet did not give enough light to write by. At last Dick Carson gave up skinning his knuckles and pushed the door open without invitation.

Robert felt a pang of conscience at the sight of the writing on the letter. He put the note down as casually as he could on his makeshift table and apologized for having nothing to offer his messenger.

'Forget it, Robert, there's not enough to go round as it is, except on Cardigan's yacht which makes me slaver to think of. Anyway, I must get back. It looks as if the Russians might move.'

'Soon?'

'Tomorrow perhaps. A spy brought intelligence this morning. Join us if you want to. You know the colonel won't object.'

Robert nodded.

'Thank you. I'll be down at dawn. I – I don't have a horse.'

'I'll speak to the colonel. Have you any food for yourself? Short commons tonight.'

Robert thought of the palm-sized piece of pork.

'Enough, thank you.'

'Dawn, then,' Carson said, and was gone.

Robert picked up Sarah's letter and looked at it. He felt distinctly uneasy about her, as if he had let her down in some way, awakened her trust and then abused it, opened her mind and then abandoned her to fend for herself. He had not seen her since she had let him read Edgar's letter from Constantinople, but she had impressed him then as being much stronger than he, much more enduring, much more sure. Her stature seemed to have grown, her very presence to be in some way more impressive. She was not at all the girl he had danced with in the spring. He shook his head and unfolded her letter.

ss *Hercules*
October 24th, 1854

Dear Robert,

I know we said good-bye when last we met, but I could not leave the Crimea without a word to you. I sail tomorrow and pray for a day as pleasant as today has been. With good weather I should be home for Christmas or at least the New Year.

I shall think of you all a good deal, and will become a faithful reader of *The Clarion* in the absence of first-hand information. If there is any way in which I can be of use to you, please do not hesitate to ask.

God bless you,
Your friend,
Sarah Drummond

It was most unsatisfactory. Unsure what he had looked for, Robert knew it was not that sensible and conventional tone. He poked his steaming, bursting fire with his boot toe and thrust the paper between the slats of wood where it flared briefly and suddenly into a pure, clear apricot-coloured flame. On an impulse, Robert thrust his hand into his pocket and pulled out a small folded paper, much worn and creased. He opened it and held it so that the curl of hair it contained might fall into the flame of the burning letter. The hair did not slip but seemed to cling to the paper. Robert swore to himself and folded it up again, returning it to his pocket. He gave the fire another kick and went back to his stool and his candle. He picked up his pen.

The Russians have a new weapon. When their dead fall in the lines outside Sebastopol, they are not burying them but leaving them where they lie, to rot. Then they bring out the bodies of those who are killed within the city walls and add them to the nauseous heaps. The stench is beyond belief.

He stopped, put down the pen and sat for a moment staring unseeingly down at what he had written, his right hand on the pocket containing the packet of hair. Then, with a sudden resolution, he stood up, took a stride to the wall, and thrust the little package hard between the planks of which the hut was built. It was still visible, wedged tightly between the boards of splintery wood so he thumped at it two or three times with his fist. Then he bent and scooped a fingerful of earth from the floor and packed it hard into the crack so that the whitish line of paper was covered. When that was done he stood back and surveyed his handiwork and then, with a faint sigh, went back to his seat and his work.

# Twelve

In her sleep before dawn next morning, Sarah heard thunder. She rolled over drowsily half her mind instantly awake and apprehensive to think of the weather she must face down the Black Sea. It seemed quite distant thunder booming away somewhere over the hills, and she lay waiting for her body to feel the toss and heave of the stormy seas below her. There was none. She opened her eyes into blackness and heard, this time with all her mind, the distant roll of gunfire. There was a knock on the cabin door. Little Mary stood there shivering, dressed in everything she possessed with a shawl clutched about her shoulders.

' 'Tis battle, ma'am!'

Sarah fought at the last shreds of sleep.

'For how long, Mary?'

'Half an hour or more, ma'am. I woke at four, bein' that anxious about our goin' and I must have lain there but twenty minutes or so before I heard it. You can see flashes of fire above the hills, ma'am, terrible they looks!'

Dragging a blanket from her bunk about her, Sarah went to the window. The first grey and pink streaks of dawn were glimmering above the harbour, illuminated now and then by a fiery glow from the ground which was accompanied by the crash of cannonade.

'What are we to do, ma'am?'

'I shall dress, Mary, and you will make me some tea and then we shall have to wait and see what happens. Perhaps Captain Edgar will send us a message.'

Mary was close to tears.

'P'raps we shan't get away, ma'am! P'raps we shan't get to Miss Blanche!'

Sarah smiled out into the streaky darkness of the early morning.

'Perhaps we shan't, Mary.'

The battle of Balaclava has begun. I am very much afraid your departure must be postponed. I send you a horse so lose no time but come up here as quickly as ever you can.

Edgar

Mary stared in mystification at Sarah's smile and pink cheeks. She did not understand her mistress at all. She had helped her to dress, then had brought her tea and the only slice of stale bread that remained to them, and Miss Drummond had not seemed to heed either, but had moved about the cabin humming to herself like a person with something pleasant ahead of them to do. And now, it being almost seven, and within an hour of their planned departure and she, Mary, almost frantic that Miss Drummond would not seem to concentrate on their going, this message had been brought from Captain Edgar, and Miss Drummond had clapped her hands, yes, actually clapped her hands like a child at Christmas! Mary gazed at her.

'Shall you come with me to the battle, Mary?'

Mary shrank back.

'Oh no, ma'am, if you please, I'd not care to, not at all.'

'Then I must leave you, Mary. Do you eat the bread yourself, and tidy the cabin and make the bed for we shall not be going tonight.'

An unbidden wail escaped Mary. Sarah turned to her and took her shoulders.

'Do not fret, Mary. If you wish so much to go to Miss Blanche, go you shall, and as soon as may be arranged.'

'And – and you, ma'am?'

Sarah tied on her bonnet and picked up her cloak.

'Nothing is decided, Mary. Not any more. But you shall go if that is what you wish.'

The door closed behind her and her hurrying footsteps died away along the deck. Some minutes later, leaning over the rail outside the cabin, Mary could see the dark shape of a paddle-box boat moving away from the side of the *Hercules*, and in it her mistress, upright and graceful in her bonnet and cloak. It was still only seven-fifteen in the morning.

The road out of Balaclava was packed. Troops were trudging away from the village bundled up in whatever rags and tatters of uniform they had been able to assemble, dimly moving dark masses in the early mist. Officers overtook Sarah and her escort as they trotted onward, all with the expression of men who know something serious is impending.

They were making first for the cavalry camp on the heights at Kadikoi. Lord Raglan had sent word that he would be pleased to see Sarah on the Sapoune Heights beyond the camp, across the Sebastopol road, whence she would have an excellent view of the action. It appeared that above Balaclava there was a great plain, perhaps two miles wide, entirely enclosed by hills, with a long ridge running down its length and dividing it into two valleys, the North and South. Lord Raglan and his staff had taken up a position at the western end of this great amphitheatre of land on some heights at least six hundred feet above the valley floor with a clear view down the South Valley, but a slightly less clear one down the North owing to the ridge of land running between the two.

As Sarah reached the head of the valley, a brilliant autumn sun broke through the veils of mist, and a gasp rose from all those gathered round her. The scene below, before obscured in morning fogs, revealed itself in startling clarity. Above, the sky turned azure, clear and pale as a thrush's egg; far into the distance the waters of Balaclava harbour glittered in the sunshine, and below the army, scarlet and gold and immaculate from this distance, moved and wheeled on what seemed from above to be a smooth green carpet of grass. Bursts of firing sent plumes of smoke whirling round the earthworks which the British had built at intervals down the valley, and from which the Russians seemed to be having no trouble in driving the Turks.

There was quite a group up there on the heights. Sarah saw Mrs Duberly, gracefully seated on her horse, with her celebrated yellow curls brilliant in the sunlight, and received from her a very slight bow of acknowledgement. Mrs Duberly did not care for the presence of other ladies. Beyond her, and the men grouped around her, Lord Raglan and his staff, among them Captain Duberly, had positioned themselves on a small plateau on the hillside's very edge and were surveying the scene below through glasses. Further away still and behind the commander's position, were groups of men in civilian clothes and the occasional woman in extravagant dress.

'Tourists,' Dick Carson said.

'I can hardly believe it! I knew there were some down in Constantinople, but here! What have they come for?'

'To be entertained while they picnic.'

The air was as still as it was clear. Between the bursts of firing down below, Sarah could hear the clink of bits and spurs, wafts of speech, the yells of the Turks as they were driven from the redoubts.

'My dear Sarah.'

Edgar was at her elbow, pale, but his eyes were full of excitement.

'I am so bitterly sorry that you must stay another day or so. I dared not leave you in the harbour in case by some unlucky chance the Russians were to take Balaclava. You are good indeed to be so calm at the frustration of your plans.'

'*Your* plans,' she said softly.

'I must leave you. I must join the brigade. It takes half an hour at least to get down to the valley even for the most intrepid horseman.' He paused a little and looked down at the toy battlefield below him, and when he turned back again to Sarah, his mouth could not repress a smile. 'I saw Nolan of the 15th Hussars yesterday and he said to me, "Is not this fun? Is not this a most glorious life a man could lead?" and I answered him doubtfully then, but today – today – ! Do not leave the heights, Sarah, do not move till I come back to you.'

She put a hand on his sleeve.

'Shall you be in danger?'

He looked away.

'You forget I am only the paymaster.'

'Then why – ' she began, and checked herself. 'God keep you, Edgar.'

He raised his hand to her with a look of deep affection, and then urged his horse over the verge of the heights, to begin on the sheer and rocky stumble to the valley below.

Robert had been with the cavalry since four. Aware of Lord Lucan's practice of getting his men out a full hour earlier than was necessary, and anxious not to miss the chance of a mount,

Robert had rolled himself out of his inadequate blankets in the blackness before dawn, and had plunged out, breakfastless, into the bitter air. Carson he discovered had been as good as his word, and a cob had been found for him, a stocky solid beast with huge round hooves and a heavy head. It lacked any kind of elegance but promised well for stamina. Robert sought out Colonel Lowe to thank him.

'If it assists you in your task, Chiltern, there is nothing to thank me for, and all I ask in return is that you do not make the source of your transport public, nor stay too close by us. It is thought Raglan will watch the battle from somewhere half-way to paradise, and we shall fight it out on the valley floor. I only hope he realizes how hilly that floor is. I suggest you adopt a position somewhere between the two. Here.' He pulled from his pocket a folded paper. 'I was sent this among other newspapers from England. It was written by someone who clearly sympathizes with your Mr Hope. Don't let it enrage you, and take care of yourself.'

Some two hours later, fortified by the gift of hard-boiled eggs and rum from an officer of the Light Dragoons, the light was at last sufficient to read by. The clipping Colonel Lowe had given him proved to be from the *Illustrated London News* of June 11th that year, and included a charming engraving of the house Lord Raglan had occupied at Scutari in the spring. Around the picture ran an article championing the British stand over the Turkish question, and Colonel Lowe had scored the margin in one place with pencil.

'Thank heaven we are not a nation of Brights and Quakers. If we were there would speedily be an end of us, and Russia would be free to possess herself, not of Constantinople only, but of Manchester – and London!'

Robert smiled grimly down at the cutting. It might be laughable, but it was also salutary. Was there not a hideous danger of becoming so involved in the daily misery and maladministration of life here that one forgot about the larger issues involved? To become so absorbed by the trees that one forgot they belonged to a wood? Robert glanced about him at the cavalry lines. Officers were riding up and down shouting orders and complaints about imperfections of dress, the wrong helmet, crooked belts, muddy boots, staff officers failing to sport the cocked hats proper to them. Robert sighed. Even at this moment, this suspended and eerie moment before battle began in earnest, it seemed that buttons came before principles.

Sarah was weeping. Up there on her cliff she had seen Sir Colin Campbell's men, a mere six hundred Highlanders, rise out of the ground in a double file of scarlet coats and kilts and drive back four squadrons of Russian cavalry. It had been an incredible spectacle watching the Russians riding across the North Valley towards Balaclava, apparently ignored by the British cavalry whom they passed within a few hundred yards, and the watchers on the heights had begun to scream out involuntary warnings of the danger pressing on the English harbour. Robert, several hundred feet below her on the hillside, and able to see the hillocks and ridges in the valley that kept one group of cavalry from seeing another, heard these frantic screams high in the air above him, and realized, with a sickening sense of what it might mean, that Lord Raglan saw the battlefield as if it were as smooth as a billiard table.

Sarah had screamed with the others, howling into the bright blue autumn air with a frenzy born of impotence. Then she had seen that thin scarlet line of Highlanders hold firm at the valley mouth before the harbour, and she had seen the Russians waver and flee before it, and the contemplation of such courage and success had reduced her to tears. There were many weeping round her too. People put their arms about each other, sobbing and smiling. A message ran among the watchers – Lord Raglan's stump of arm was twitching, a sure sign that he was worried or frustrated.

Sarah dried her eyes and peered down again among the drifting veils of smoke. The Russians had turned away now from the eastern end of the valley, from Balaclava, and were coming thudding up towards the cavalry and the heights where she watched. Dick Carson, ordered to stay by her until relieved, to his intense frustration, felt a small lessening of his irritation to see how tense she was, how oblivious either of him or the other people near them, craning forward, her fists clenched, her face still streaked with tears.

'It'll be the Heavy Brigade,' he said with some satisfaction, watching the Russian progress, 'the Heavies will get them.'

She did not look round.

'I should hate you to miss any action on my account, Captain Carson.'

'Thank you, Miss Drummond. Honesty compels me to agree with you. But it looks as if the Light Brigade won't be called on just now, and by the time it is, I'll be riding with them.'

'Sometimes – sometimes orders must be difficult to obey. It is hard for you to stay here.'

Dick Carson cleared his throat.

'In one sense, yes, I fear Miss Drummond. But we're all under 'em you know, all under orders. There's only a handful of men down there who aren't. One of them being our friend Mr Chiltern.'

'Robert!'

Dick Carson saw a rosy colour flame into Sarah's cheek.

'He's got a horse, Miss Drummond, and a wad of paper and if I know anything of him, he'll be down there in the thick of it taking notes.'

Sarah continued to gaze down at the jogging grey block of Russian horsemen moving towards them.

'Do – do you think he will be in danger?'

'Most probably. It wouldn't be like him to turn from it. He's an awkward dog but I've not seen him shrink yet. I'll wager you he's down there by the Heavy Brigade with his pen poised.'


When the Heavy Brigade charged, Robert was as close to them as he dared to be without obstructing their passage. While the Russians rode up the valley, Robert had guided his horse downwards towards the British cavalry, impressed to find his mount as sensible as it looked. It would not be hurried, but picked its way steadily among the slithering stones, head bent and big hooves squarely placed. When he reached the bottom of the slope, Robert had eyes to spare for the scene around him, and was horrified to see that the Russians were not riding up flattish terrain as it had looked from three hundred feet higher, but were descending upon the Heavy Brigade from over the central ridge of the valley. If the British were to charge, they had to do so uphill, and that over terrain pitted and holed and strewn with rocks.

It was impossible. Screwing up his eyes against the sunlight, Robert saw the solid mass of the Russian cavalry above him, a great impenetrable grey square. Below, the Heavy Brigade were still being ordered precisely into line, Robert could see clearly the furious impatience of the faces under the shakos. There was a moment of breathless, unearthly silence, and then, with a sound so thrilling that Robert forgot everything else at that second, came the trumpet call to charge. A roar rose like all the wild beasts of the world together, interspersed with the Irish yells of the Inniskillings, and the brigade went past Robert at the gallop, the ground shuddering beneath their feet, their sabres wheeling in glittering circles. They smashed into the Russians with irresistible force and above the howls and cries, Robert could hear the violent and endless cursing of the troopers as they hacked hopelessly at Russian overcoats too thick to penetrate and shakos too solid to be pierced.

Kicking impotently, Robert tried to urge his horse forward, but that practical animal would not be moved. There was nothing for it but to stand in his stirrups and listen to the clatter of metal on metal and the screams and yells, and to peer through the whirling mass of dust and smoke at the spectacle of a thousand men chopping and hacking at each other with swords and sabres and even with their bare hands. He could have wept. If the chance had been offered him then, he would have sold his soul for a sword to gallop in after them with, wild with the same rage, mad with the same savage courage.

In under ten minutes it was all over. The enemy were streaming away in flight up the causeway ridge, and the blood-soaked Heavy Brigade were sorting themselves out.

'Pursue them!' Robert shouted to no one in particular, 'Follow it up! Why don't the Light Brigade pursue them! Why let them escape! Why does no one order them?'

He was unheeded. He looked about him at the troopers, dazed with effort and success and bleeding copiously, collapsed on their horses' necks like men stunned. Beyond them, in the trampled earth, he could see men lying, limp forms in the muddle of mud and broken weapons. Dismounting from his sturdy horse, Robert pulled the reins over its head and led it firmly forward towards the nearest of the crumpled figures. He bent over the man. His leg was pulpy and hideous, but he was breathing heavily. Robert bent to slide an arm beneath his trunk.

'I'll get you to the field hospital,' he said.

The cob stood as still as stone while Robert heaved the man across his saddle. It was no easy task, for the man – a captain it would seem from his jacket – though young and lean, was big-boned and heavy and faint with the pain of his smashed leg. He was fair, with darker brows drawn together in suffering, and a neat moustache above his tightened lips. A scabbard hung empty at his side and his head was bare. As Robert rolled him on to one hip to ease the pressure on his wounded leg, his eyes opened briefly, grey and tormented, and his gaze travelled quickly over Robert's civilian clothes.

'Don't – don't risk yourself – '

Robert smiled at him.

'I've been longing to.'

The young captain only grunted, then his lids slid down as his limbs deadened with unconsciousness. Robert swung himself cautiously into the saddle and dug his heels into the cob's flanks. Slowly and carefully, the heavy horse began to move forward down a narrow gully ahead, Robert guiding it with one hand, and grasping the young officer's jacket with the other. The soldier's head lolled alarmingly, the hair swinging, his chalk white face thrown up every so often by the rhythm of the horse's movement. Robert wondered uneasily if he had any chance of getting him alive to any help. There was a field hospital not a quarter of a mile away below the hillside on whose summit Lord Raglan stood, but the route was made difficult by the terrain, and by the frequent bluffs behind which any kind of danger might lurk. He put a hand down to the man's brow, and felt it cold and wet.

There was a sudden clattering of hooves, and from a small defile to his right, between two high outcrops of rock came a couple of Russian cavalrymen, massive in their grey overcoats. Robert looked hastily about, but the shallow gully down which he was riding was empty of soldiers, even though he could hear English voices amid the battle clatter not fifty yards away over the rocks to his left. He looked down at the soldier; he was weaponless, he had lost his sword, and Robert had nothing but a clasp knife and his pencil.

Of its own accord, the cob had halted. Robert sat still, one hand on the reins, the other still grasping the captain's jacket. He looked ahead and saw that the Russians had now been joined by a further two, and that the four were strung out across the gully, and that the original pair were smiling. He did not like the look of their smiles. Briefly, he thought of retreat, and then realized that retreat would only result in pursuit, and the likelihood of being cut down from behind. To advance seemed little better since he had nothing to defend himself with but his bare hands. The young captain stirred a little and his eyelids flickered; blood from his leg was smeared down Robert's boot and dropped steadily to the stones below.

The Russians started to advance. Robert sat still and waited. They had perhaps twenty yards to come and they rode with agonizing slowness. For one wild moment, Robert thought their line would simply divide and pass by him, a part on either side, but he then saw they intended to surround him, two at the cob's head, two at his tail. They stopped, and one of them laughed softly. The cob's ears went back.

Robert, moving only his heels, urged it onwards. Obediently, it took two steps and then the Russian pair ahead closed in, one man holding his drawn sword across the cob's nose. One of the Russians spoke to Robert, and although his words were incomprehensible, his tone was jeering.

Robert said, 'Let me pass,' and kicked the cob again.

This time the horse ignored him, deterred by the blade against its nose. From behind, one of the Russians said something sharply, and the man in front of him who had not drawn his sword, leant over and fingered the gold braid on the uniform jacket of the wounded captain. He looked up grinning at his companion, who smiled back, and took his sword away from the horse's nose and raised it into the air. The pair behind cheered.

A blast of fury exploded in Robert's brain. They were going to kill a wounded man, were they, merely because he was an enemy officer. He heard himself give a roar of the purest rage, and at the same moment wrenched the cob's head round towards the swordsman, his heels grinding into its ribs. Startled, the cob jerked forward, its heavy shoulder thudding against the Russian's leg. For a fleeting moment, Robert released the wounded man's jacket, and swung his left arm with all the strength he could muster at the swordsman's wrist. At one moment the blade was slicing downwards, the next it was wheeling free in the blue air, and as the cob thundered forward, flinging up stones with its great hooves, Robert heard amid the shouts of his antagonists, the metallic clatter of the sword hitting the rocky ground.

The cob was now going for its life. To ease it, Robert leant forward over the wounded man, glancing backwards now and again at the Russians in close pursuit. It was obviously only a matter of seconds. The cob had a double burden; the Russians' horses were considerably bigger and their riders now thoroughly angry. Robert concentrated on the end of the gully some hundred yards away. It seemed like a talisman – if he could reach it, he was safe. Even as he watched his goal, it began to fill up with horsemen, horsemen riding in towards him – horsemen in red coats!

He raised his left arm and shouted. As the men in front of him broke into a gallop, he heard the slackening of the thudding hooves behind him. He glanced round once more and saw the Russians were not only slowing up but turning. By the time the half dozen men of the Royals were level with him the Russians were making off back up the gully. The cob slithered thankfully to a halt and stood heaving, its heavy head drooping as it blew. Robert slid to the ground and stood leaning against its flank.

'Mr Chiltern, ain't it?'

He nodded, panting.

'Ain't you armed, sir?'

Robert felt in his pocket and held up a pencil. Laughter broke out all around him. He looked up and indicated the man still bleeding across the cob's withers.

'We must get him to the field hospital. That's what I was doing. Are we far?'

They shook their heads. The nearest man bent over the wounded captain.

'Captain Nugent of the Inniskillings, sir. I'll show you the way.'

Robert straightened up and moved to the cob's head, pulling the reins over his ears.

'Lead on, then.'

Up on the heights, the picnic baskets were opened. Sarah accepted a wing of chicken, but refused wine. All the while she ate, she remained gazing fixedly down at the valley, and when Edgar arrived to relieve Captain Carson, she was unaware of his coming.

He was fighting extremely mixed feelings. He had sat in his saddle all morning with the rest of the Light Brigade, waiting for the summons to assist the rest of the cavalry. No summons had come. The men of the brigade were seething with impatience and were hardly to be restrained when the Heavy Brigade achieved such success. At this moment Colonel Lowe had ordered Edgar up to escort his sister and to summon Dick Carson down. Without a flicker crossing his countenance, Edgar obeyed. He begrudged Sarah no care, but it was hard to be plucked from the stage of the battle so to speak, and to fail to receive the smallest sign of welcome or gratitude from her.

Silently he took his place by her side. At one moment, she turned and took his hand and said, 'I am thankful you are not hurt, Edgar,' and then she dropped it again and turned back to the spectacle below.

Thus it was, side by side, and almost in silence that they witnessed the charge of the Light Brigade. They saw Captain Nolan of the 15th Hussars take Lord Raglan's order to charge, apparently, the Russian guns, and they watched with tightened throats as he guided his horse so skilfully at breakneck speed down the precipice, and they saw him race across the valley floor towards the cavalry commanders. And then, after what seemed an interminable wait, they saw the six hundred men of the Light Brigade ride jingling forward, perfectly turned out, perfectly in line, slowly steadily trotting onward, stirrup to stirrup in the bright, clear silence of the morning.

'They cannot mean to ride at the Russian guns!' Sarah said.

Edgar looked along the valley at the Russian artillery, thirty squat guns lined up – and waiting. He looked back at the Light Brigade, precise and steady and still trotting forward, their lines even and unbroken. They had covered fifty yards perhaps, not more, and there must have been a mile or more to go.

He said, 'It seems they do,' but his words were lost in a crash of gunfire. The Russians had opened up. They saw Captain Nolan leave his position in the front line and dash like a madman across the front of the whole brigade, only to be torn open by a shell and fall shrieking from his horse. Despite himself, Edgar gasped and his eyes filled with hot and sudden tears.

'He said it was glorious – only yesterday – he said it was the most glorious life a man could lead – '

Sarah seemed not to hear him. Her eyes were fixed upon that unwavering trotting band, always moving onward, while the enemy shot crashed into them, closing up neatly the gaps that fallen horsemen left, never hesitating, trotting on – on – As they advanced along the valley, the fire became heavier, grapeshot and roundshot pouring in from both sides and men began to fall in groups, and then the thirty great guns at the end opened up, and the unbearable quiet trotting at last broke into a canter and then to a gallop, tearing down the valley at breakneck speed, right up to those terrible guns – and then through them, right through them and into a thick pall of smoke like a curtain.

'Eight minutes,' Edgar said.

He glanced at Sarah. She was as white as paper, staring down the valley at the blanket of smoke through which the few brave unwounded had vanished. And then a sudden silence fell, as abrupt as the noise that had preceded it. Below them, the valley was littered with twitching men and horses. Sarah could see some of the animals struggling to rise, only to fall back with screams that sliced through the sudden quiet, and all around them the twisted bodies of soldiers lay still or attempted to crawl from where they had fallen. The green grass, so smooth and even from the heights where they watched, was blotched with blood, brilliant in the sunlight, and among the wreckage of limbs down there, they could see the white splinters of shattered bone.

Edgar took Sarah's arm. They were both trembling like leaves.

'Will you not sit down a moment?'

She shook her head.

'That was madness. *Madness*,' she whispered. 'There was never anything so brave, so gallant, so – so *terrible*. It was an insane order to give – '

'Hush, my dear Sarah, hush, I should not have let you come,

indeed it was wrong of me. It was not right to let you see such a thing. I shall take you back to the ship, you must be gone this day, battle or no battle, forgive me –'

'No!' she said vehemently.

Edgar was startled by the savagery of her tone. He stepped back in surprise. She turned at last from the view of the valley and faced him.

'I am not going back. Not to Constantinople, not to England, not to Blanche. I am not even going back to the *Hercules*. I am going down to the harbour and I shall beg a passage on one of the hospital transport ships and I shall go down to Scutari and offer my services to Miss Nightingale when she arrives from England. That field down there is thick with broken men, thick with suffering and I will be a spectator no longer!'

He reached to take her arm again, but she snatched it from his fingers.

'No, you shall *not* soothe me, you shall *not* try to persuade me differently. I have endured enough, bowed enough and from now on I shall do as *I* think I should. I can bear my uselessness no longer and you must bear my decision. Don't touch me, Edgar, don't treat me as a silly fool. My mind is made up, quite made up, I think it has been made up for ages, but only now do I have the strength to obey it, and nothing you can do shall stop me!'

He reached out for her a third time.

'Dearest Sarah, do not speak so! You do not know what you are saying, you are agitated by what you have seen, you are not yourself. Let us talk it all over calmly, later, when you are more yourself, when the awful visions you have just seen are not so vivid. Decide nothing now, I beg you, dearest Sarah, decide nothing now!'

She whirled away from him and resumed her position, staring down the valley.

'I have never been *more* myself, Edgar, never in all my life. I have always been something other people wanted. Now I know what I want. I shall not disgrace you, Edgar, you need say nothing to anyone. It will be supposed I am gone home as planned. But I am going to Scutari, Edgar, I am going to nurse.'

I now know why this sea is called Black. We have been tossing on it now for eight days and it has been inky dark and treacherous all that time. Captain Noakes said last evening that we were not above a few days from Scutari, but I remember that some of the ships that crossed from Varna in the summer took seventeen days to accomplish a journey only half the length of mine, so I think he may be bent on encouragement rather than accuracy.

He insisted I should have a cabin. There is no surgeon on this ship, he could not be found when we left Balaclava, and so I have his little cupboard and his hammock is slung in it at night for me. I have not been in the hammock much for the work to be done upon the ship could take more hours than are sent each day. I am horrified how quickly wounds grow maggoty and the wounded have often no strength to do anything but lie on the rotten boards of this hulk and suffer. We have so little fresh water on board that I order buckets of sea water to be pulled up for washing, though even when the wounds are cleaned there is nothing but such filthy rags as the men can spare themselves to bind them up.

The smell is terrible, but it seems one grows quickly used to anything. Most of the men are too weak to move, and there are no chamber pots. The decks are washed down as often as possible, but they are so packed with bodies, it is a hopeless task, and I fear the filth is winning. There is little to eat beyond the usual salt meat and biscuit, and that is a poor diet for a healthy man, let alone a weak and wounded one.

I have a strange and conspiratorial friendship with Captain Noakes. It was pure chance and great luck that he should be standing on the quayside when I rode down from the battlefield, and even greater luck that he should have heard of Miss Nightingale and feel sympathy for my desires. Edgar never tried to dissuade me further, indeed I hardly gave him the chance, but stayed all the rest of that day among groups of people to preclude any private conversation. I could not look at him for his poor, familiar, stricken face went to my heart so. I cause him bitter pain, quite as much as Blanche did, perhaps more, but I am so sure, more sure than ever I was of anything before, that what I do is right, that I find that is a stronger force than my cruelty.

I have brought nothing with me, there was no time. I was even forced to leave my journal behind and can only write now because of the generosity of Captain Noakes. He has provided me with a pen of his own, and a pile of endpapers cut from sailing manuals – he is a kind and resourceful man. Edgar gave me money as we parted, quite in silence, and it would have pleased me not to take it, but that would have been a silly and over-romantic gesture. He says he will send more. I went on board in my riding habit and cloak and bonnet – a very strange figure I must cut! – and I sleep in my clothes and wash in sea water. There is only one other woman on board, a soldier's wife, but she has a fever, poor woman, and is as helpless as the men she would wish to comfort. I found her the second day out from Balaclava lying on the open deck, soaking wet while the rain lashed down upon her and her skin burned with sickness. We have erected a clumsy screen for her on the gun deck, a poor and hardly private place, but the best we can do.

It is a mercy I am not sick at sea. It is becoming difficult to tell who is sick with fever and who has no stomach for the sea. They shout for water all day, all night. There are five men and myself to help them and no one else, and there must be above four hundred! There seems to be no resentment, not even surprise among my five assistants, of my presence. Were there ten times our number, I doubt it would be enough. Above a dozen die each day and must be pitched overboard. . . . That part quite overwhelms me.

This ship must be very old, forty or fifty years at least, built for the wars against Napoleon. It is all heavy black timbers, and the decks below the gun deck are low and stifling and almost entirely without light. All day and night the timbers and yards creak and groan and the sails slap and crack in the wind and there is not a spot to step on that is not foul. We have seen sunlight once only in more than a week, the day after the battle, but the rest of the days have been dark and wild and we are tumbled about in the treacherous waters as if we were no more than a walnut shell.

But I would not go back, I would not retrace one step. There is only one part of me that remains at Balaclava still, and that is my heart. Robert has that, even if he has no use for it. I know he came through that day for I heard him warmly spoken of down by the harbour for all the help he gave to the wounded on the field. I also heard there that poor Captain Carson was killed in that mad and terrible charge. I wonder who else, I wonder if any of the officers who have shown me such infinite kindness in the last months are now being shovelled into graves or lying on the deck of such a ship as ours? Have there ever been so many heroes all at once before? Have men ever been so noble and so brave?

Morning has come. I can see a steely light in the east, and make out the choppy roughness of the waves. Soon I shall wash as best I can, and smooth my hair with the comb Captain Noakes so tactfully made me a present of, and then I shall go down to the deck to see if that poor brave man with both legs shattered has survived the night. He has seven children, of whom he mutters in his delirium, but when he is calm he is so patient and enduring that he seems like a candle burning in darkness. How I wish I was a surgeon, how I wish I had a practised skill!

Time to begin. Breakfast will be biscuit and rum and water. To think I once shrank from drinking rum! Captain Noakes tells me I am lucky to get any for the huge consignment ordered for the British Army from Matthew Clark, the wine merchants in Cannon Street, still sits in their warehouse. Much good may it do our poor soldiers there! I must wash a petticoat today and somehow contrive to mend a great tear in the skirt of my habit which I caught going down a companionway.

God keep you, Robert.

# Thirteen

The waterfront at Scutari was, if it were possible, doubly as revolting by November as it had been the previous spring. From a safe distance out at sea, it still had enormous charm, being a row of rakish and picturesque buildings, some squat and washed with ochre or white, some tall and festooned with complicated wooden balconies, and all set against the hillside covered with tiled roofs and random walls, surmounted by the great barrack hospital. The sea that lapped against the quayside itself was dotted with Turkish caiques, broad bellied fishing boats painted in brilliant colours with lanterns swinging at the bows, and among them, every so often a huge British hospital hulk or supply ship floated like a whale among minnows.

On closer inspection, the vivid and romantic impression disintegrated into horror. The sea was choked with rubbish and the bloated carcasses of beasts, the quayside was a sea of evil-smelling mud littered with broken boxes and sodden sacks and the walls of those white and yellow houses were leprous with neglect. The alleys that ran back into the town were narrow and filthy, there was no paved thoroughfare anywhere, no corner that was not damp and stinking and infested with rats. November brought wild winds and rain to Scutari and thousands more men, wounded in Balaclava's sequel, Inkerman.

One of every four or five houses on the waterfront was a ship's chandler of some description. With the influx of British ships into the harbour during the summer, the needs of shipping had become steady and profitable business, and many of the fishermen who had resigned themselves to the customary profitlessness of the winter, found that it was a simple matter to put their knowledge to practical use and supply the demand.

One such fisherman, an idle and shrewd Greek, had not only filled a store room with ropes imported from Egypt, but had realized that Scutari was quite as full of people as it was of ships, and had offered two dingy and dirty rooms at the top of his house to lodgers. After a succession of soldiers' wives and their children whom he had bodily flung out when it became apparent that they had no funds, the rooms had been taken by a stout and determined sailor's wife, who said she should take them for a month. She proceeded to astound the Greek by not only paying him in advance for the first fortnight, but by also vigorously and repeatedly scrubbing the floors and walls.

When Mrs Coles took the rooms in the ships' chandlers in late October, she had not quite known why she was doing it. She had accompanied her husband, Captain Coles, out to Turkey but it had not struck her for one moment that she might lose him. He was a sailor after all, and not even in command of a fighting ship. The *Truro* had been only a transport ship, later used to ferry the sick down from the camps and then the battle-fields, and it had not occurred to Captain Coles, or to his redoubtable wife, that there was any danger in that whatsoever. It was hard and ceaseless work for both of them, but it was hardly perilous. And then, in the first week of October, anchored in Balaclava harbour to take on yet more sick, Captain Coles was struck with cholera. His wife nursed him with all her tremendous common sense, but within three days he was dead, and his body, sewn in the hammock he had used since he was a boy of twelve, was thrown into the Black Sea.

Mrs Coles was reduced to a state of uncharacteristic numb-ness. A fellow sailor, captain of another and similar vessel to the *Truro* took her on board and carried her down to Scutari, supposing that as she was not destitute and now had no reason for staying, she would wish to return to Cornwall. Once in Scutari, she thanked him and refused all further offers of help. She slept that night wrapped in her cloak in a corner behind the waterfront, her carpet bag under her head, and her small store of gold in a linen bag sewn inside her underbodice.

Within a couple of days, she had installed herself above the Greek chandler's shop. Why she did so, she could hardly say herself, but she felt a curious reluctance to go home before she had resigned herself to the loss of so good a husband; for three days she scrubbed and swept and felt soothed by the occupa-tion. On the fourth day she went into the bazaar and bargained furiously for a low rough bedstead, a pile of stiff, coarse, dark blankets and an amazing chair in scarlet lacquer that had come, without doubt, from the East. The purchase of the scarlet chair was a triumph, because its brilliance had caught the eye of several soldiers' wives loitering around the alleys. When Mrs Coles had succeeded, she planted the chair in an empty corner and sat in it, to get her breath back.

A woman who had been eyeing her for some time now came up and stood before her, twisting a dingy white apron she wore over her clothes. Mrs Coles stared at her challengingly and settled herself more firmly in the scarlet chair.

'You from the 'ospital?'

Mrs Coles sniffed.

'What hospital?'

The woman came nearer and squatted at Mrs Coles's side.

'The Barrack 'ospital. Thought you was one of them Nightingale nurses. Thought you'd give me work.'

Mrs Coles looked at her sternly.

'Don't you know of Miss Nightingale then?' the woman went on. 'I bin 'ere a week. I was down at the 'arbour the day she come in with all them nurses. They say she's upset the 'ospital doctors good and proper wantin' invalid food and clean beddin' and that. She's lady, Miss Nightingale is.' She leaned closer to Mrs Coles, and breathed stale liquor into her face. 'She's brought a fortune with 'er. Thirty thousand pounds, they say. I thought she'd give me work. I'll beg if I go 'ome.'

Mrs Coles contemplated the woman in the apron.

'Is – is this Miss Nightingale lookin' for more nurses, then?'

'They're dyin' up there like flies. You'd think she couldn't 'ave too many, wouldn't you? They say she don't like you to drink, though how a body's to survive wi'out, I can't say. Still, if you don't 'ave money, you can't 'ave drink so I want a bit of work. There's too many whorin' already, otherwise that'd be the easier way. Would you come up to the 'ospital with me?' She eyed Mrs Coles's respectable and neatly mended stuff gown. 'It'd 'elp, like.'

'Have you no 'usband?' Mrs Coles demanded.

'Killed at Balaclava, wasn't 'e? Not a month since. You a widder?'

Mrs Coles nodded.

'You'll come up to the 'ospital, then? We'll get work if you come.'

Mrs Coles put her hand against the place under her bodice where the linen pouch rested. It was still quite plump but it would obviously not replenish itself.

'Who are you?'

The woman grinned.

'Sarah Anne Evans.'

Mrs Coles rose and laid hold of the arms of the scarlet chair.

'I'm Mrs Coles, widow of the late Captain Coles. I'll think it over. I'll be up by the 'ospital before dusk if I decide to come.'

Mrs Evans put a hand on the chair. 'I'll 'elp you take that 'ome. Mebbe you've room for two –'

'You touch my chair and I'll brain you with it.'

Mrs Evans stepped back.

'No offence meant I'm sure. Only tryin' to 'elp I was. 'Ow are we to manage if we don't 'elp a bit?'

Mrs Coles hoisted the chair into the air.

'I'll bid you good day, Mrs Evans.'

Back in her lodgings, a letter awaited her. It was from Samuel Noakes, a man who had been a good friend to both the late captain and herself, and who presently commanded the *Truro*'s sister ship the *Tamar*. He said briefly that he needed her help. He had someone with him who was in trouble and he would be with her again by nightfall. Samuel Noakes had been a loyal friend and had done them many a favour, therefore if what he asked was in any way within her power to fulfil, she would do it. She put the scarlet chair beside the fireplace, coaxed a small fire out of bits of broken crate picked up on the waterfront, and put all thoughts of Sarah Anne Evans and Miss Nightingale out of her mind.

# *Fourteen*

It was a cold and miserable morning in early December when Miss Nightingale was informed that a person wished to see her. She was as usual, deeply occupied, but paused long enough in her task to ask what sort of person it was.

'Oh – a lady, ma'am. At least, she speaks like a lady though she's hardly dressed as one. Very shabby she is, and thin, poor soul, but she seemed so anxious to see you, ma'am, that I'd not the heart to say I wouldn't ask you at the least.'

Miss Nightingale sighed. She was not unsympathetic, but the person below hardly sounded the robust and sensible sort of woman whom she could have made such excellent use of. She considered the list of bedlinen she had just drawn up, and amended the number of sheets to double. She would be most grateful, she said, if she need not be troubled personally this morning.

Agnes Clay nodded and withdrew. She had had little hope that Miss Nightingale would come herself, and had said as much to the poor girl down at the hospital entrance. But the girl had been so insistent that she had not been able to bring herself to disappoint her outright. Now she must do so after all.

The girl was still waiting where she had left her. She wore some sort of dark stuff skirt and jacket, much mended, and a bonnet quite devoid of any trimming under which neatly braided dark brown hair could be seen. She was standing quite still, her shabby cloak over her arm, watching – without flinching, Agnes Clay noted – while a stream of half-dead men was carried past her on clumsy makeshift stretchers.

Agnes touched her arm.

'Forgive me, my dear, but Miss Nightingale's that occupied she can't spare a moment just now.'

The girl turned deep blue eyes on her full of pleading.

'Oh please! She cannot – cannot turn me away when I have come so far to see her! Why will she not see me?'

Agnes drew her aside to an alcove where the traffic in and out of the hospital did not make conversation so difficult.

'What is your name, dear?'

'Drummond. Sarah Drummond. I have come all the way from Balaclava – I was with my brother there – I have come all the way down the Black Sea to help Miss Nightingale. She cannot turn me away! Oh I beg of you, let me see her! If I saw her, she would know how much in earnest I am!'

Agnes surveyed her. She certainly bore no resemblance to the well-dressed young women who had besieged Miss Nightingale recently with offers of help and subsequently proved themselves such broken reeds when asked to do anything more than lay a white hand on a fevered brow.

'But you're no nurse, Miss Drummond –'

'I can learn! I spent two weeks on a hospital ship with no surgeon and I'm sure that counts for some experience! I promise you I am in great earnest. I know what kind of tasks I must undertake, I am quite prepared. Oh I beg you, let me see her! I will only take a minute of her time, but I am sure she would relent if I were to see her!'

Agnes considered.

'Listen, my dear. Miss Nightingale's had a lot of applications like yours before, and they've all but one or two, come to nothing. The work's too hard for young ladies, and Miss Nightingale hasn't the time to waste seeing to them any more. You wouldn't want to undertake most of the tasks here, I promise you wouldn't.'

Sarah's fists were clenched and her eyes were brilliant.

'But I've *done* them, don't you see? I was on that ship with above four hundred men and I *know* how conditions are! I'm not fresh from London, I've been with the army since the spring, you see, I *know* –' her voice faltered and she put a hand out to steady herself against a wall.

Agnes put out an arm to help her.

'You're not well, dear,' she said reprovingly.

'It's nothing,' Sarah said faintly. 'It will pass. I've had a touch of fever, only a touch, that's all.'

Agnes drew her to sit down on a projection of stonework in the wall.

'Now then, dear, you sit there a moment. What's all this about fever?'

Sarah was breathing very quickly.

'It's nothing, I promise you, just a little spell of sickness. I am so much better, indeed I am, it need not stop me nursing! In a day or so I shall be well, quite well –'

'When did you get to Scutari?'

Sarah looked up at her.

'What day is it?'

'The third of December.'

There was a pause.

'Then – then I have been here nearly a month.'

'A month!'

Sarah was silent. Agnes stooped and put an arm about her shoulders.

'Come on, dear. Where have you been?'

'I was quite well the day we landed. The captain was most kind to me, he took such trouble . . . he found me lodging for the night in a house by the harbour, a house kept by a Greek but where a sailor's wife was already lodging, such a kind woman, without her I might have – I only meant to stay one night and then to come straight up here, to see Miss Nightingale, but I must have fallen sick in the night for I knew nothing for days, nothing at all, and even when I came to myself I was as weak as a kitten, and so confused, so feeble. Mrs Coles nursed me so kindly, I have always met with such kindness. But the moment I was stronger, I wanted to be here, to see Miss Nightingale. I kept begging Mrs Coles to let me come, and today at last she said she thought I might, and so I have come, just as I set my heart on doing – ' She seemed to struggle with tears for a moment and then said vehemently, 'You *cannot* turn me away! This is what I have come for! You cannot let me go away. What should I do if I cannot do this, and this is all I want to do?'

Agnes held out a hand.

'Come then, dear. We will go back to the Lady-in-Chief together. I'm not promising anything mind, but at least you'll know that I'm speaking the truth.'

Sarah pressed her hand gratefully.

'I never doubted that.'

Agnes smiled.

'Follow me, dear.'

The doorway of the hospital, though chill and bleak, had at least had the advantage of natural light. Now, keeping close to Agnes's hurrying figure, Sarah was plunged into an evil-smelling gloom as she was led along a dark and airless passage, only lit by occasional smoking lamps, and packed so closely with the wounded in their bloody rags that it was difficult to find space enough to step. A faint chorus of moans came from these limp forms, and often hands rose eerily from the shadows to pluck at their passing skirts.

'How – how many men are there here?'

Agnes paused a moment.

'There's four miles of corridor in this place, my dear, not to mention the wards and every inch is packed. These men only came in last night so they've no bedding yet, but they'll be better off by nightfall. Some of the men themselves are well enough now to give a hand but I promise you it's a paradise to what it was a month ago!'

In the tiny corner room that served her as bedroom, sitting room and office, Miss Nightingale was still at her lists. She did not look up as they entered, but continued to write, saying only, 'I know I am late with my rounds but if I do not put these orders in today, we shall run short of sheets before Christmas.'

She was dressed entirely in black, only relieved by white cuffs and collar and apron. Her dark hair was hardly visible under a white cap surmounted by a black silk square, but her clear pale profile was admirably revealed by these nun-like adornments. It was a severely beautiful face, with a straight nose and a firm, precisely cut mouth. Agnes and Sarah waited in the doorway.

At last, Miss Nightingale put down her pen, and turned towards them.

'And so?'

Agnes put a warning hand upon Sarah's arm but it was gently removed.

'Forgive me for interrupting you, Miss Nightingale, but I will only detain you one moment. I know you have no use for unskilled workers, but I am not quite in that category. My brother is with the —th Hussars and I saw the action at the Alma and at Balaclava, indeed it was Balaclava that set the seal upon my determination to be of some use in this terrible war. I beg you will at least consider my application to help you, I beg you will not dismiss me as a girl with romantic notions. I spent two weeks on a hospital ship coming here so I know what is ahead of me –'

Miss Nightingale had raised a hand. Sarah fell silent.

'Agnes, would you leave us? Perhaps you would start my round for me?' She turned to Sarah. 'May I know your name?'

Sarah blushed furiously.

'Forgive me. My name is Drummond, Sarah Drummond. I would have come to you at once, the very day I landed, but I caught some slight fever on the ship. You must believe I am in earnest, you must believe I have only the deepest wish to help wherever it is most necessary.'

'Do you come from Northamptonshire? The Drummonds of Oakley?'

'Yes. Yes, that is my home. My parents are there now.'

'And you came out here with your brother you say? Please sit down, Miss Drummond. It cannot be good for you to stand, especially if you have been unwell. That chair is hardly luxurious but it will be better for you to sit.'

Sarah took the upright chair gratefully.

'I came to Constantinople in the spring with my brother – and my sister. Nobody seemed to think the war would be anything like it has turned out to be, Miss Nightingale, indeed we all thought we should be home for Easter. We thought of the whole thing as red coats and gold braid and bands and marching and – I – I feel very ashamed of what I thought then, very foolish. But it has gone on far beyond, and my sister has gone home for she could not bear it longer, and my brother wanted me to go with her but I could not, you see, I felt it would be so wrong. I hesitate to speak of duty since I am so inexperienced, but a sense of duty *is* what I feel, and an intense desire to help, to be of use.'

'Do you come with your family's sanction?'

Sarah looked down.

'No. No, I do not. My parents must know where I have come

by now, but I have heard no word from them. My brother did everything to persuade me not to come.'

Miss Nightingale rose and went to the window.

'When I was very young, I asked my parents to allow me to go to Salisbury Hospital for three months to learn nursing. My sister had hysterics and my mother and father were angry and deeply offended. It was as if I had asked to be a kitchenmaid. That is how your brother feels, how your parents and your sister will be feeling.'

'Yes.'

'They may not forgive you. When I eventually got to Germany and spent three months nursing there, I was quite stunned when I returned. They would hardly speak to me. I was treated as if I had come from committing a crime.'

'I think – I think I could bear that better than I can bear to be so useless, so idle, such – such a plaything.'

Miss Nightingale came back to her seat.

'Have you always felt this, Miss Drummond? All your life?'

Sarah shook her head.

'No. I knew nothing about such things, I was so sheltered, so ignorant. But these last months have changed me so much that I cannot recall what I was before. You must not think,' she said, her voice rising with her earnestness, 'that because my feelings are new, they are not genuine. I think they are what I have been waiting for. I feel as if I had found myself.'

'I do not doubt your earnestness for one moment, nor do I doubt that you would be able to bear the tasks required of you. You mentioned that you came here on a hospital ship. I imagine that you brought a companion?'

'No,' said Sarah, 'I was quite alone. I left Balaclava the very day of the battle, I would not stay another miunte. I had been shut up on board ship for months, and suddenly my mind was made up to go, to come to you. I had prayed for a sign and suddenly I seemed to have it, so I left my brother, and a little maid who was to be sent down to Constantinople to join my sister, and I came.'

'And you assisted the surgeon on the passage?'

'There was no surgeon. He could not be found. I fear that many lives were lost by his absence, since all we could do was to dress wounds and give water. I had never dressed a wound before in my life, but there were five orderlies on the ship who soon put me right. They seemed almost – almost glad to have me there, I think.'

'You sound doubtful, Miss Drummond.'

'I feel it. I cannot believe that they could have been pleased to obey a raw recruit such as I was, but it seemed that they were. Whatever their feelings, however, there is no doubt at all of my gratitude to *them*.'

Miss Nightingale made no reply, but sat for some moments in silence contemplating Sarah. The wind tugged fretfully at the window and a thin rain began to patter on the glass.

'Miss Drummond, I am not going to let you nurse.'

Sarah sprang up with a cry of anguish.

'Miss Nightingale you cannot mean it, you cannot! If it is my recent illness that concerns you, it will be quite gone in a few days more, I will wait those days, weeks if you require it, but do not turn me away, I beg you, do not turn me out – '

Miss Nightingale had risen herself and now advanced to take Sarah's hands in hers.

'I am not turning you away.'

'Not? But you have just refused me, just said that I might not – '

'Yes. And I repeat that. I will not let you nurse. I will tell you why. I brought nearly forty nurses with me, all of them middle-aged women as respectable as I can keep them whom I pay between twelve and twenty shillings a week. Clearly I could not ask you to work on such a basis and to do so would be to waste your talents. I am finding plenty of labour available here, I really have no shortage of nurses. But what I need, Miss Drummond, are organizers, and I have one special area which needs organizing so badly that my daily work is much impeded by the difficulties it causes at present. You seem not only intrepid to me, Miss Drummond, but capable, resourceful and humble. Will you seat yourself again so that I might tell you of my problem?'

She released Sarah's hands gently and resumed her seat, waiting quietly until Sarah too had subsided once more upon the chair.

'This hospital is as I am sure you know, Miss Drummond, a disused barracks and one of its many peculiarities is that it is built upon a slope. On the side of the building where the ground slopes steeply, a long covered wall has been erected, and the space below that is divided into cellars. They are very dreadful, those cellars, Miss Drummond. They have almost no ventilation, and all manner of unpleasantness drains down into them from the sick rooms above in the hospital. But there are people living down there, Miss Drummond, people in the most abject misery. We believe there are probably two hundred women and as many children in those terrible cellars and they are all in rags and covered in vermin. They are the families of the army, the wives who were allowed to accompany their husbands, and the army makes no provision for them at all. They have nothing to do but drink, Miss Drummond, and to clamour daily at the hospital for everything, for food and water and clothing. But we cannot attend to them. My work is with the soldiers, but my heart bleeds for these women, Miss Drummond, for their condition is not of their own making. Now what I would ask you is to undertake to help me, to relieve me from the importunity of these women, to look after them. There are funds available, and gifts from England arrive by every boat now, but we have no time to administer them. Will you help me?'

Sarah stood up.

'I should be glad to.'

Miss Nightingale smiled.

'You will not find yourself alone. Lady Alicia Blackwood came to me on just such a mission as yours but a few days ago, and she will be thankful to have some support in this task.'

Sarah picked up her cloak.

'Perhaps you might spare an orderly to show me the way, Miss Nightingale?'

Miss Nightingale shook her head.

'Not today. You must go back to your lodging and rest for two days more, then Lady Alicia will send for you. I shall inform her of your coming myself. Are you in want of anything?'

Sarah held out her cloak.

'I must pay a visit to the bazaar for something a little warmer than this, but apart from that I am well provided for.'

Miss Nightingale smiled once more.

'Then I encourage you to conserve your strength as much as

183

you are able. There seems to be no task which does not take a heavy toll of its performer here. Miss Drummond, I will bid you farewell for the present, and I thank you for your perseverance in seeing me.'

As Sarah left the little room, she turned once more to thank Miss Nightingale and smile, but the Lady-in-Chief had resumed her writing again and was working already as if no interruption whatever had occurred.

# Fifteen

Sarah refused to let Mrs Coles accompany her down to the cellars. Mrs Coles was extremely agitated, knowing full well what kind of women her charge was likely to encounter down in that evil gloom, but Sarah was adamant.

'It undermines my authority, dear Mrs Coles. If I come with a protector, you see, they will not take me seriously. They will think me someone frivolous, only interested in acts of charity, not in them or their plight.'

Reluctantly Mrs Coles had given way. She had lent Sarah her own voluminous boat cloak, filled her with as much breakfast as she could be persuaded to eat and had said that if Sarah was not back before dusk, she should come to fetch her.

The Greek chandler provided Sarah with one of his small and filthy sons as guide. The child was thin and bruised and cheerful, and hurried Sarah through the labyrinth of alleys at the utmost speed, chattering to her confidentially and leading her by a corner of her cloak. He did not release her until they stood beneath the towering yellow walls of the Barrack Hospital above a dark and sinister entrance that seemed to lead down into the bowels of the earth. The stench of the hospital was bad enough as it was, seeping out through those rotting walls, but the smell that rose from the depths below the hospital was sickening to a degree. Sarah drew up a fold of Mrs Coles's cloak and held it across her nose and mouth. Then she fumbled for a coin, placed it in the boy's dirty little outstretched palm, and went quickly down into the darkness.

The stink made her gasp. Down there at the bottom of the broken brick staircase, dark though it was, almost impossible to see, it was all too evident that human beings were in occupation. It was perhaps a blessing Sarah could not see the floors and on what she trod, but in any case, she was soon distracted from any such consideration by the sounds around her; whimpers and cries, cackles of laughter, shouts and curses filled the darkness. Not only was humanity present, but it was present in some numbers.

By the time a few minutes were up, Sarah's eyes became accustomed to the gloom. She was in a huge low room, into which a little dull winter light filtered through grilles somewhere up near the ceiling. That ceiling gleamed with wet as did the walls and there was not even the smallest attempt at a fire anywhere in the chamber. All around the walls lay huddled heaps, little clumps and bundles of humanity, impossible to distinguish among, and scattered just anyhow upon a floor of earth oozing with wetness and littered with filth. Across a couple of corners ragged curtains had been clumsily erected to give some kind of makeshift privacy, and at various intervals in the walls openings led off into black tunnels lined with slimy bricks. The smell was appalling and the air was filled with cries and mutterings.

Sarah drew her cloak tightly around her and set out across the floor. No one paid her the smallest heed. She went right round the room, peering earnestly into every group, and found everyone to be either very young, very sick or very drunk. All were in rags, all were grimy and shivering. It was astonishing that any were alive. In one corner, a creature hardly a woman but dressed in a cheap and stained gown of scarlet, was evidently and painfully dying, coughing helplessly and violently and blazing with fever. A baby clung to her, and a small child, apathetic with hunger, crouched dull-eyed and shaking with cold, by her broken boots.

The tunnels revealed even worse miseries. Sarah found a woman in the last stages of labour on a pile of rags so filthy as hardly to be cloth at all, two skeletal children frantic and clutching each other in a room no more than a dark cupboard, and a huge pipe, its evil flow stopped up by a wet bundle that proved to be a dead baby. Twice she had to pause and vomit. No one stopped her, no one appealed to her. Starvation and filth and drink had made them all senseless to everything, careless of everything. She counted forty children in need of immediate medical help, seven women in the last weeks of pregnancy, over thirty delirious with some sort of fever, more than a hundred affected by liquor in varying degrees, and at least a dozen dead. There were several babies too weak to suck from breasts too undernourished to feed them, a horde of beady-eyed children darting and slinking in the gloom like rats, and behind one of the curtains a little family, cold and hungry like the rest, but with an air of dignity about them that held Sarah for a moment, the ragged screen in her hand.

'When did you last eat?'

The mother struggled to rise, and failed. The baby on her knee began crying, weak and thin. A boy of eight or nine perhaps, green-white with lack of food and rest, turned his face to Sarah.

'Yesterday. Yesterday me mam –'

His mother kicked him feebly and muttered inaudibly.

'Beg pardon, ma'am. Yesterday, ma'am. Found some bread by the kitchens, ma'am. Enough for me and me sisters, ma'am, but not for me mam. She ain't eaten in four days. Not since I found them potatoes, ma'am.' He looked to his mother for approval.

Sarah knelt by the woman. She was probably not thirty yet, but her face was chalky and pinched with want and her hair, dragged back from her bony forehead, was scanty and dull.

'I have come to help you. Do you understand me? I have come to feed you, and give you work, and help you to be warm and clean. I have money to help you, money from England, from Miss Nightingale. Do you understand me?'

The woman gazed, exhausted and without hope. Sarah turned to the boy.

'I am going to find food and firewood. Before night I will come back. Do you want to come with me and help, or do you wish to stay with your mother?'

The boy shrank against his mother's thin shoulder. He said nothing, staring with huge dead eyes at Sarah. His mother put out her hand to him. She whispered, 'He's afeared, ma'am.'

Sarah got to her feet.

'I shall be back before nightfall.'

The woman gazed back at her without conviction.

Climbing up the steps to the blessed relief of the air above, Sarah encountered Lady Alicia Blackwood.

'Miss Drummond, never was I more glad to see anyone!

Miss Nightingale told me I should find you here. She declared you to be the only person besides myself and Mrs Bracebridge who had applied to her to help whom she considered to be really in earnest. We have a terrible task, do we not?'

An icy wind was whipping round the corner of the building. Sarah pulled her cloak as tightly to her as she could.

'I don't think they are all past hope, surely? I saw one woman, and spoke to her a little, whom I'm sure would be respectable if she could, and I don't doubt there are others like her.'

'We must take them out, my dear. We must indeed. They are sorely needed in the laundry and in any case will only become demoralized down there. The prostitutes and the drink get daily more prevalent.'

'There was a baby –' Sarah began.

Lady Alicia closed her eyes briefly.

'Don't tell me, my dear. One could not believe such things if one did not know them to be true. Doctor Blackwood came out here with the appointment of military chaplain, but never did he think for a moment we should find such horrors. Still, we have found them and they must be dealt with.'

Sarah said hesitantly, 'I hope I have not been presumptuous. I have promised firewood and food by nightfall. It seemed one could make no beginning otherwise.'

'Indeed one could not. Now, my dear, let me tell you what is to be done. We have a free gift store – Mrs Bracebridge is trying to run it – a perfect medley of things from England, but we have lamps there, and rations, and there are always men loitering round it who might be gainfully employed collecting firewood. Shall you see to that?'

'Yes,' Sarah said gratefully, 'I shall be glad to.'

'Dr Blackwood has been full of excellent schemes. He allows some of the women with babies to apply to the kitchens every day for food so at least some are nourished.'

Sarah remembered Miss Nightingale's comment on the women clamouring for food and drink, but said nothing. She longed to be gone.

'And I intend to set up a new laundry, Miss Drummond. The old one is worse than useless. Someone in the hospital will direct you there, and perhaps you may estimate how many women we could take from the cellars and employ on the work. I am going down to the cellars to see how many workmen we may need for the basic cleaning and erection of partitions. May I leave the other matters in your hands?'

With a nod and a word of thanks, Sarah was gone. Not ten feet away, the Greek chandler's son materialized at her side. He latched on to her cloak once more.

'The shop,' Sarah said to him, 'the laundry. The free gift store.'

He gazed at her, his dark eyes blank.

She pulled out her purse and made a motion of paying for something, a small pantomime of bargaining. Then she took the corner of her cloak from him, and scrubbed it and wrung it out and hung it on an imaginary line. The boy grinned with recognition and seized her cloak again, setting off at his steady trot with her stumbling in the mud at his heels.

She learned so much that morning she felt that even in Balaclava she had only scratched the surface of understanding. She went through ward after ward of the great hospital expecting somehow to find warmth and cleanliness and comfort, and found instead, despite a certain order, muddle, pain, blood-soaked bedding and shirts, cold, wretchedness and vast wooden tubs in every room which served the men as chamber pots and which rendered the air almost as unbreathable as it had been in the cellars. Many of the nurses, whom she had been tempted to see as the salvation of these sick and wounded men, were drunken and promiscuous, such doctors as she saw, grey with fatigue. The operations were performed only behind a curtain and the curtain was an innovation of Miss Nightingale's.

The kitchens were almost as filthy as the wards, and rudimentary to a degree. In a vast grease-stained room, clammy with steam and alive with rats, huge cauldrons bubbled with stale water in which each man's portion of meat boiled in pieces of rag. Above the usual kitchen clatter and the steady cursing which seemed a part of every corner of Scutari, Sarah could hear wails and screams. She pushed her way among the Turks who stirred the cauldrons with wooden poles, to the doorway and found there a gaunt and ragged band of women, most of them clutching pathetic babies in tatters of shawls, howling for food. A British soldier with one leg only, leaning on a stick, was shouting at them hoarsely.

'Dr Blackwood's ladies?' Sarah said.

'The same, the devils. Varmints they are, every one. When we give 'em food, they screams it ain't good enough.'

Sarah tried to speak above the babble, but made no headway at all.

'Wastin' your breath, you are. They wouldn't listen if they could.'

'Where is the free gift store?' Sarah said.

The man lifted his stick and pointed it away behind the hospital. The little boy began to jabber and tug at her, desperate she should know he knew himself.

'Down there, miss. The Turks think "free" means they can lay their dirty hands on whatever they fancies.'

The store proved to be a bedlam. A large and draughty shed lined with rickety shelves, it was filled to bursting with candles and bedding, sacks of flour and arrowroot, bags of dried peas and cabbages, bundles of knives and spoons, socks and towels, crates of soap, tottering stacks of bedpans. It was an uproar of noise and muddle, rats and Turks darting in and out like fish. Sarah could not find Mrs Bracebridge in the confusion, nor indeed anyone who spoke English except four dozy soldiers smoking in a comfortable nest of bales.

'I need your help. Would you please come and give it?'

Two of them affected not to hear her. One rose slowly to his feet, the other to his knees.

'I want to help in finding and carrying wood and rations. I need buckets and arrowroot and milk. Also scrubbing brushes and kindling. Will you show me where they are?'

The man on his feet kicked his lounging comrades.

'Gerrup, do.'

Sullenly they stood in front of her. She remembered Miss Nightingale's fund collected by *The Times*, also the small supply of money that remained to her personally.

'I am not asking you to do it for charity. I am merely asking you to do it *now*.'

Half an hour later, her own arms full of blankets, Sarah led a strange procession away from the free gift store. Stumbling behind her, four soldiers carried pails and bundles of kindling, a churn of milk and a sack of arrowroot. In her pocket she had a complete inventory of all she had taken, and a list of what she further required as well as a large bar of carbolic soap. It was three o'clock in the afternoon and she had eaten and drunk nothing since seven that morning.

The following day it snowed. If it had not been for the small fires and newly imported lamps now glowing in the cellars, it would have been as black as night down there. The jumping shadows thrown made the place more sinister than ever, illuminating the slime on the walls and the pinched and filthy faces of the wretched inhabitants. They crawled from their corners towards the feeble flames and Sarah could see from their dress, that there were men among them, as demoralized by drink as the women.

The arrack sellers were a curse. They lurked about the entrance to the cellars, and filtered down into the gloom whenever they could evade authority. The spirit, distilled incompetently in hovels all over Scutari from the rotting peaches left over from the summer, was cheap and lethal. It caused hideous pain especially about the eyes and head, but before the suffering began, it provided a few hours of distraction powerful enough to be desirable. Sarah found that the son of the woman she had spoken to on her first day, once he had a little bread and soup inside his puny frame was an excellent spy. He would crouch on the stairs down to the cellar, almost unnoticeable in the gloom, and sprint like an arrow to inform her once a spirits pedlar was in view. She would then, grasping a large green umbrella, which was part of a particularly incongruous consignment of presents from England for the free gift store, march determinedly up the steps and belabour the culprit soundly with her weapon. Once a man dropped his wineskin in panic, and Sarah had the satisfaction of stamping its contents hissing out upon the mud. After half a dozen of such episodes she was no longer surprised at her own resourcefulness and strength.

Little Samuel Wilkes, her ally in these episodes, grew quickly to become her devoted slave. He was waiting for her each morning as she came down the staircase, followed by a resigned but still resentful train of soldiers bearing whatever was necessary for that day – milk and soap always, pieces of cloth, wicks for lamps, bundles of firewood, salted meat, cabbages.

'Samuel! Good morning. And how is your mother?'

'She ain't so bad, ma'am. The baby's fed at last. It couldn't take much, ma'am, on account of bein' so sickly, but it's sucked a bit, ma'am. And our Annie's slep' at last a bit, ma'am, an' not cried all night. Plenty did keep cryin', ma'am, but when your own cry, that's when you can't sleep, see.'

The Wilkes had so far been Sarah's reward. Scrub and feed and scold as she might, the demons of drink and dirt were quite as healthy and powerful as ever. But Jane Wilkes, behind her tattered curtain, with her son and her daughter and her baby, had from the first shown that she would respond to the trouble taken with her.

She had been in service, she told Sarah, back in the forties, in a house in Belgrave Square. She had been only a kitchen-maid, but she had come from Putney, bringing with her village standards of decency and self-esteem. A footman had sprung on her one night in the middle of a New Year party upstairs, and she had fought him off with teeth and knees and elbows, far more fearful of what her carter father in Putney might say, than of the consequences of the footman's advances.

Then she had met Sam Wilkes. She had spent a rare free afternoon in Hyde Park with a fellow kitchenmaid, watching the military bands, and Sam Wilkes, splendid in uniform, and made bold by having a fellow soldier with him, had pretended to trip her up with his boot toe, and had ended up following her to Belgrave Square. He'd gone on coming to Belgrave Square every evening he was free, leaning against the area railings above the kitchen and throwing pebbles at the window until Jane, in a panic that Cook might hear him, was forced to run out and promise him anything if only he'd be good.

The promise of anything had of course eventually been young Samuel, conceived in Richmond Park and born illicitly in a barrack room of Sam's regiment. There had been four regimental families among the soldiers in the room, and seven children, and Jane was used to no privacy because she'd never had any. Young Samuel was born with no screen but a few chairbacks and an army greatcoat, Annie three years later, the same. But if she couldn't give them privacy for their bodies,

Jane was determined to give it to them for their minds. If she could give them nothing else, she would pass on, as far as she was able, the simple, striving, decent code of life she had learned in Putney.

'I wouldn' have give in, see,' she said to Sarah when telling her of Richmond Park, 'if I 'adn' 'ave loved 'im. Not like some. 'E was always good and kind, see, 'e couldn' leave otherwise we'd 'ave starved. You gets used to livin' in one room with a lot of sojers. You 'as to. And they're wonderful to the children, real kind and that. Sam was always kind. Now I've lost 'im, I wouldn' want to live 'cept for the little 'uns. I 'av'nt seen him since the Alma. 'E were drowned there. I seed them all go down and then I couldn' see for the smoke, but he never come up agen. The baby was only eight weeks then, ma'am. Born at Varna, 'e was, on the beach. If you 'adn't come, like, 'ed 'ave died too, just like 'is daddy.'

She did everything Sarah told her to, quietly and docilely. She ate the arrowroot into which Sarah had surreptitiously slipped a little port of her own purchase, went meticulously over her children's heads with a lice comb, washed all their garments she could in a tin can of water heated over a fire, and kept, as far as she was able, a distance between herself and the other inhabitants of the cellars.

'Soon as the baby's stronger,' she said to Sarah, 'I'll take the children 'ome. I'd rather be goin' with Sam, ma'am, but since 'es dead, I'll go 'ome to Putney. Dad'll not turn me away, not now's I've been married, decent-like, and I'm a widow.'

There was many a night that Sarah, climbing wearily away from the muddle and misery of the cellars, wretchedness that thrived on apathy, blessed Jane Wilkes and her children with fervent gratitude.

# Sarah's Journal

It is snowing again. It has snowed heavily all the past few days and there is, they say, more to come. The Tsar is reputed to have said that January and February are his best generals for they have killed far more of his enemies than his armies. It is difficult to believe that it could possibly be colder than it is now. I have bought fur boots and a fur jacket in the bazaar, all made of very poorly cured skins so that I smell like a tannery, and a strange woollen cap with earflaps, and I spend all my days in this curious garb, and latterly the nights also. I am wearing them now, and I have bundled myself up in two blankets, but even so, were it not for generous Mrs Coles's fire, I believe I should freeze. I am surprised my ink has not succumbed to ice.

I never spent a stranger Christmas. Yesterday was my turn to do duty at the free gift store and we had such a battle over a three hundred yard piece of flannel that I thought the material would be in shreds before I could sell it. There was a list of two hundred wanting it, and sixty were triumphant and the cries of the disappointed were truly deafening. We are told a consignment of bonnets is on the way and I do not look forward to its arrival, unless there are at least five hundred! The rats were particularly hungry and we found quantities of flour and goat meat gone. I am so covered with flea bites today that you could hardly put a pin between them. Perhaps it is just as well that I am wearing far too many clothes to scratch!

There is no doubt that the poor women become daily more troublesome. They were so beaten down with squalor when I first went down to the cellars three weeks ago that they were at least a little grateful for the interest taken in their welfare, but now they have been fed and sorted out into some kind of order, they are getting bolder daily, and more demanding. I find it very difficult to refuse them anything, their conditions are still so very terrible. We have tried to give some a little privacy, we have erected rough partitions to encourage them to retrieve a little self-respect, but the cellars are still dark and disagreeable and the abominable stench down there only a little better. Above half have the cholera, and we must ever be on

our guard to see that the sick do not lie down with the unin-
fected. Three are to be confined next week, and we are making
a mattress for these births. All babies up to now were born on a
heap of rags only fit to be burnt. What a beginning to any
life. . . .

I spent all of today down there. We erected a sort of makeshift altar, and Doctor Blackwood preached with no pulpit but a
broken chair back. We hunted among all the cellars to assemble
our congregation and persuaded all but the very sick or the
very drunk to attend (I drove away three Greeks selling arrack
– they are as much to blame as the poor women who crave it
so). It struck me most forcibly, watching that ragged and pitiable
gathering in the smoky lamplight, how God-fearing many are,
especially the men who have joined their wives in our odd little
community. The Bible is for many of them, a backbone. They
cannot read it for the most part, but they know great quantities
by heart.

Two died today. One was that poor wretch who has been
three parts dead since I knew her, and who no one knew anything of. They put her in a coffin marked 'a woman'. It shook
me to the core of my being to see her carried away so labelled.
'A woman' only, nothing to anyone. What an arrival I say of
babies born on a pile of rags – what a departure to go nameless
to the grave. A baby died too, but two days old. Lady Alicia
said to me that she thought those who died quickly were the
lucky ones, and despite all our efforts, all we do, I can only
agree with her.

I dined today on bacon, and dried apricots from the bazaar.
We made a great stew for the women who usually seem readily
to accept the goat masquerading as mutton, and some declared
it was inedible and thrust their plates beneath our noses
demanding to know whether we should eat such stuff. Ten days
ago they would have eaten shoe leather. . . .

Lady Alicia's plans for a 'hospital' and an extra laundry and
a nursery for the children so that the women may work are
almost completed. The laundry will serve the soldiers' hospital,
which managed, in all the months before Miss Nightingale
came, to wash only seven shirts. There is so much to plan for,
so much to do – never have I known hours, days, weeks go by
so fast, so fast !

My parents have written. It is just as Miss Nightingale said it would be. I have apparently caused my mother to faint and brought shame and disgrace upon the name of Drummond. My father does not know how to hold up his head in the county. Blanche is expected daily and it is imagined that she will be made to suffer just as my mother did. If I come home at once and confess to having made an hysterical mistake, I gather all will be forgiven me. If not, my father will not vouch for the consequences.

I read it all quite stony-hearted. Then I re-read it, and tore it up and scattered the pieces in Mrs Coles's fire. My only fear is that some reprisal shall be taken on poor Edgar, and so I have replied to that effect, and no more, beyond sending home such cuttings as I could find championing Miss Nightingale and her work. All England it now seems, with the exception of my parents, is torn with pity for our soldiers and their neglected women, but then, Oakley Park ever was a backwater.

I should like a word from Edgar. I have heard nothing from him, except in a letter from Colonel Lowe who states that he is as well as could be expected in such a winter. It was a kindly letter, and he strove so hard to support me although misgiving must be what he truly feels. He said Inkerman was a mere Pyrrhic victory, a dreadful dawn slaughter in the fog and he was glad I was spared it. Sebastopol is proving indestructable and the siege drags on and on. We have lost so many soldiers through sickness it seems that the army now camped around Sebastopol is almost entirely new recruits, many of them Colonel Lowe says, pitifully young.

Of course he could not know how I longed for news of Robert. There was only a mention, though it was of a sort that made my heart glow with pride. 'Your friend Mr Chiltern,' he wrote, 'will deserve a medal after this campaign if anyone does. His courage and compassion are truly remarkable.' I wonder if he is hungry, if he is cold? There was hardly flesh enough on those long limbs when we left England, now he must be a mere skeleton. Will he have grown a beard? All the men who come into the hospital are bearded, but some have to be thawed before they can be fed for the hair has frozen into an icy clamp. Robert must look very grim with a beard and that piercing gaze of his. Has his editor at last begun to give him the credit he is owed, has he at last begun to praise him for his perspicacity and clear sightedness? Has he enough clothes, has he boots, has he shelter? Does he ever, ever think of me?

# Sixteen

January brought weather more bitter than any Sarah had ever known. Her tiny room on the waterfront became glazed internally with ice, and the fire which Mrs Coles kept faithfully burning for her return each night stood but a slender chance against the savage cold. She slept in her clothes, boots and all, after a nightly self-imposed torture of stripping off before her tiny fire to shake what vermin she could from her garments and to don the clean linen Mrs Coles delighted to provide for her. It had been a mistake to buy those poorly cured furs from the bazaar since they brought with them a colony of fat fleas already in residence who seemed, like all Turkish fleas, to regard flea powder as a delicious form of sustenance. Sarah's skin became scarlet with bites and the irritation they caused at night drove her almost demented; from her room next door the watchful Mrs Coles could hear the thuddings and tossings of her itch-crazed sleep.

Each day began early. In the dark dawn when each breath was painful to draw in the bitter cold, Mrs Coles would rise and brew a cup of coffee for Sarah, strong, bitter coffee as black as ink. She would tiptoe into Sarah's room bearing her steaming offering and a tallow wick which revealed by its wavering ochre light the poor bare cell in which Sarah slept. There was a low bed with a mattress of straw stuffed sacks, a stool, the strange and wonderful red lacquer chair which had come from the Scutari bazaar, and a table piled with the ragged assortment of papers which now constituted Sarah's journal. She had kept a journal, she told Mrs Coles, since she was five and had first learned to write, and would purchase every New Year, a morocco-bound volume to contain the doings and thoughts of her life. One such volume, bound in dark green leather and monogrammed in gilt, lay still in the cabin on the *Hercules*, she said, and she was sorry to have left it behind for many reasons – many, many reasons.

'That particular book was, you see, a present from my brother.'

Mrs Coles knew a good deal about that precious brother. He had written at last, his letter had come after much longing for it, and she had taken it in to Sarah on one of her dawn visits, slipping a spoonful of scarce sugar into the coffee that morning by way of celebration. Sarah had sat up in bed, pink with eagerness, her hair tumbled on her shoulders, bundled up in the strange hotch potch of furs and coarse blankets.

'Oh, Mrs Coles, give it to me! Please, quick, oh give it to me!'

It had obviously been a sad disappointment. There was money in it, quite a lot of money, and once the notes had fluttered from the paper, there was but a single sheet remaining and even from across the little room Mrs Coles could see quite clearly that sheet was only half written upon. Sarah had read it with a kind of desperation and the pinkness had quite fled from her cheeks, and then she had let the paper slither to the floor and all the money in it and turned her face away so that Mrs Coles could not see it. Mrs Coles had wanted to comfort her. She had been a wet-nurse herself several times and all the strong motherly instincts aroused by that occupation had risen powerfully again and she had tried to hold Sarah in her arms and soothe her. But Sarah would not let her. She shook her head and would not turn her face.

'Come, dearie, come. That's no way to take on! Tell Mother Coles, tell me now, tell me do.'

But Sarah would not turn and would not speak. She put out a hand, one thin hand roughened by the work it did, and Mrs Coles caught it and felt her own pressed hard. Then Sarah sprang out of bed with a sudden energy and stooping gathered up the money on the floor and held it out.

'Take it, Mrs Coles, take it all. I would never survive without you, not for a day. Take it and buy us what we need, buy something for yourself, anything, anything at all –'

Mrs Coles was shocked.

'Oh no, dearie, no! I couldn't do that! 'Tisn't mine, dearie, 'tisn't right.'

'Then it may lie upon the floor,' Sarah said, 'for I have no use for it. I shall simply walk on it if you do not take it. There is nothing I want it for, nothing at all, except perhaps some ink. Buy me some ink, Mrs Coles, and spend the rest as you think fit.'

She had knocked over the coffee then in error, and had been visibly distressed at the waste and her seeming carelessness of Mrs Coles's trouble. She had washed hurriedly, smashing the ice on the bowl of water that stood upon the stool with her bare fist before Mrs Coles could get to do it with an old chair leg as was her custom. The ice had flown about in jagged splinters and Sarah had plunged her face in the icy water with such vigour that Mrs Coles had been momentarily afraid she meant to harm herself. Then she had braided her hair quickly and neatly – she would never let Mrs Coles do it for her – and wound the braids into a knot and pulled on her cap, all in a matter of moments. Then she was gone, running down the broken staircase to the icy street, no coffee inside her, no word of farewell, the air in the room behind her still stirred with the speed of her going. When she came back that night she had gone straight to Mrs Coles and held her in her arms and kissed her warmly. But she never spoke of the letter from her brother and Mrs Coles never found it. It was her belief it had been thrown upon the fire.

After the piercing black air of the dawn, the atmosphere of the cellars had to be got used to anew each morning. The piles of filthy rags that had served as beds were now all ashes, the beaten earth floor had been scrubbed as well as was humanly possible, but the walls still oozed damply and the pipes from the hospital above, though they discharged fewer horrors than they had done into the cellars, were hardly reliable. The rough partitions that had been erected afforded more privacy than the ragged curtains they replaced, but the shouts and cursings, the wails of babies and bursts of laughter were not confined by these thin walls of unplaned wood. Drunkenness was still rife, pedlars of arrack still lurked about the entrance to the cellars but it was less the accepted way of life. Babies were now born in privacy, deaths happened in some seclusion. The work to maintain what standards had been achieved and to improve them, was cease-less.

Each morning Sarah descended in the darkness to this twilit world already in uproar. The steps down were of brick, each tread uneven, and she had to go down with care, her mittened hand upon the slippery walls. Lamps and tallow candles would already be alight, giving off their own rancid smell since the oil used was from animals, and figures would be moving about in the dim and smoky light. Samuel Wilkes would be waiting for her, alert as a terrier. Sarah would pause at the bottom of the steps, and close her eyes for a moment and adjust her senses, surprised every morning, to the smell of poverty and humanity and cold and then she would set off down the rows of cubicles, to rouse those women who were to work in the newly set up laundry.

There were shouts to greet her.

' 'Tis the lady!'

'Gerrup, do, you lazy varmint!'

'Mornin', miss!'

'I'm not well, miss, I can't come. Can't move me legs – '

'Drunk you was! Miss, I'll tell you! Couldn't stand last night, shoutin' she was!'

'You pay what we're worth, miss, and we'll come!'

'You're not stoppin' 'ere. You're goin' as the lady says!'

Each morning she collected Jane Wilkes and fifty other women. Huddled in shawls, some sporting new and tawdry bonnets they dared not leave behind, children in their arms and dragging at their skirts, they would gather at Sarah's command. It often took her an hour. They were given porridge and thin coffee, the children were handed crusts of bread if they were still hungry, and by six they were at work.

The laundry at least was warm. At one end improvised play pens had been set up into which the babies and small children were thrust in relative safety, and at the far end great fires were lit under the boilers. Drying lines were stretched between the two, line upon line of shirts and sheets, towels and bandages, sweating and steaming until by ten you could not see across the chamber. Against one wall great stone sinks had been erected for soaking and scrubbing, with tubs of raw yellow soap beneath them, gifts of carbolic from England.

It became quickly evident that some work in the laundry was far more taxing than any other. The back-breaking work at the sinks, the dangerous and almost intolerably hot work at the boilers was clearly far more exhausting and disagreeable than the easier tasks of sorting dirty linen, hanging wet garments, or refolding dry clean bedding for use in the hospital. Sarah was aware of the grumbling and also, after days spent in that steaming inferno, of the justification of many of the complaints. She took turns herself at every task, enduring several scalds, painfully inflamed hands, and an aching back so acute that sometimes she could not sleep.

At the beginning of February, the women trooping in for work found her busy posting a list upon the laundry door.

'Wha's this, then?'

' 'Ere, lemme look!'

They craned forward, pushing and shoving.

'You'd better tell us, miss. Can't read it, light's that bad.'

Sarah finished hammering in the nails.

'It's a list of payments.'

'Payments? But we know what we're paid! Precious little an' all it is too. D'you mean it's to be less?'

Sarah shook her head. No, it was not to be less. In some cases, but not all, she explained, it was to be more.

There was instant uproar. She stood with her back to the door and watched them shout at her, some of them raising their fists and shaking them, all pressing in on her, mouths open, a nodding sea of bonnets and shawled heads and broken teeth.

'It is perfectly fair,' she said.

The clamour subsided a little to hear her.

'It is entirely fair. The tasks such as folding sheets are far easier and more pleasant than that of keeping linen moving in a boiler. It is much easier to wash a nightshirt than blood-soaked bandages. Therefore we will reward those who do the difficult and disagreeable tasks accordingly. That is all.' She took a deep breath. 'Please go to your places.'

Muttering, but no longer shouting, they dispersed. Throughout the morning, Sarah moved among them as she always did, and observed the remarkable enthusiasm with which the worst tasks were now tackled.

'It is wonderful what the promise of more money will do,' she confided to Lady Blackwood when the midday break came round. 'I only hope it does not simply mean more arrack. I have never known them work with such energy.'

The afternoon went with astonishing speed. The hampers of linen sent up to the hospital that evening were almost twice the usual number, and without the customary prompting, the worst items for the next day were left to soak overnight in the sinks. Sarah went home triumphant.

'Mrs Coles, it's wonderful! They at last seem to understand the meaning of an incentive, they seemed so pleased to work in this way! I wonder I did not think of it before. I shall have no shortage now of volunteers to do the worst tasks, we shall be able to cope with any emergency from the hospital now, easily. They seemed so happy today, so glad!'

Mrs Coles placed a plate of goat stew before her. She crackled as she stooped for she wore Edgar's money pinned at all times inside her gown, frugally eking it out in case he should forget to send more.

'Eat that up, dearie, every mouthful. You're as thin as a lath as it is though it's good to see some colour in your cheeks even if it is them devils have put it there. Don't you trust 'em, dearie, don't you be pleased too quick. They're slippery as eels, they are, that's how they've learned to be.'

Sarah looked up and laughed, and dipped her spoon into her dish.

The following morning, Samuel Wilkes was waiting for her on the waterfront, not on the cellar stairs as was his custom.

'Why, Samuel! Is something wrong? Is your mother ill?'

'No, ma'am. She's all right, ma'am. But the Lady-in-Chief wants them lists you keep, them lists of stuff you 'as from the store, and she wants them before you goes into the laundry.'

He leaned towards Sarah and added confidentially.

'Pity you ain't got two 'eads and four 'ands, ma'am. You'd a done a much better job on that store than that Mrs Brace-bridge. She's a muddler, she is –'

'Samuel!' Sarah said sternly.

He grinned up at her.

'It's the truth if I says it or I doesn't. I reckon it's because of them muddles the Lady-in-Chief wants them lists.'

Sarah had not been in the hospital for six weeks, and the change was remarkable. The smell was still there but much reduced, scrubbed floorboards were visible between the straw stuffed mattresses that were now available to almost every man, and there was an air of much greater vitality about the place. Sarah had heard all the stories of Miss Nightingale's ceaseless battles with the hospital authorities, but it seemed that she was, in some measure winning.

Her interview with Miss Nightingale was brief.

'I am most grateful to you for coming, Miss Drummond, and much obliged to you for the punctiliousness of your inventory. They are far more of a curse than a blessing, these frightful contributions, and it seems almost impossible to keep a proper account of where everything goes. I am also much impressed by what you are doing in the cellars, Lady Alicia has kept me well informed. It is an extraordinary relief to find in Scutari that someone is as good as their word.'

Sarah had been about to go when Miss Nightingale checked her. She held out a sheet of paper covered with a list of names.

'Miss Drummond, would you be so good as to find Agnes Clay for me? She is with the amputation cases this morning, and this is a list of the men who I think may now take something a little stronger than arrowroot. You would oblige me so much.'

As always, Sarah found her knees flexing in an involuntary curtsey as she accepted the mission. There was something about Miss Nightingale that made a commonplace farewell seem inadequate.

Little Samuel was thrilled to be in the hospital. His mother, ever fearful of the degrading influences rife in Scutari, liked him to be by her when he was not accompanying Sarah or running some errand, and thus he had no chance to enter that fascinating repository of wounded heroism.

He pattered at Sarah's heels as she crossed the wards, grinning and cheerful, longing all the time to stop and tell the men lying against the walls that he was a soldier's son, and that his father had been drowned at the Alma. When they reached their destination, Sarah told him to stop.

'You must wait for me here, Samuel. I won't take you in here unless your mother says I may.'

Samuel protested. He'd seen plenty of sights in Scutari, in the cellars, even on the field of the Alma. He'd seen dead men as well as men with limbs missing. Amputation was nothing.

'I say you may not, and I mean it,' Sarah said. 'Operations are different. If you disobey me, you shall not come with me again.'

The ward was very much changed. When she had last seen it in December it had been quite literally, awash with blood. She recalled that first sickening morning when she had been led through by the Greek chandler's son, and had seen the operating table screened by nothing but a curtain, and the queue of hapless victims waiting their turn for the ordeal. There had been blood on the floor, the walls, the bedding, the clothing, on hair and hands and faces. The surgeons had looked like butchers, and the only nurse had been drunk.

Now, there was no sign of an operating table at all. The huge room had been newly lime washed, and blood, where it was evident, was now confined to bandages. Straw stuffed mattresses lay neatly, heads to the walls, and at the foot of each one lay every man's possessions, a kitbag stencilled with his name, rank and number if he still had it, just boots or a coat if that was all he now possessed.

Sarah saw a group of nurses, dressed in grey cotton gowns, at the far end. A cauldron of something was steaming on a hook above the fire, and the flames made a brilliant glow beyond the grey and white of floor and sheets and blankets. She walked down the ward, reading out the names on the kitbags as she went, saluting each man personally, smiling at them all. Roberts, Smith, Poulson, Baxter, Cross, MacDonald. Most of them grinned back, some waved to her. Marshall, Flanagan, Thompson, Pike, Wheeler. Everyone of them was without an arm or a leg, sometimes without both. What on earth would become of them, limbless, and back in some slum or village? Cartwright, Morgan, Dent, Wilkes . . . Wilkes.

Sarah stopped by the mattress. The man on it lay with his armless left shoulder wadded with a bloody bandage and his right arm flung above his eyes. Ridges in the blanket showed that he had one leg, his left leg – and a half. He was green – pale and as thin as a skeleton.

Sarah knelt by his mattress.

'Are you Sam Wilkes?'

The man nodded. He didn't move his arm. In hospital someone always seemed to want to know your name, your number.

'Were you with the Twenty-Third? At the Alma?'

Again he nodded.

'Have you a wife Jane? And a son Samuel? And a daughter Annie and a baby?'

Sam Wilkes took his arm away and revealed eyes exactly like his son's.

'Jane,' he said hoarsely, 'Janie – '

Sarah put her hand on his wandering one.

'They are quite safe. I know where they are. They are safe and well, all of them.'

Sam Wilkes turned his face away.

'Nah,' he said. 'Lost 'em at the Alma.'

'No,' Sarah said, 'they lost you. They came down here on a sick transport. They stowed away. They are in the cellars under this hospital. Jane and Samuel and Annie and the baby.'

Sam Wilkes looked at her for a moment with wild hope, then his eyes dulled again.

'Nah, lady,' he said.

Sarah got to her feet.

'I'll show you.'

She hurried back down the length of the ward and found Samuel seething with impatience outside. She seized his hand.

'Listen to me, Samuel. Something very important has happened. Very important and happy. Your father is in there. Your *father*. But he won't believe I have found you. Come with me. Tell him it is true.'

She was cheered this time as she went down the ward, the little boy pulling impatiently at her hand. Only his father lay as inert as she had left him, his arm back across his eyes.

Sarah pointed.

'There, Samuel! That one.'

Samuel peered. He shook his head.

'Not that one. 'E ain't so pale, me dad. 'E's bigger too – '

Sam Wilkes took his arm from his eyes and stared. Samuel crept nearer and bent over him.

'Where's yer arm gorn, Dad?'

Tears were beginning to spill down Sarah's face, and a cheer like a salvo broke out all around her.

By nightfall, Jane Wilkes was nursing her husband herself. His arm had been shot away as he crossed the Alma, holding his rifle high above his head to keep his powder dry, and his leg had been wounded by a cannon ball as he struggled out of the river on the far bank, and gone gangrenous. He possessed his right arm and his left leg and now his family. The Lady-in-Chief sent word that she would find him work when he was deemed well enough to do it; he was neat fingered and there were plenty of things a deft man could do in a hospital.

Jane Wilkes was torn between unutterable gratitude and an acute sense that if she were to nurse her husband, she should not be able to repay her debt to Miss Drummond in any way at all by redoubled work in the laundry. Sarah, elated to ecstasy by the Wilkes' reunion, waved her protestations away.

'Think nothing of it, Jane! You have worked there wonderfully for a month, and when Sam is well enough, you shall work again. But by his side is where you should be now, and besides, the laundry is so much easier now, so much simpler to handle. The new scales of pay have made it a very different place.'

Indeed, it was true that Sarah no longer heard grumblings and complaints, but that first day's enthusiasm was quickly extinguished. A sort of sullen doggedness seemed to settle over the laundry for some days, and then the mutterings began again. Those allotted the easier tasks began to complain that they were deprived of a chance to earn more. Those at the sinks and boilers clung tenaciously to their work. Sarah chose to ignore them all. The laundry was done, the hospital was served, Sam Wilkes was stronger every day, the women must learn to endure. Everyone should get their chance. At the end of a week they should all change round, everything would be perfectly fair.

Monday came. Instructions were given that every person should change to a newly allotted task, a different pay scale. The laundry erupted. Sarah found herself in the midst of a shouting, screaming mob, many of them brandishing the stout

207

sticks used to stir the linen in the boilers. They were being imposed on, they would not have it.

'Please stop! Please be silent! What I have suggested is perfectly fair, perfectly just! If you will entrust your grievances to a spokesman I will be delighted to explain. I cannot speak to all of you, it is not possible!'

The mob heaved and surged, still resentful. Then it broke apart and revealed a figure in its midst, a figure who had been screaming like a mad thing, a figure surprisingly neatly dressed in a dark gown and a white apron.

'Mrs Evans!'

An expectant, excited silence fell.

'What are you doing here? I thought you were with the hospital ships! At Balaclava. Why are you here?'

Mrs Evans licked her lips. Her eyes were bright and eager.

'I'm a widow now, ain't I? Trooper Evans died in that charge, didn't he? Wrongly ordered they was, the Light Brigade, shouldn't never have gone. He was blown up by the guns, blown in pieces, nothing left at all but his buttons. So I come here, crep' off the ship. I wasn't going home to starve, not me. The army isn't going to find me so easy to get rid of, not like that high and mighty Colonel Lowe thought he could.'

'Stop it,' Sarah said furiously, 'stop it at once! How dare you speak that way, how dare you be so insolent?'

Mrs Evans took no notice but hurried on, her voice shedding its assumed gentility as her excitement grew.

'I 'bin 'ere in the laundry a week or more. I told 'em not to tell you. I saw it was you, I knew you all right. You wanted me sent 'ome didn't you, to punish me for 'elping your precious sister. Well I ain't goin', I'm stoppin' 'ere, right 'ere. And we'll teach you you can't order us to do this and that, tell us what we'll earn. Who are you to say anyways?' She moved a few steps nearer. 'You should see yourself, my lady. A beggar wouldn't look at you twice now, oh no. That Mr Chiltern, no wonder he'd rather have had your sister, who'd want a scarecrow like you now? All skin and bone and big ideas, that's all you've become. He'd laugh to see you now, laugh in your face. Look at you! You'd like to 'it me now, wouldn't you? Spit in me face, that's what you'd like, but you're too much the lady ain't you and you're too much the lady to deal with us. We wants our rights. We'll work as we please for top rates! All of us! We won't eat what you give us, it's not fit for dogs. Who are you to say different? Eh? Who are you, my fine lady, now?'

She stepped forward one pace. Quite involuntarily Sarah retreated.

'Do not listen to her! Do not pay any heed to what she says! Why do you believe her, why do you listen? She has only been here a few days and you have worked here a month, five weeks, why listen to her –'

Mrs Evans was laughing. Her mouth was open, displaying her stumps of teeth, and from it came her mirthless laughter while her small hard eyes took in all Sarah's vulnerability, all her lack of power.

'It ain't no good askin' them, no good at all. They listens to me because I speaks sense, that's why they 'earkens to me. And they know what *you* are, 'acos I've told 'em. I've told 'em how you schemed to get me sent 'ome on the ship, I've told 'em 'ow I was starvin' on that ship and you was scared to touch me, to offer me any 'elp. I've told 'em 'ow you ran to your brother and tried to get me shipped 'ome. They know 'ow you'd do anythin' to stop your sister 'avin' wot she wanted 'acos you's mad with envy for her looks and 'ow you tried to take out your spite on me. I've told 'em all, told 'em everythin'. There's nothin' they don't know.'

'I didn't! I didn't try to get you sent home! I helped you to stay with your husband –'

Mrs Evans came quite close and thrust her face up to Sarah's, unleashing a gust of spirit stinking breath.

'Oh yes? 'Elp was it? Is that wot you calls it? I asks to be your lady's maid and you jerks your skirts from me 'ands? That's 'elp is it!' She turned to the crowd behind her. 'Remember that, will yer? You kicks a woman when she's down and you've 'elped 'er, that's wot you've done. Well, my fine lady, *my* chance 'as come now. You and your family's been the ruination of me and I'll not forget it. When I was down, you 'elped me by kickin' me. You's down now, ain't yer? Slavin' in these cellars is a far cry from dinin' with my lord this and ridin' with my lord that, ain't it? You've lost your looks and your sister and doubtless your brother too. So it's down *you* are, and it's for me to 'elp you now. And so I shall, so I shall, just as you 'elped *me*.'

She lunged forward, her hands like claws, and caught Sarah a violent blow across the shoulders. Sarah staggered, chalky-faced, but did not fall, clutching behind her for support. At the sight of Mrs Evans's brazen courage, there was a low hiss of support from the mob of women behind her, and they surged forward like so many birds of prey, clawing and muttering.

'No!' Sarah screamed. 'No, no, no!'

Their screams rose above hers. Howling now, their hands out like talons, they pressed forward, eyes glittering, bonnets nodding. Mrs Evans braced her shoulders against the pressure at her back and then, smiling still, and screaming with the others, she let them drive her irresistibly forward to fall pummelling and scratching upon the now prostrate Sarah.

# Seventeen

It was late February when Colonel Lowe arrived in Scutari. He landed one afternoon on a day which was one of the first to show that the blackness of the Crimean winter might at last give way to something gentler. A pale blue sky, bleached as if through long storage, lingered until the early evening and a faint silver sunlight glimmered on the Bosphorus.

If it had not been for the nature of his mission, James Lowe would have felt himself much heartened. He had passed a hundred supply ships on his journey down the Black Sea, bringing fresh meat and vegetables to Balaclava and the encampments round Sebastopol, as well as sheepskins, blankets and huts, waterproof boots, flannel shirts and furs. News of these long-awaited comforts had been of passionate interest in the camps before he left and he had remarked to Robert Chiltern how glorious a change they would make for the men. Robert, gaunt himself now, and darkly bearded, had laughed.

'Glorious, I grant you! Quite glorious! This cornucopia of good things just when spring comes is no more than typical of this whole campaign! Where were the huts and boots in the snows I wonder? Where was the fruit and soups when half the army lay dying of dysentery and scurvy? You can rejoice if you like and I will join you. Who could resist the thought of a change from that salt junk? But I won't commend Parliament and I won't forgive the commissariat. The men are to be washed away with plenty in spring!'

Sympathetic though he was to such scepticism, the sight of the shiploads of abundance was undeniably wonderful. And when he reached Scutari and the weather relented to show the first frail glimpse of spring, James Lowe felt his heart lift despite the task before him. Scutari itself was hardly better than it had been, the waterfront still a stinking chaos of mud and debris and dead dogs but the sky *was* blue, the sun *did* shine, and the great yellow barracks was now a hospital from which more men emerged alive than dead. Only two in every hundred died there now, rumour ran, a mere two, after the terrible figure of forty not four months ago. What was more, Sarah Drummond had been a part of that triumph, Sarah who had run away after Balaclava to offer her services to Miss Nightingale. Colonel Lowe stood below the barrack walls and thought of Sarah's hand in such success and felt himself glow with vicarious pride.

His servant was despatched to find lodgings. He did not expect to stay in Scutari above a few days, indeed his compassionate leave would not allow for a longer stay, for even though Lord Raglan had been gracious, even insistent, in allowing him to leave, he did not like to be away from his men for long. The siege of Sebastopol was proving insufferably tedious. It was four months now since Inkerman, the last significant battle, and neither side had advanced an inch. The monotony of the days was terrible, so terrible that even the capture and killing of a centipede found ambling up a hut wall provided major entertainment. Morale was frail after the bitter winter, and now it was battered further by boredom. Colonel Lowe did not like to take his eye off his soldiers for long.

The hospital presented a spectacle of cheerful busyness. He was conducted down a long whitewashed ward, neatly lined with mattresses laid out on scrubbed planks, and put into the care of a stout and respectable looking woman who was ladling broth into bowls for distribution down the room. She smiled good-humouredly at Colonel Lowe, handed her black iron spoon to an orderly to continue her task and came to see what he required.

'Forgive me for disrupting routine.'

'Not at all, sir. I like to be here to see they're given fair measure but I can do that as well from a yard away. May I be of service?'

Colonel Lowe looked around him. There was evidence of a good deal of clean linen and very few of the men were bandaged. Most it seemed, were half sitting and regarding the soup bowls with healthy interest.

'Mostly dysentery cases, sir,' Mrs Clay said, following his

gaze. 'On a light diet you see, till they're able to take something stronger.'

'They look excellently cared for.'

Mrs Clay smiled.

'You wouldn't recognize the place if you'd seen it when we came. Landed with the Lady-in-Chief I did, back in November. First sight was enough to make you want to turn tail and run.'

'I've no doubt of it. This hospital has been one of the few successes of this war. Now, I wonder if you can help me. I am in search of someone who came here, oh, four months ago, in November it was, to help Miss Nightingale. A Miss Sarah Drummond. Can you tell me where I might find her?'

Mrs Clay turned and beckoned to an orderly nearby.

'She's not here, sir. She came to the hospital, I remember well, thin as a lath she was after the fever. Miss Nightingale sent her to look after those poor women in the cellars, and she's started the laundry there and done us proud –'

'Fever? Fever, you say? What fever?'

Agnes Clay shrugged.

'Who knows, Crimean fever most likely. She was nursed by some kind soul, lives with her now I'm told. Now, Smithson, you're to take the colonel down to Miss Drummond's lodgings. Above the ship's chandlers, the Greek chandlers, on the waterfront. Terrible place, Scutari, no names, no streets, no numbers. Hers are the top rooms, at the back.' She gave Smithson a push forward as if to set him in motion. 'Reckon she'll be glad to see you, sir. Had a hard time, she has, but she's not given in, not an inch.'

There proved to be many Greek chandlers on the quayside and it was inevitably the last one that they were seeking. The weak first sun of the year was subsiding into the cold and inky sea as Colonel Lowe put a coin into Smithson's outstretched palm, and turned to climb the rotting outside staircase from the street. It looked hardly promising. The steps were rough and broken and there was no outer handrail to prevent the climber in the dark from catching a foot in the crumbling treads and pitching sideways into the vile alley that ran between the chandlers and the adjacent house, an alley dark and dreadful and scuttling with rats. With the sun's going a sudden rank chill had fallen, an echo of the apprehension Colonel Lowe felt as he put his hand upon the wall to steady himself and began to climb upward. He might rejoice to see Sarah, but he dreaded his mission.

The staircase ended abruptly in a small square platform with a broken rail and a doorless black entrance to the house. Colonel Lowe paused for a moment, marvelling at the perils Sarah must encounter daily as she left or entered her lodging, and then he leaned within the entrance and called.

'Miss Drummond? Miss Drummond, it is James Lowe! I am come from Balaclava. Miss Drummond?'

Somewhere inside a baby began to cry, and a dog, aroused by his voice, howled in the alley below. A curse and the thud of a kick silenced it. Colonel Lowe was puzzled. Mrs Clay had said someone lived with Sarah. He took a step off the platform and into the black passage inside, and called again. Still no answer. He glanced at the sky outside and saw that dusk was falling quickly. Soon it would be quite dark and he had no lantern. He stepped deeper into the passage and waited for a moment while his eyes became accustomed to the gloom, then he put his hand upon a narrow door that gave on to rooms at the back of the building, and pushed.

Inside, there was a small, almost empty room. There was a mattress against one wall, tidily covered in sacking, and an old ammunition chest doing duty as a table, and a stool. The make-shift table was covered in a piece of clean coarse cotton, with a bottle serving as a candlestick, and two metal plates and spoons laid opposite to each other. A tiny grate held a neatly laid fire, and on the floor beside it was a pile of kindling. A gaudy piece of shining fabric, green and scarlet and gold, had been spread over one of the stools and on the walls hung various garments, garments of stout grey woollen material suspended limply from nails driven into the cracking plaster. There was no sign that any of these things could possibly be Sarah's.

Across the room however, was a further door, ajar. Colonel Lowe went quickly across and knocked on the splitting panels.

'Miss Drummond?'

Silence still. He pushed the door open. It was an even smaller room than the first, and had no fireplace. Against the partition wall lay a rough low bedstead with a mattress of stuffed sacks, but there was a pillow covered in white cotton and a pile of neatly folded blankets of hard brown wool. By the single small window was a table and an extravagant scarlet chair with claw feet and golden dragons, battered and chipped but redolent of past splendour. On the table lay piles of paper, piles of ragged papers of different shapes and sizes, all closely covered with Sarah's regular handwriting. Averting his gaze with difficulty from these possible revelations, Colonel Lowe pulled out the red lacquer chair and sat himself down to wait.

It was an hour before he heard her. The room had darkened entirely and was uncomfortably cold, but he did not like to light someone else's fire, especially when there was so little fuel evident. So he had paced and stamped to thaw his feet and thought a hundred times that he could hear her voice in the confused babble rising from the quayside. Then at last he caught the scrape of feet upon that perilous staircase and saw the swinging shadows flung by a lantern and Sarah's voice, talking to a companion, rose clearly up to him.

He called out to warn her. He heard her stop, and gasp, and then her footsteps began again hurriedly and in a second she had come flying through the narrow doorway in the lurching lamplight and he had held out his arms and caught her.

'Oh Colonel Lowe, I cannot believe it ! How wonderful, what a miracle ! Oh you cannot believe what a joy it is to see you, you cannot, you simply cannot !'

A woman had followed her in, a middle-aged woman in a grey cloak, holding a lantern in one hand and a huge covered market basket on her arm. Sarah pulled her across.

'Colonel Lowe, you must meet Mrs Coles. Mrs Coles, this is a very great friend, who has been more than ordinarily kind to Edgar and to me. And, Colonel Lowe, Mrs Coles has been the greatest support to me imaginable and has cherished me as if I were a child in the nursery !'

Colonel Lowe did not relinquish her hand. She had put it into his when she released herself from his arms and he held it firmly.

'Miss Drummond, I am at an utter loss. I expected to find you with Miss Nightingale, up at the barracks, but I am told you were turned away. Sent to some cellars. What cellars?

What is Miss Nightingale thinking of? And what do I hear about your having the fever? And why are you living here, why on the waterfront? Surely – '

He stopped. Sarah, with her other hand stretched out to Mrs Coles, was looking at him admonishingly.

'I do assure you, Colonel Lowe, that this is a very respectable and salubrious lodging compared to many. Is not that so, Mrs Coles?'

'It's not what you should have by half, dearie, in that the colonel's quite right.'

Sarah swung round to take his other hand and smile up into his face.

'Will you stay and eat with us? Mrs Coles is a famous cook. There can't be a soul on earth so ingenious with goat seven days a week as she is.'

He looked doubtful. The fire was so very small, there were no signs of any provisions anywhere, it seemed hardly right to inflict another appetite on them.

'Never fear, sir!' Sarah cried, pulling the cover from the basket, 'There is plenty! Look for yourself!'

He peered in. There was a black iron cooking pot with a lid, a loaf, potatoes, fruit, a cabbage, packets and bundles.

'I've to take it with me each day,' Mrs Coles said apologetically. 'I dursn't leave it for fear of the rats. So when I goes with Miss Sarah, I takes all the vittles with me.'

'Then I shall be delighted to stay.'

He had never seen Sarah in such high spirits. She flew about the rooms, insisting he occupied the scarlet chair, lighting the fire and candles, cushioning his seat with blankets, while Mrs Coles hung the black pot above the fire and set the bread on the table with a yellow cheese and some oranges. He had seen Sarah as gay once before, upon the *Hercules*, but that had been a false gaiety, the feverish spirits of someone who would mask what they truly felt. But this was different. He sat upon his dragon throne and watched her as she laughed and talked, and despaired of what he must tell her.

'Where were you when I came? I expected to find you here.'

'Oh no, I am never here in daylight unless I – no, I am out from dawn till dark. Miss Nightingale set me to help organize the poor forgotten women of the regiments. They were living down in the cellars below the hospital, in such conditions as I can hardly tell you of, poor creatures – '

'Poor!' Mrs Coles said derisively from the fireplace. She turned and brandished her ladle at the colonel. 'Poor! Wicked creatures they be and no mistake. All but killed her a month back and she only trying to do them good, paying them what they ain't worth a quarter of!'

'Hush,' Sarah said in a low voice.

Colonel Lowe leaned forward.

'No! Not "hush". Tell me. What is this? I hear at the hospital you had a fever, now I hear you have been half killed! What has happened?' He rose and caught at Sarah's arm. 'Tell me what has happened!'

'Please do not be alarmed. Look at me! I am quite well, you can see for yourself. Am I not?'

He looked at her fondly.

'It appears to me miraculous that you are alive at all, let alone well. Since you ask, I do not think you seem well. Too thin, too pale for my peace of mind, but in excellent spirits.'

Sarah took her arm away and pinched her cheeks.

'There! Does that please you better?'

'What would please me is to hear the truth of these last months.'

She sat down on the nearest stool.

'There is very little to tell. I fell ill when we came ashore after the battle and the ship's captain brought me here. If it hadn't been for Mrs Coles I do not know what I should have done – '

'She was delirious nigh on a week, sir, raving, it was pitiful to hear her. But she would go to Miss Nightingale, it was all she was minded to do, she wouldn't heed me, sir, she would have her way. And then when Miss Nightingale'd sent her down among them devils, and she'd started the laundry and gived them all bite and sup and payment, they turned on her and near killed her. So I wasn't takin' no more chances, sir. I goes up with her mornin's and I comes back with her evenin's, and should any so much as lay a finger on her I'll cudgel 'em black and blue. She wouldn't have Miss Nightingale told of the trouble, she wouldn't even let that Lady Blackwood punish Mrs Evans as she deserved, the wicked, lying woman, and all she's had is her dismissal which is a deal more'n she deserves to my mind. Hangin's too good for the likes of her. In bed a week, Miss Sarah was, black and blue with bruises she was but she wouldn't hear Lady Blackwood's suggestion to go home, wouldn't hear of it. Don't you look at me so severe, dearie either, for who's to tell the colonel what's true as I well know you won't?'

He reached out again and took Sarah's hand.

'Is it all true?'

She looked at him for a long while, and then she looked away, and nodded.

'I can scarcely bear it,' he said, 'or believe it. To think I half encouraged you to come here, to think I said to Chiltern that I thought you should be allowed to fulfil your own destiny! I never imagined, never thought for one moment that you would be so cruelly, wretchedly treated.'

She tore her hand away.

'I am *not*, I am *not*! These violent things have happened but I am not dismayed by them! Would I still be here if I was? Would I have asked for clemency for Mrs Evans if I had wished to be revenged upon her? Would I, with Edgar sending me money, have hesitated to go back to England if I had not wanted to stay? Do you not see? I am useful, I am busy, I have a role to play, I am happy, *happy*!'

He retreated to the scarlet chair. It seemed incredible that she should not recoil from what she did, what she had been through, but it seemed rather that she embraced it. He looked again about the bare and comfortless little room and tried to see it as a dwelling any woman could ever become fond of. But she was not, it seemed, like other women, not any more. He turned back to her eager face and was thankful that in the midst of her anxiety to calm his fears and give evidence of her own contentment, she had asked for no news of Edgar.

Mrs Coles stood up.

'We've but two plates, sir, and the vittles be poor enough, but you're to sit here and eat with Miss Sarah.'

He protested. He could not deprive Mrs Coles, he was sure they usually ate together, he would wait his turn. Mrs Coles shook her head and took the grey cloak from the wall.

'I'll not hear of it, sir, it ain't right, not right at all. I've a deal of things to see to among them monkeys in the bazaar and

I've all night to eat if I've a mind. I'd stay and serve you, sir, but it's best you're on your own.'

When the door had closed behind her and her steps could be heard carefully descending to the street, Sarah sprang forward, her eyes alight with a new eagerness.

'Ah, bless her, Colonel Lowe, bless her! Now I may ask you all I could not ask before her! She has taken against Edgar for some reason, though no brother could be more generous, and thus I could not ask about him freely while she was by since as you saw, she has most decided opinions!'

She pulled the brilliantly draped stool close to his chair and seated herself.

'This is very inhospitable of me I know, for you must be faint with hunger and I can assure you that the soup will be as excellent as it smells. But I am greedy for news and my hunger makes me selfish, so before we eat, please tell me all you know of Edgar, how he does. Does he speak of me? Has he forgiven me? Did I cause him wicked pain? It is the only blight across my contentment here – at least it – yes, it is the only blight. So tell me all, all you know!'

There was no escape. He looked at her steadily, leaning forward, her grotesque fur coat fallen open to show a shabby dress of black, her hands clasping the arm of his chair, her face quite brilliant with her desire to hear him speak. He put one of his hands over hers.

'That is why I am come, my dear Sarah.'

She did not speak. Her blue gaze seemed to burn like cold fire for a moment, and then it dimmed and diffused as if a cloud had crossed her mind.

'Sarah, my dear, brave Sarah, I am come to tell you that Edgar is no more. He died three weeks ago, of cholera. He was ill only two days, it was very sudden, very swift. He died in the hospital at Balaclava.'

A shudder ran through her, a shudder so convulsive that he thought she must fall. But she remained on her stool, gripping his chair arm still, her gaze fixed upon his face and her mouth set tight against her tears. Then he bent forward, and lifted her in his arms, and took her on his knee like a child, to comfort her.

I am well punished for my headstrong selfishness, I am indeed. Never once did I think he might die, that he might have un-utterable need of me, so bent was I on doing what I would do. If there was any service I would have wished to render him, any comfort I would have given myself, it would have been to nurse him if he were dying, to hold his hand, to watch him in his loneliness. Well, I have failed him. I have left him heartsore to die without any comfort, any companionship. I came to the Crimea to be his companion, to look after him, that was my fixed purpose, and I have failed him.

I did not know remorse could be so keen. It gnaws at you like a rat inside, you can feel its teeth tearing at you, never letting you forget. I never shall forget, never, never. I do not deserve to. I have been nothing but a trouble to him, worse than Blanche, oh far, far worse than Blanche, for I flaunted my rebelliousness at him, I taunted him with it every day, and then I left him without a backward look.

And I burnt his letters. I *burnt* them. I burnt them because I was proud and thought him stubborn in his refusal to condone what I did or encourage my endeavours. I took his money and threw away his dear handwriting, a part of him, because he would beg me to think again, to think of him, to think of our parents. Oh if I had only thought of him, if only, if only!

But all I ever thought of was me. I must have my way, gratify myself, satisfy myself. Even in my great longing for Robert that is what I am doing, is it not? I do not think if I would be good for *him* – at this moment I think I could only be a grief to him, to everyone – I only think what *I* need, what *I* want. Even now, when I would give everything in the world to have him here, to comfort me, to tell me that even the least part of what I have done is right, I am thinking of myself. Why should he come, why should anyone come?

Why did Colonel Lowe come? Good, kind man, so gentle, so anxious to spare me pain. Why should he take such trouble, leaving his men who need him, refusing to let an official letter be sent to me to break the news as I deserve, softening the blow?

I do not merit such kindness, I long to know how to repay it, even in the smallest measure.

What am I to do with all this grief and bitter remorse? Not one atom of it will bring him back, nor tell him how sorely I now feel. If I had stayed in the Crimea, I should have been with him, perhaps I might have saved him, or at the very least have eased him! I would pray if I thought I should be heard, but I shall not be, I cannot be. Oh, Edgar, forgive me, forgive me, hear me and forgive. . . .

# *Eighteen*

Two weeks wore on, and Colonel Lowe did not return to Balaclava. Information had followed him speedily down the Black
Sea to say that a great clearing up campaign had begun and
that his men, and indeed all the men of the army, heartened
now by the dawning spring and proper supplies of food and
clothing, were attacking the mountains of refuse about the
camps with commendable vigour. Robert wrote to tell him
how gladly the men fell upon the chance to work.

All of every day the sky is striped with pillars of smoke as the
men set fire to those awful piles of decaying things. You would not
recognize Balaclava. The men look immediately so much better,
so much heartier, they begin to seem an army again, rather than
a ragged mob. The telegraph line will reach Balaclava any day,
and the railway line to the camps on the heights is nearly done.
The two corpses which have lain half-buried outside my door
since December were carted off today to my unspeakable relief –
if they can do the same to the remains of that dead camel thirty
feet from my hut shortly, I shall think myself in the lap of luxury.
Some potted game came my way yesterday. Manna could not
taste more wonderful.

So do not hurry back if the delicacy of your task forbids it. You
know Raglan won't hold it against you – remember how he
refused to let the cavalry join in at the Alma because he could not
bear the thought of Lord George Paget being killed and thus
breaking pretty Lady Agnes's heart? He talks now of an expedition to cut off Russian supply lines to the east, but it is only talk –
I wish it were not for I should dearly love to go along – and it does
not seem we shall do anything for at least another month. To
think of another summer here possibly – could one bear it?

I know you will pass on my condolences. Your staff wish to
know if Edgar Drummond's effects should be sent down to Scutari,
but perhaps they would only prove distressing.

> Yours ever,
> Robert Chiltern

Encouraged by this, and similar news from fellow officers, Colonel Lowe could linger. It eased him to do so, for Sarah was so stricken at his news, so full of self-reproach, that he did not like to leave her, even in the capable hands of Mrs Coles. He had been dismayed at her reaction, so much more complicated than simple grief, and would have left her only with a most unquiet mind himself. There was little he could do, however, for her zeal in her work seemed almost redoubled by her grief. She was still at the laundry by five each morning, and did not leave it until twelve hours later when he would wait in the raw spring twilight to escort her back to the waterfront and Mrs Coles's savoury stews.

The whole situation distressed him acutely. Over the first shock now as he was, the shock of finding a gently nurtured girl such as Sarah with raw hands and broken nails and the traces of bruises still from blows she had received, he felt his protectiveness grow steadily from day to day. He was no longer surprised at her hardiness but increasingly upset by it, all the more so perhaps, because she seemed to accept it so comfortably. He tried to recall her as he had first seen her in Constantinople a year ago, plump then, her hair glossy and intricately woven, in a dress of some pale shining stuff with a pink ice on a glass plate in her hand and young men lounging round. He could not in all honesty say that her new thinness suited her entirely ill, but he longed to see her becomingly dressed again, warm, cosseted, given flowers – and pink ices. He had diffidently suggested a new dress to her for clearly she was not pressed for money, but she had shaken her head abstractedly and said there was no need.

'There will come a time, you know, of course there will, when I shall be quite frenzied with delight at the thought of new clothes. At least – I hope I will. But not now, it does not signify now. What should I wear them for, what place would they have here? We are all such a rag-tag lot you know, all of us but Miss Nightingale who looks as neat as a pin no matter what she does. As long as I am warm, I am comfortable and I only regret my appearance if it offends you to see me so down at heel.'

Mrs Coles always welcomed him conspiratorially. Some nights

he would firmly decline to stay and eat, other nights she would either wait upon them both as they dined off the ammunition box, interposing volubly and decidedly in their conversations when she wished, or else would don her grey cloak and take her basket to the bazaar. Amply provided with money by Colonel Lowe, she found sheets and towels for Sarah, a sheepskin for the rough floor by her bed, a looking glass, a brazier for charcoal to warm her cell-like bedroom. Sarah seemed quite distraught at his kindness; each new gift appeared to cause her more pain than pleasure. She would cry out that she did not deserve it and her eyes would be full of tears.

By the middle of March, he felt he must return. The huge cleaning-up operation around the camp had been performed with such zeal that there seemed a danger, it now being almost completed, that the men would sink back into the lethargy inflicted by the monotony of the siege. Military reviews were planned he heard, and rumours, confirming Robert's, of an allied attack planned on the Russian coastal base at Kertch, continued to filter down to Scutari. Robert wrote once more with a scathing description of the way allied and enemy officers sauntered about together during periods of truce, exchanging cigars and conversation, and added that he believed the men were becoming restless again.

The times of truce are for burying the dead and soon that's all there will be to do. You have been away above a month and I can only hope this bodes no ill for matters in Scutari. Tell me, or better still, bring me news of how things are!

There was, however, one more thing to be accomplished before he returned. The weather had now settled into steady spring warmth, sheepskins were discarded, patients from the hospital, among them Sam Wilkes, were to be seen hobbling on sticks in sheltered corners and Colonel Lowe resolved to embark before the freak winds of April came to agitate the Black Sea. As he was to go, he begged Sarah that she might leave her work for one day only, and ride out with him to the country beyond Scutari. The air and the holiday could only do her good, the laundry could hardly suffer in a single day.

She contrived somehow to borrow a habit, a habit of dark green cloth with silver buttons and rows of black braid stiffening the collar and hem.

'It seems a ball gown to me! I can hardly believe myself in anything so fine! You were quite right, you know, I think I did not know how sick I was of that black frock until I took it off.'

He had also done some borrowing himself, of a pair of handsome ponies, the property of a fellow officer lying mending from stomach wounds in the hospital. The day was chilly still, with the raw yellow light of spring, but there were few clouds in the pale sky, and the last blots of snow had melted from the fields.

They left Scutari down a stony track, edged with rough grey boulders and small starved fields. There were windowless cabins every so often, some washed white, some left grey stone, and outside them were scratching hens and goats and black-eyed children. Brown buds on bushes and trees gave promise of the leaves to come, and there were skylarks above and the occasional frog croaking in the roadside puddles. There were few people on the track beside them, just the odd slant-eyed peasant in his sheepskin waistcoat driving his donkey along while a whisk of black behind a boulder indicated where his woman hid from the eyes of foreigners and men. The little wind whipped colour into Sarah's cheeks and ruffled the ponies' manes and the only sound, beyond its singing and the voices of the high larks, was the dry slither of hooves among the stones of the track.

They rode all morning; the leisure seemed unspeakably sweet. At noon they turned off the track towards a group of trees overlooking a shallow valley and sat down with bread and wine and sharp white cheese, among the rocks. There was a stream below them and beyond it a great rough field of tawny grass.

'It reminds me –' Sarah said, and stopped.

Colonel Lowe waited, but she said no more, shaking her head to herself as if in self-reproof.

'You seem – happier today.'

She looked across at him.

'I have no business to be, but it seems I am. I shall never forgive myself, never, but I think the time has come to stop inflicting my remorse on all around me.' She rose and came across the space of grass between them to seat herself beside him. 'I can't thank you enough, never, not if I had eternity to do it in, for your kindness to me, the time you have given me, the friendship. I wish there was anything, anything at all, that I could do for you to show you what I feel, how deep in gratitude I am.'

He reached out and took her hand and kissed it.

'There is, my dear.'

She looked up immediately.

'There is?'

'Oh yes, there is. The best way you could reward me – for repayment is not what I want, the last thing I seek – is to allow me to protect you further. I think you must now have done what you set out to do, must have proven to yourself that you could be as useful and as capable as you wished to be, and the time has come for you to be again what you were brought up to be. I am so much older than you, I know, I could wish at this moment that I were only half the age, except that I think I can serve and shield you better now than I could have done at five-and-twenty. Will you let me do so? I have never married, I have never until now loved well enough to marry. But now I do. Sarah, my Sarah, if you will only let me call you such, will you let me love and cherish you as I long to do and as you richly deserve?'

She had not looked away all the time he was speaking, but now she did. She gazed downward at her green lap for a full minute, and when she looked up again her cheeks were fiery.

She whispered, 'You must think me so – so shameless, so greedy – '

'No! A thousand times no! It is because I wish to give you whatever you will let me for the rest of my days that I ask you to marry me! Greedy? Never! It has been my delight to think of your comfort. Only say that it may always be so!'

'I – I am greedy! Oh, you will see that I am! I am shameless because I have taken your great kindness, your thoughtfulness, your gifts and never thought what you might – oh so properly, so understandably – assume from my taking them. I cannot marry you. I wish – I wish for so many reasons that I could, but I cannot. I will be your friend, always, the most loyal and loving friend – '

'But I want a wife. I do not want you merely as a friend. I want you as my wife.'

'I cannot!' she cried.

'I would not – curb you,' he said, 'I would not stifle you. If you wished to be – more than just a wife, if you wished to go on and – do whatever it is you wish to do, I would not oppose you.'

She seized his hands.

'You could not help yourself! Do you not see? You are so kind, so good, so strong. You wish to shield me, protect me, you said so. What I have done in these last months upsets you, I see it does. How could it be otherwise? It is not how you expect a woman to be!'

He gave a faint smile.

'Am I really so old-fashioned?'

'No! I did not mean that! It is your nature to cherish. Look at your men, how much thought you take for them! It would be the same with me, it must be, and I have now learned to take thought for myself.'

'Is – is that all?'

'Yes,' she said, and blushed again.

'Except,' he said in the kindest tone, 'that you do not love me.'

'I do! I do – but not as a husband.'

He stood up abruptly and walked away a few paces to stand flicking a long grass stalk against his boot and to gaze away at the soft hills. Then he came back to her and she rose to stand before him.

'I have no business to ask these questions but I cannot seem to help myself. You must refuse the answers if you wish.'

'I shall not refuse.'

'Is it because I am so much older than you? Are you afraid that I shall leave you long alone?'

She smiled at him.

'It most certainly has nothing to do with that.'

He bent his head briefly in acknowledgement.

'And – and is it because you love another?'

She said quickly, 'Oh no, no, there is no one.'

'Then I must simply accept your refusal. I hope that this half hour will put no barriers between us at least, even though it has brought us no closer?'

'Oh no! No, how could it! I still think you the best and kindest of men, I should be desolated if we might not be friends still. We may – please, may we not?'

He took her hand and kissed it once more, then he smiled and nodded and went away to saddle the ponies for the ride back to Scutari.

They arrived back as the shadows began to blacken between the houses, and the silhouettes of spire and dome and shaggy storks' nests on pinnacle tops stood out sharply against the greeny-yellow sky. Colonel Lowe had meant to escort Sarah for the last time up that decrepit stairway and then bid her farewell before seeing if a ship was leaving the quayside that very night rather than the morrow as he had planned. But she begged him to stay for one last evening, pleaded with him, saying that she would not hear of his going so abruptly.

'If you leave in this dramatic way, how can we meet again as friends?'

He followed her inside. The black iron pot, now as familiar to him as any of his own possessions, was bubbling comfortably on the fire, the ammunition box was laid with bowls and spoons and bread. In the centre stood a bottle of champagne.

'Should I hide it?' Sarah asked sombrely.

He smiled with difficulty.

'Mrs Coles and I had schemed together, you see. No, we shall drink it. Its properties will be quite as heartening as they might have been celebratory.'

'Open it immediately, then.'

He took the scarlet lacquer chair as had become his custom and grasped the bottle firmly. Sarah had laid aside her borrowed hat and was now tying Mrs Coles's apron over the green habit before she stooped to stir the contents of the pot. Wrestling with the cork, he watched her profile against the red light of the fire and knew he had been a fool not to leave her here as he had planned and go, cleanly. All he was doing now was prodding an inflamed tooth. The cork came out abruptly, splashing froth and wine on to his hand. Sarah gave a little exclamation and came swiftly to his side, a glass in her hand.

'Here.'

Silently he poured the pale liquid into the tumbler she held. He saw her hand was not quite steady but he dared not look up at her face bent so close to his. He wished he could think of something to say, some diverting topic.

Sarah produced the second tumbler.

'Fill this,' she said, 'and then I command you, absolutely command you, to drink it *all*. Quickly.'

'Oh?'

'Yes, I do. It is my turn to give orders. The day before the battle of Balaclava you came on board the *Hercules* and made me drink because you guessed, quite rightly, that I would benefit from it. I now do exactly the same to you, except that you must take great manly gulps and swallow it all. *Now*.'

He could look at her then, and smile.

'Yes, ma'am.'

She watched him steadily until the glass was empty, then she took the bottle from his hand and refilled it.

'Now you may begin again.'

He was laughing in protestation. 'No indeed! Champagne is not water!'

'You need not drink at the same speed, I merely wish to see you continue steadily.'

She turned away to the fire to lift the lid from the pot and taste the contents.

'Goat again, I think. Or perhaps just very old sheep. Still, I doubt even Lord Cardigan's French chef aboard *The Dryad* could be more consistently successful with goat than Mrs Coles. Will you write to me still? Please say you will. There is no one left to write now, no one to give me news of what happens, news of the regiment. I don't like to feel my links are all cut now, that I don't belong.'

James Lowe swirled the wine round in his glass, making the agitated bubbles hiss faintly.

'Do you never hear from Robert Chiltern?'

Sarah put up a hand to tuck a wayward strand of hair behind her ear.

'No,' she said. She wrapped the corners of her apron round the handles of the pot and lifted it on to the table, her face rosy from the steam. Then she picked up a bowl and began to ladle the stew into it.

'Odd. He has written to me twice while I have been here. He didn't mention his health so he must have beaten the cholera. He had it quite badly.'

The stew flew from the ladle, splashing across the rough cloth Mrs Coles had spread over the table. Sarah said nothing but stared down at the spreading brown stain, the ladle dripping forgotten in her hand. James Lowe reached out and took it gently from her, replacing it in the pot.

'Not Sarah,' he said quietly, 'but Rosalind.'

She looked up at him, confused and troubled.

'Rosalind?'

'*As You Like It*. Rosalind faints to hear Orlando has been wounded by a lioness. Sarah spills my supper hearing Robert Chiltern has the cholera.'

She was blushing fiercely. She turned away and sat down on a stool, her face in her hands.

'I thought it might not be true, that you loved no other.'

She said, her voice muffled by her hands, 'Nothing will come of it, he has no thought of me. It was Blanche, not me.'

He sighed.

'Ah well. I believe I would almost rather you refused me because you love Robert Chiltern than because the idea of marriage to me is intolerable.'

'I – don't know what to say to you.'

'You say, "Dear James, in a year's time I shall be very happy to see you again." Everything will be calmer then, more ordinary, more real. Your own feelings will be less painful.'

'No.'

'I shall come all the same. And in the meantime I am going, we have both had enough for one day.'

'When – when you get back to Sebastopol, you will say nothing, won't you, nothing at all to – to anyone?'

He shook his head.

'My dear Sarah, am I really likely to?'

'I am so sorry, so *sorry* –'

'So am I. For all of us. And not least for my poor men whom I must now get back to. Will you give me your hand?'

She rose and held out both her hands to him. She looked very much as if she were about to cry, but he dared not stay and comfort her. So he took her hands and pressed them, and kissed her cheek, then he picked up his hat and stick and went softly down the broken stairway to the quay, leaving her standing there disconsolately in the dusk.

# Nineteen

If it had not been for the mercifulness of the soldiers, Robert might indeed have died of cholera. When he fell ill he was refused admission to the military hospital because he was a civilian, and therefore there was nothing he could do but crawl back to his hut and trust to the strength of his constitution. Soldiers who had found him generous and sympathetic during the rigours of winter discovered him there, shaking and gaunt under his blankets, and themselves procured opium and milk from the bazaar to dose him with. The opium was rolled into small balls of greyish paste and fed to him regularly during the critical hours on a spoon, a method learned by a sergeant who had seen cholera constantly during years in India. It had frequently worked then, and did so now. Robert emerged from his hut skeleton thin, and heavily bearded, but with a thankfulness to be alive which made even the now drearily familiar landscape around Sebastopol appear inviting. The sun was out, the vague rumours of an expedition to cut off Russian supply lines seemed to be crystallizing into plans and there were military reviews and cricket matches organized for the coming month. Robert stood outside his hut and listened to the sporadic booming of the guns from Sebastopol, and realized that winter was over, that he was miraculously alive and that he had now been war correspondent for a full year.

In the first week of April, Colonel Lowe returned to camp bringing with him letters for Robert. They met at a vast military review organized by the French to show off their infantry, dragoons, field artillery and two regiments of Chasseurs d'Afrique, magnificent in sky blue and black. Robert was in a restless mood since not only was he feeling much stronger, but his request to the military authorities to accompany the expeditionary force to Kertch had been refused. He took the letters James Lowe held out to him almost as if he did not observe them.

'They say they'll search every ship to make sure I am not aboard even if the generals have to do it personally. Sir George Brown has even sworn that he'll put me in irons if I so much as put a foot on board and he is quite capable of carrying out his threat, the old brute.'

'I'm glad to see you well enough to be angry.'

'I was most tenderly nursed, sir. A woman couldn't have done it better.'

James Lowe looked away across the neatly wheeling groups of men below them.

'I don't know about that. Miss Drummond was much distressed to hear you had been ill.'

Robert said in a low voice.

'How is she?'

'Remarkably well.'

'And nursing?'

'No,' Colonel Lowe said shortly, 'no, she is not. She was sent by Miss Nightingale into the cellars of the hospital to deal with a crowd of drunken scoundrelly women, the wives of the army.'

Robert was visibly startled.

'I don't believe it!'

'You may as well for I've seen it with my own eyes. She and some others have turned a hell-hole into something very close to respectability. She has delivered babies, held the dying, reunited a family, set up and organized a laundry for the hospital, survived a riot. She is living with the wife of some sailor in a pair of rooms you wouldn't call cupboards at home, no one of her own kind near her, no comforts. She wore the same gown every day I saw her. She works from dawn till nightfall and her hands are like a kitchenmaid's. And she's happy, can you believe it, happy!'

'Good God,' Robert said softly.

James Lowe kicked irritably at a clump of grasses before him.

'It made me extremely *un*happy to see her. Do you realize that she was set upon by those harpies when she tried to institute a regular system of payment? They might have killed her! What can Miss Nightingale be thinking of?'

Robert was silent.

'It's all very well, Chiltern, for us soldiers, we men. But she's a woman. Can you imagine it? Set on by a troop of screaming drunken vixens?'

'Don't –'

'I'm glad to see some reaction from you.'

'I feel plenty of reaction. I'm simply getting used to Miss Drummond's – magnificence.' He looked down at the letters he held as if he saw them for the first time. 'I do thank you for these. I think I've had enough of this showing off for now. I think I'll ride up to the trenches and see what the Russian reaction is to this display of French strength. Is there any chance of you putting in a word for me over this expedition to Kertch?'

'I'll try.'

Robert touched his cap.

'I'd be vastly obliged, sir. It's very good to see you back. The men have missed you sorely.'

James Lowe watched him stride away and saw that among most of the groups he passed, a hand was raised in greeting. The commanders might abhor his presence, but it was evident that Sarah was not the only one to succumb to the force and warmth of his personality. Colonel Lowe turned back resolutely to the review, and raised his field glasses.

Robert did not ride up to the Russian lines, for it was perfectly evident from a considerable distance that the enemy was content simply to watch this display of strength being performed under their noses. Instead, he went back to his hut to examine the letters. One, he had noticed was from Hope. That was not such a surprise as it might have been. Hope, after a silence of weeks, had taken to writing in quite a new vein, realizing as he had been forced to do, that Robert's reports found increasing favour with *The Clarion*'s readers. Copies of the paper were now delivered regularly even to Windsor Castle. Hope wrote:

It is my happy task to commend your last despatches. We were all much alarmed to hear you had been taken ill, though I think you must exaggerate the 'inhumanity' of the military authorities. Despite your success, my dear Chiltern, you must not see yourself as some sort of martyr. We rejoice greatly to know you are restored to health.

I fear I have no influence to get you on the expedition to Kertch officially. I suspect Delane of *The Times* is equally helpless, though my spies tell me Russell will attempt to stow away. I leave that suggestion for you to adopt as you will. I can fully understand your impatience as the siege wears on and we should of course be glad of the reports of some action.

I know you will be glad to hear that I am sending you an assistant. He is George Lacey with whom you worked a good deal in the past. If you are to be away from Sebastopol, I feel you should have a replacement in the field. Lacey will of course work at your direction.

Robert swore and threw the letter across the hut. Typical Hope! *The Times* had sent out W. H. Stowe to assist William Russell and thus Hope, whose jealousy of *The Times* was the mainspring of his professional life, was not to be outdone. It was insufferable. The thought of a fellow reporter was odious to Robert. He cherished his independence, his solitary and to him, satisfactory state. He did not want to share his knowledge, his success or even his hut, with George Lacey. Lacey was an amiable enough man, a shrewd and patient reporter, but his very presence would curb Robert's achievements. The military authorities were ill-disposed enough to journalists as it was, but the larger their number grew, the more obstructive the commanders were bound to become. The notion was not, as usual, for Robert's benefit, but for Hope's glory.

Sighing, he picked up the second letter. It was from his father. He put it down again, profoundly disturbed. Apart from a letter formally wishing him well when he set out fourteen months before, he had had no communication at all from his family apart from a hurried note from his sisters written on the day of his birthday and probably, he deduced from its air of hastiness, without parental knowledge. He could imagine that his mother would have liked to write and did not feel she could cross his father in doing so. His father's letter in January of the previous year had simply said that he was glad his son was going with the army, but was regretful that it had to be only in the capacity of journalist. Now, more than a year later, he had written again. Robert broke the seal.

High Place
Marsham
Suffolk
28th February, 1855

My dear Robert,

It seems I have cause to congratulate you after all. I made no secret of my bitter disappointment that you, as my only son, should refuse to enter a profession which has meant so much not only to me but to generations of our family before me. I shall always regret your choice, always, since your success as a journalist only proves to me what a soldier you might have been. Colonel Lowe has expressed as much to me in a recent letter, and I know no man whose opinion of such matters I respect more highly. He says you have an ability to handle men he has rarely seen in anyone, and an aptitude for initiative and endurance that would be a benefit to any regiment.

But this is not why I write to you. I break the silence because I do not wish to be estranged from my only son. I may regret to the end what you have chosen but I do not wish it to come between us. It has been a sad year with us here and your Mother pines for news from you. She has had much to bear this last winter for I am much broken in health and find it a great pain to draw breath some days. I have not hunted once, the horses are as fat as butter tubs. The weakness came upon me quite suddenly last autumn but I refuse to believe it is the flatness and dampness of the land about here that brings my coughing on. Doctor Bridges insists that is so, and commands me to go to Switzerland for the spring and early summer. I do not want to go, but for your Mother only I shall.

I have not once been up to Westminster this past session. There is much needs doing in the constituency, but I cannot do it longer. The task must be taken on by a younger, fitter man, and that soon before affairs become sadly behind hand.

Will you meet us in Lucerne? We are to be there for three months, until the end of June. I have taken a house, large enough for all of us, and my feelings about leaving Marsham for three months would be much alleviated by knowing that I might see you and that you might be pleased to take some burdens from me. We shall look to you.

Your Affectionate Father,
Robert Chiltern

235

Robert sat down on his camp stool quite suddenly. His father had never written or spoken to him in such a way in all his life, had never admitted to any weakness, had never asked for the smallest kind of help. They had all leant upon him, wife, daughters, son, trusting to his strength and justice and self-discipline, believing in him, relying upon him. He was as tall and thin as his son, the Whiggishness of his politics tempered by his own severe brand of humanity, and apparently as much master of himself as he was of the six lives that clustered round him.

Robert looked down at his handwriting. It appeared as strong and firm as ever, but the phrases it wrote were quite unfamiliar. He had only once seen his father emotionally moved before and that was the interview he had had after coming down from Cambridge to announce that he would not be a soldier. He had stood in the library at High Place, looking resolutely out past his father's angry face to the flat Suffolk fields, yellow in the July sun, and said that he meant to make his mark some other way, to change how people thought, to make things better if he might. At first his father would not believe him and called him a puppy, a naive and dreaming boy, and then he had seen his son would stand as firm as he was accustomed to do himself and he had grown angry. He had shouted, Robert remembered, shouted out his disappointment and frustration and rage, and Robert had had to fight his own panic at the sight of this first loss of control he had seen from his father in twenty years.

Now came the second. What it must have cost him to write that letter, sitting at his desk in the library, with his lurchers, as ever, camped upon his feet, and his lungs bursting and his conscientious and energetic mind burdened with the knowledge of what he had failed to do for his constituents this past winter. He must have choked down so much pride to write, he must feel so keen a need. He had of course no support at home, he had been too long the rock to expect Robert's mother to take the role over now, saddened and frightened as she would have become by the estrangement between father and son, by the husband's illness. The letter was a cry for help. He looked down at it once more, much moved and disturbed and saw that it was not only a cry for help, but an offer for the future. Would the constituency have him for a moment? Would his father, faced

with another defiance from his son after he had held out such
an olive branch, be willing to exchange his own Whig views for
Robert's own passionately held new Toryism? They were
enough alike, father and son, to see and admire in each other
inflexible principles. Would that sympathy see them through a
difference in such principles?

Robert rose slowly, gazing unseeingly out at the April sun
gilding the battered land outside his door, his mind still absorbed
in these new apprehensions and excitements. How ill was his
father? How soon now could George Lacey come? Would his
father help him with the cost of an election, even if he cam-
paigned as a Peelite? Should he set off for Europe at once, so
that at least his father might know how gladly he grasped the
hand held out to him? Colonel Lowe must be informed, perhaps he at least might know more of how his father was, how
serious was his ailment. Robert sat down again and read the
letter through a third time. His hands were by now not at all
steady. Then he put it by, as tenderly as if it were some wounded
bird, and took up his pen to write a note to James Lowe and
beg him for a half hour of his time.

A reply came two days later. Colonel Lowe much regretted that
all intercession on Mr Chiltern's part to gain him permission to
go with the army to Kertch had been quite fruitless, but that
he should be pleased to see him at any time that evening. Robert
had spent an unquiet time in the interim, full of confused and
perplexing feelings and so abstracted that the men who, laughing, had brought him a copy of the signed photograph of herself
Mrs Duberly was generously distributing among her admirers,
were anxious that he had been without women for so long that
he had forgotten the sensations they customarily aroused. He
had taken the picture, looked at it remotely for a second or two,
and then handed it back saying only, 'The wrong lady, you
know.'

Then he had mounted his stalwart cob, his faithful companion since Balaclava, and ridden to the cavalry camp.

Colonel Lowe's hut had been transformed in his absence. A
floor of boards had replaced the mud that had been his carpet
all winter, two braziers burned cheerfully against the chill of
the evening, one at either end and the narrow camp bed had

been replaced by a much more substantial affair, besides the addition of chairs, a solid table, and several brightly burning kerosene lamps. James Lowe was seated at the table alone, with a pile of books, weapons and other objects before him. He rose when Robert entered and held out his hand.

'I'm glad to see you. This is a dreary enough task. I'm trying to decide which, if any, of Edgar Drummond's possessions I should send down to his sister, and which back to England.'

Robert surveyed the heap on the table.

'He didn't have much, poor fellow.'

'It wouldn't have been in character you know. A Bible, the military lists, his pistols – lovely pair those – boots, shirts. Not much. His uniform was burned I'm afraid. They get a little over-zealous down at the hospital.'

'What's that, sir?'

James Lowe picked up a small thick volume bound in battered dark green leather.

'It's Miss Drummond's journal.'

'Journal!' Robert sounded startled. 'How did it come to be here?'

'She must have left it on the *Hercules*, and I suppose he took it for safe keeping. It will of course have to be returned to her. Do you think I should send all his things to her?'

'No, sir.'

James Lowe sighed.

'You are probably right. I shall get them sent back to Northamptonshire then.'

Robert put his hand on the journal.

'And this?'

'Someone trustworthy shall take it down to Scutari, I suppose. I find the whole business distressing and distasteful. If it wasn't for knowing the family, I should simply let officialdom do it all, but I feel I hardly can as things are.'

'I might take the journal for you, sir.'

James Lowe looked up.

'*You*, Chiltern? I thought you were hell-bent upon being a stowaway. Why should you go down to Scutari?'

'I've heard from my father.'

Slight self-consciousness flickered for a moment in Colonel Lowe's eyes. He turned and shouted for his servant.

'You'll take some wine with me, Robert?'

'Gladly, sir.'

'I have to confess I've had a hand in it, Robert. I've written to your father and told him how highly the men here think of you, and what a splendid campaign I feel you've fought on their behalf. It seemed tragic he shouldn't know – and be proud of you.'

'I – I do most sincerely thank you, sir. You have been more of a benefactor than you know. There was silence between us for years you know, he was so disappointed in me.'

Wine was brought and placed on the table in the yellow ring of lamplight. Moths began to flutter in from the darkness and dance thickly around the flame.

'One of his few mistakes, Robert, to feel that. I don't believe he's disappointed now.'

'How ill is he, sir?'

'It's consumption, I believe. I don't know how severe. I can't think he'd even mention it if it were not severe.'

'He's asked me to go to Switzerland. He's taking a house there for the early summer.'

'And shall you go?'

'Yes, sir. *The Clarion* were sending out an assistant reporter anyhow. He can stow away instead.' He put his hand out and touched the journal again. 'So I shall pass Scutari you see.'

'Did your father mention Parliament?'

'Obliquely.'

'And your reaction?'

'Beyond anything I'd ever hoped for. But he mightn't like my politics.'

James Lowe leaned across to refill his glass.

'If you go to him I think you will find he can swallow your politics. It's a good moment to go, you have really done your task here. The worst is over for the men in the sense that they have at least enough clothing and food and medicines now, even if not enough occupation. You are seeing the fruits of your endeavours and I think your success will carry a lot of weight with your father. He is a man of great humanity, you know.'

'Why did he not stay with the regiment, sir?'

'Your grandfather died and his seat in Parliament fell vacant. Your father is not one to run two careers, he would feel one of them was bound to suffer. And he was so entirely sure you would join the regiment.' He smiled. 'In a sense you almost have. You will be sorely missed.'

'I'm reluctant to go, whatever the future holds.'

'A great deal, I'm sure, Robert.' He stood up.

'And you, sir? When all this is over?'

'India again. If they'll have me.'

'Give up the Hussars?'

Colonel Lowe smiled.

'I couldn't bear to go back to barrack life and parade grounds, I'd rather train cavalry for the real thing. The North West Frontier is very real.'

Robert stood too now, and held out his hand.

'I wish you all the luck in the world, sir.'

James Lowe inclined his head.

'Come and see me before you go. Will you take this?'

Robert looked at the dark green volume.

'Of course.'

'You will be much amazed to see her, Chiltern. In personal terms, I believe she has done much more than any of us. She makes me feel that maybe women are stronger than men in some ways. More enduring perhaps.'

'*She* has become very strong it seems. It doesn't surprise me.'

'No?'

'She once said to me that to go back to England would be like being shut up in a box. I think her life before this weird adventure was like being in a box too. She was full of qualities that there was no room to use.'

James Lowe took a last swallow of wine and put his glass down.

'There must be thousands like her,' he said, 'all over England, all over Europe. Thousands. All shut up in drawing rooms, capable of so much.'

Robert picked up Sarah's journal and dropped it into his pocket. 'I still think she's rare though, sir. I'll bet if you let half of them out of drawing rooms they'd scream to get back in. She hasn't looked back, has she?'

'You may find she has a lot to teach you, even you.'

Robert patted his pocket absently.

'Yes, sir.'

Colonel Lowe smiled.

'You won't be so sceptical when you get there.'

Robert smiled in return but seemed to be revolving something in his mind. He moved at last towards the hut door which the colonel's servant opened as he approached.

'A week or so, sir, and then it's good-bye to this dirty little angle of land.'

'Godspeed, Robert.'

Robert seemed to collect himself then and salute, and left the hut with his usual brisk stride. In the thick blue light outside, Colonel Lowe saw his long black shadow fall across the hut window, flicker past the red-tipped white cones of the tents beyond and then vanish into the dusk.

# Sarah's Journal

It seems so odd that the spring which fills the rest of the universe with energy, leaves me full of such lassitude. I have things so comfortable now, and the warmth is so penetrating I have not had to light my brazier in three nights but I wake each morning so full of physical limpness that I feel like a rag doll from which the sawdust is running. I am certainly not undernourished, thanks to Mrs Coles, and my work has become immeasurely easier now that the sickness is controlled and everyone's health and spirits so much better. Can it be that things are *too* easy? That I liked it better when there were such awful difficulties to be overcome? It does not say much for my affection for my fellow men if that is really so, for I could not wish to see them still as I found them in December. I do not wish that, but I do wish I was still at the base of the mountain, not progressing comfortably to the summit. I seem to like to have a mountain ahead of me.

One thing is certainly very cheering. Only two days ago Major Heversham, who once lent ponies to Colonel Lowe and me, set out for England, and he took with him all the Wilkes family. He was badly wounded in the stomach at Inkerman and brought to Scutari, and when I went to thank him for the ponies, I told him about the glorious luck of finding Sam, and he has taken a particular interest in them ever since. He is a good-hearted man, and a keen horseman, and says there will be plenty of work around his stables for Sam, and work in the house for Jane and a lodge cottage for them all. It is all very wonderful and I smile every time I think of it.

Miss Nightingale has gone to the Crimea to look at the hospitals there. It is strange and astonishing what an effect her going away has had here, how sorely her influence is missed. Her subordinates are either too lax or too zealous in her absence. Perhaps I am missing her as keenly as the others, missing the sense of knowing she is there to direct and scold and praise. I keep finding myself daydreaming at my window in the evenings, gazing out at this scruffy and disgusting little town with a most silly and sentimental affection and feeling how sorry I shall be to see the back of it for all its filth and smells and squalor.

I suppose I am really apprehensive about what is to become of me. Sebastopol is daily expected to fall (it has been daily expected to fall since December however) and once that has happened the army will all go home and the hospitals will be shut up and I shall be shipped back to England with all the other women who have toiled here. Of course I shan't go back to Oakley, at least for no more than a visit. I have had but one letter from my father, very stern and disgusted with me, and two from Blanche, all frocks and parties. It appears the young officer who was taking his broken shoulder home on the same ship as Blanche and the Bagshots proves to be both a baronet and very attentive. His shoulder doesn't seem to prevent him dancing or riding or dashing up and down to Northamptonshire every minute. What time Blanche has from her wardrobe and her gaiety she presumably gives to him. They don't want me back. What should I do with them or they with me if I went?

No, I shall go to London. Miss Nightingale set up a nursing home near Cavendish Square before she came out here, so why should I not do something of the kind? I now know a number of the most kindly and influential people and thanks to Edgar I am not without money. Why should I not be part of this new movement to make nursing a respectable profession, or even better the notion of a profession for women even respectable in itself? Did not Robert once say to me that everyone ought to be able to look back on a day and think it a day well spent? I *do* think that now, almost every day and I should like there to be thousands like me.

Yesterday, however, was not a well spent day. Perhaps that is what has made me so reflective today, longing all the time I worked to be back here in this rose and blue twilight to write, in private, to think. They found the body of Mrs Evans in an alley by the slaughterhouse, dead, it is thought, of drink and malnutrition, still in her apron though sadly dirty now. Some soldiers found her, and if she had not had Trooper Evans's buttons on a string round her neck, they would have left her there in the mud and offal because death is still such a commonplace here. But they saw she was a soldier's wife, so they bundled her into a bit of sacking and brought her to us that a coffin might be made and I saw her laid out in the little death chamber of the cellars while they measured her.

She never wished me anything but ill, but somehow it was not me myself she hated, but what I was, what I stood for. I broke her rules of how a lady should behave, just as I broke James Lowe's. She wanted me to be exploitable, charitable, generous and an innocent to her world of guile and self survival. I was her enemy when I began to know about her. When she frightened me on the ship, that was correct, that was how things should be. When I resisted her in the laundry, when I challenged her over Blanche, I was behaving as she would have done, not as I, a lady, should. Would she have come to this pitiable and savage end if it had not been for her involvement with us all? Was it Trooper Evans dying or the Drummonds that killed her really? She was a black-hearted woman in many ways, but so ignorant, so frightened of others' cleverness, how could she be otherwise? She was present through the last fifteen months like a rotten apple in a barrel of good ones, and yet she had no power to win in the end, not even really the power to survive without help.

Robert was so right. How can life be better for anyone, everyone, unless help comes from those with the influence, the power to give it? At best, Mrs Evans could only be ordinary. She had no chance to be better than that, more remarkable.

I don't suppose a day passes but that I remember something Robert said, some dream of his, some wish. Much good it does me to think of him when there is not the smallest chance of my seeing him, or even if I did of it being more than the most commonplace of meetings. Our great bond, that terrible winter and those poor suffering men, is largely over, and I must turn my mind from it, from him, *wrench* my mind from him and put it to thoughts of going home to England. When Sebastopol falls, I must not be at a loss. I must have a plan.

It is nearly dark. I wonder if the lilies of the valley are out at Oakley – we always gave them to Mamma on May day and she always said that the scent of them gave her a headache. It gives me a headache to think of that life of hers, one sofa, one drawing room, one great monotony. I haven't seen a flower in months, yet I haven't thought of them until now. What you do not have, you do not miss. Except one thing, of course, one thing. . . .

# *Twenty*

On 20 May, George Lacey arrived in the Crimea, laden with comforts for Robert from England, and longing for action. Within three days, using himself as a decoy, Robert managed to get Lacey hidden away on the transport ship *Hope* when the expedition left on its one-hundred-and-fifty-mile journey to the straits of Kertch. The Russian fleet in the sea of Azov was its objective, all the enemy's magazines, naval stores, grain and military equipment and Robert could hardly bear to see the *Hope* depart without him whatever magnificent alternatives seemed to await him on the shores of Lake Lucerne. He had bidden good-bye to James Lowe the previous evening at a meeting too poignant to be prolonged, and then had packed his few tattered possessions, his pistols and his precious papers into an army kitbag and slept for the last night in his bare and familiar hut. Most of the troops had departed for embarkation the previous day presuming Robert would accompany them as he had always done before, and he, preferring not to think of this as the end of the adventure, did not say that it would be George Lacey they found at Kertch, not him. The morning the expedition sailed north to Kertch, Robert Chiltern found a passage on a transport going south to Scutari. He wore the full-dress trousers of a sergeant of the Royal Engineers, a comfortable, shapeless 'Balaclava' jacket of grey wool and the forage cap he had acquired in camp at Varna the summer before and somehow failed to lose. Two members of the crew mistook him within the first hour for being a wounded soldier on his way to the hospital in Scutari and gazing down in some surprise at the red stripes on his overalls, as if he saw them for the first time, Robert realized that he would have to find himself some civilian clothes before presenting himself in Switzerland.

By early June, the days in Scutari were fiercely hot. Fat blue flies clotted round eyes and on foodstuffs, the lanes around the town first dried and then cracked and disintegrated into fogs of dust. The long wards of the hospital were shuttered against the sun and men lay on sheeted mattresses without covering in the heat.

Down in the laundry, the temperature made it an inferno. The cellars remained mercifully quite cool in their half-buried darkness but nothing could reduce the temperature of the boilers. Tempers rose with the heat and quarrels broke out savagely among the women working with the scalding linen. Sarah spent all day in a flimsy cotton gown purchased from the bazaar which she peeled from her body at night like a banana skin, and washed in a bucket, to hang it drying later in the window for the morrow.

The atmosphere was not only hot but restless. Several of Miss Nightingale's friends who had helped her so staunchly through the winter, were going home, lingering only a few extra weeks in the scorching Turkish summer to see Miss Nightingale fully restored after the bout of Crimean fever which had prostrated her. Replacements for these ladies in the store and the cellars were being sought among the European community in Constantinople, among governesses to diplomatic households or sensible dependents of expatriate households. It was suggested to Sarah that she might like to accompany one party home in July. She shook her head.

'I think not, not unless Sebastopol has fallen. I would rather wait until the army returns.'

Mrs Coles was discouraged to hear this. It seemed more than likely that Sarah would keep her by her when they returned to England and she could now hardly wait for that time to come. She had had enough, redoubtable though she was, of bazaars and dirt and Turks.

'It'd do your health good to go, dear. Doesn't do a body any good at all to boil away in this hot-house. You don't want to fall ill again now, do you?'

'I shan't, Mrs Coles. I'm too busy to be ill. When there's no more for me to do usefully here, I shall go. But not till then.'

Mrs Coles shrugged and sighed. The days were dragging on into the cauldron of high summer. It would be June 18th tomorrow, the fortieth anniversary of Waterloo, a day she always remembered because her father had been a soldier of the line there and had reminisced annually to his children about the fighting in thick black smoke amid fields of standing corn. Eight months now she and Miss Sarah had shared these two little rooms and seen them turn from igloos to ovens. If only Miss Sarah had listened to that colonel, they might have been in England now, Miss Sarah buying a trousseau, Mrs Coles in some vaguely defined but indubitably respectable position in her household. She sighed again. Miss Sarah was in her room again, scribbling furiously. She'd used enough ink in these last few months to float a ship, and burnt enough candles to light a cathedral. Mrs Coles tapped on the adjoining door, and coughed.

'Can I get you some tea, dear?'

Sarah looked round for a moment.

'No, no thank you. Nothing, thank you.'

Mrs Coles sighed and picked up her market basket. A visit to the bazaar always gave her a sense of purpose, even if it were only the unnecessary repetition of proving how superior English wits were to Turkish ones.

June 18th dawned as bright and blue as its predecessors. The mornings were beautiful, sharp and clear with damp black shadows, but by noon the day would wilt into dusty dishevelment. Sarah rose while the dawn was moist and pink, donning her cheap cotton gown and as few petticoats as were respectable. A magazine from Paris had filtered down into the cellars some days previously, full of plates of the new crinoline, an amazing hooped affair, standing feet away from the owner's legs like a shallow bell. A dragoon officer in the hospital whom Sarah had visited once or twice reported he had seen one of these extraordinary garments among the groups of tourists parading the heights before Sebastopol. Sarah now held out the limp cotton of her gown and tried to visualize its meagre folds swinging lavishly over a hooped frame. Cool no doubt, but awkward.

She brushed and knotted her hair, washed her face in the bowl of water, always tepid in the summer, that Mrs Coles left for her, and opened the door between their adjoining rooms. Mrs Coles was up and dressed as was her custom, and was standing before the empty fireplace with a look at once tentative and defiant. She pushed a plate of bread spread with thin Greek honey towards Sarah.

'You'll eat before you go, dear.'

Sarah sat down on the nearest stool.

'What is it, Mrs Coles?'

'I've always been one for plain speaking, dear, but it's not my wish to upset you. The time has come to speak my mind.'

Sarah sighed faintly and picked up the nearest slice of bread.

'It's time we went home, dear, and no mistake. Miss Nightingale herself will be gone soon. If we wait for this siege to end, we'll still be here come Christmas and I'll not stand another winter here, dear, and nor should you. I don't mind what I do for you, Miss Sarah, because I know it's not in your mind to go home like a lady should and you're going to need some looking after. I'm not afraid of work. I'll help you in whatever you've a mind to do. But you'll be wasting your time here, I'm telling you that. I don't know what you're waiting for, but it'll come no quicker here, that's for sure. So home we should go, like Lady Alicia suggested, and that soon. There, dear. Now eat your breakfast and off you go. We'll talk it over tonight.'

Sarah put down her slice of bread with only one bite taken from it.

'I don't seem very hungry.'

'It's this climate. No appetite could thrive in it. England's where you should be.'

'I – I'll think it over.'

'Today, dear.'

'I'll try.'

Mrs Coles picked up a straw bonnet and tied its faded ribbons under Sarah's chin.

'You do that, dear. I'll see you later and we'll talk it out. You'll come to see that it's sense I'm talking.'

Robert Chiltern reached the decaying house on the quay in Scutari an hour before sunset. The place was exhausted in the thick yellow afternoon light and the owner of the chandler's shop, who had rented Mrs Coles her rooms the autumn before, a fat and somnolent Greek, lay dozing in a coil of rope in his doorway. Several neglected children scuffled in the dust and litter around him and a skeletal dog lay panting in a stripe of shadow beside the house.

Robert put out a foot and nudged the Greek. He opened one reluctant eye, observed a tattered English soldier and jerked his thumb in the direction of a derelict staircase beside the house.

'The English lady,' Robert said.

The Greek grunted and jerked his thumb again, then he closed his eye and settled himself down once more into his ring of rope.

Robert looked doubtfully at the staircase. It led up the crumbling ochre wall of the house to a black hole at the top. He put a foot on the bottom tread and a rat shot out of the darkness underneath and vanished into the chandler's shop.

Robert began to climb, feeling ever more doubtful with every step that he had found the right place. He had arrived in Scutari two days before after a stifling and tedious journey which had taken over a week longer than it should owing to a faulty boiler. For three weeks the steamship had crept across the Black Sea under a merciless sun, and Robert had suffocated for lack of occupation. He no longer even had reports to write and his impatience to be at his destination made the hot, slow crawl insupportable. Once in Scutari he had found himself lodgings, bought new linen for the first time in almost a year, and spent a day in the hospital visiting men he had known in the field. The cellars were pointed out to him, and the achievements of several ladies extolled to him. He did not go down to the cellars.

Now, the green volume in the pocket of a new lightweight alpaca jacket of peculiar cut from the bazaar tailor, he was climbing the staircase. At the top, on a broken platform, he found he had no door to knock on. He listened a moment. There was no sound within the empty frame, but daylight glimmered from an open door to his right.

He stepped quietly inside. There was a room evidently used as kitchen and dining room and someone's bedroom, sparse and tidy and furnished as austerely as his own hut had been all winter. A makeshift table under a coarse cloth was laid for some sort of meal but there was no evidence of any food. Across the little room, a door stood ajar and in the gap left, and through the cracks in the splintered panels, shone a golden glow of late afternoon sun.

Robert stepped softly across the bare boards of the floor and pushed the inner door. There was a table under a window opposite, a window full of rich yellow light, and at the table Sarah was writing. She was half turned to him and he could see part of her face bent in concentration over her page. Two long tendrils of hair had escaped from the coil at the back of her head, and she put up a hand absently to tuck them behind her ear.

'Sarah,' he said.

When she looked up at him, her face was quite blackened out by the strength of the light behind her. He could make nothing of her expression at all, but she rose slowly, holding to the back of her strange exotic scarlet chair as she did so, and he saw all her pretty plumpness was gone and that she was dressed in a garment as practical and unbecoming as his own.

She said something in a choked voice but he could make nothing of it. He went forward and took her hands and turned her towards the light a little.

'Are you glad to see me?'

She nodded furiously, her eyes shining with tears. Her face was different, quite different. It had been so smooth and even, with its delicately coloured skin and large eyes, and small mouth, a pretty doll's face. Now it was thinner, much thinner, and her eyes were larger than ever, and powerfully blue, and her mouth was firm and her skin a pale golden she would have done anything to avoid in England. She was not a girl any more and she had become remarkable looking.

'I am so surprised to see you!' she said at last, 'I can hardly believe it! I – I thought you had all forgotten me, there was so much else to think of – '

'No,' he said, and smiled.

She took her hands away and indicated the scarlet chair.

'Will you not sit down? It's hardly comfortable here but this is the only time of day the sun is bearable and I don't like to waste it.'

'And you?'

'I will fetch a stool.'

'No,' he said. 'Sit on your throne, and I will fetch a stool.'

He seated himself so that he might lean his arm on the table among her scattered papers.

'Now,' he said, 'I want you to tell me everything, every single thing, that has befallen you since you ran away from Balaclava. No, no – don't demur. I want to hear. I shall sit here immovably until you tell me.'

She began to speak rapidly and self-consciously, looking down at her lap, reciting dates and facts as if they were some task committed to memory. But when she had told him, in the baldest terms, of her journey and her fever and her rescue by Mrs Coles, she began to look up and speak with more warmth of the hospital and Miss Nightingale and the plight of the people in the barrack cellars. By the end, she seemed quite to have forgotten it was a story which involved herself at all, and was recounting it with all the enthusiasm of a fascinated observer. Robert leaned on the table, his head on his hand, and watched her.

When she had done, he got up and walked about the room for a while, his hands in his pockets. Sarah never took her eyes from him as he went up and down, his head slightly bent. He came back to the table at last and his stool.

'It will take me a long time to tell you what I think of you. I am more impressed and – and *awed* – by what you have done than I can quickly say.'

'I do not want you to say it.'

'I don't deserve to be allowed to for sure. When I have told you what I have to tell you, I think it unlikely you will let me speak to you again.'

She laughed.

'Nonsense!'

He looked at her gravely.

'It isn't I fear. I have done a most dishonourable thing. I tried very hard not to do it, but tedium and the most burning desire to know got the better of me.'

She leaned forward, still smiling.

'Confess then!'

Slowly he put his hand into his pocket and pulled out the dark green volume. He put it on her lap.

'Oh!' she said in delight, 'My journal! I thought it lost! I thought I should never see it again! How did you come by it?'

'Colonel Lowe entrusted it to me. It was found among Edgar's possessions. He must have taken it for safekeeping from the *Hercules*.'

'So – so that is your errand?'

Robert looked away for a moment.

'Only partly.'

She waited. His gaze came back to her, deeply self-conscious.

'Sarah – I read it. We had three weeks on the Black Sea and I fought against reading it for eighteen days. I know it was eighteen because I counted every one I was so passionate to read it. And on the nineteenth I could not bear it, and I devoured your journal in a few hours. I was horrified at myself and I am bitterly ashamed of the action but – but perhaps I shall not be sorry that I know what now I know.'

She said nothing. She was looking down at the book in her hands, and he could see the fingertips holding the cover were white with pressure and that her bosom under the grey cotton dress was heaving in little abrupt jerks.

'Sarah?' he said very softly.

She shook her head but still looked down and was silent.

'Then – then it is no longer the case? What I read – of myself in those pages is something – of the past then? I – I suppose I might have known it and goodness knows after all I have done, all my – stupidity and – and cruelty, I must be the least deserving fellow on earth of such a prize, *such* a prize – I cannot bear to think that if only, if *only* I had known how you – you felt then I should never have been so blind, so unbelievably wrongheaded! Sarah, Sarah, have you nothing to say to me?'

He was sitting with his knees only inches from hers and suddenly with a force that almost knocked him backwards from his stool, she had tossed the journal aside and had flung herself into his arms. She was sobbing aloud and trying to speak through her tears, her face buried in the shoulder of his jacket, while he strove to reciprocate her embrace and keep them both from sliding to the floor in an awkward tangle of limbs.

'I *couldn't* speak just now, I *couldn't*, don't you see – it was so overwhelming that you knew how much I'd loved you, how long, such days and months, and I couldn't believe that you thought of me, I couldn't imagine it would ever be anyone but Blanche –'

'Blanche!' he said bitterly, gathering her on to his knee more closely, 'I doubt it ever would have been Blanche if I'd looked to see that it might be Sarah.'

'Oh!' she cried reproachfully, freeing her face to look at him, 'It always might have been Sarah, *always*!'

'Still? Still always?'

She nodded and returned her face to his shoulder.

'You mean that?' he demanded, 'After everything I have done, breaking your heart and ignoring you and being such a damnable priggish fool?'

He could feel laughter shake her.

'Yes,' she said, muffled, into his jacket.

'Will you kiss me?'

'Beard and all?'

'For the moment, I'm afraid.'

Her mouth tasted salty, as did her cheeks and forehead.

'I shall never be so glad of anything as I am that I came by Scutari.'

She looked suddenly alarmed.

'You aren't going, are you?'

'I'm on my way to Switzerland to join my family. It seems my father is consumptive and has been told to go to Europe, so he has taken a house on Lake Lucerne. He asked me to go. I think – I think he means to ask if I will stand for the constituency now he is too ill.'

'Oh!' Sarah cried in delight, 'It's just what you wanted! First a reconciliation then – then Westminster perhaps!'

'If they'll have me. Remember I'm not a Whig and they are used to my father. I – I'm doubtful I could do it without help now, help and support of – a very particular sort. I am so anxious not to squander your magnificent talents.'

She coloured a little and put her arms round his neck.

'Of course they'll have you!'

He shrugged.

'I don't much care. What is more to the point is – will you?'

Steps grated faintly on the outside staircase, accompanied by little grunts of exertion. They froze where they were, Sarah upon his knee, their arms about each other.

'Coo-ee, dear!'

Sarah put her hand over Robert's mouth.

'Good evening, Mrs Coles!'

The puffing and panting became louder as Mrs Coles tramped into the outer room, dumped her basket on the floor and fanned herself vigorously with something that sounded like a newspaper.

'This climate, dear!' Mrs Coles's voice came stridently through the half-open door. 'It ain't fit for pigs! You could fry a chop on me, I'm that hot. No wonder them scamps in the bazaar's as bad as they are. Who could act decent in a climate that freezes you one minute and roasts you the next? I'll be glad to get out of it, I can tell you, never a minute too soon. Now dear, soon as I've unpacked these vittles, you and me's going to have a little talk. I warned you this morning, fair and square, and you've had all day to think it over. I'll put it straight to you, dear, because I can't promise to stick it out much longer. Are you coming home to England like a sensible young lady?'

Robert took Sarah's hand from his mouth and held it firmly.

'Yes,' he said to the unseen Mrs Coles. 'Yes, she is coming home to England. Via Switzerland. She is coming home as – as – ' he stopped and looked at Sarah with uncharacteristic doubt and pleading.

She leant forward and kissed him on the mouth.

'Oh yes,' she said softly. 'Oh yes!'